THE ROMAN'S VIRGIN MISTRESS

Michelle Styles

MILLS & BOON®

Pure reading pleasure

First published in Great Britain 2007
Large Print edition 2007
Harlequin Mills & Boon Limited,
Eton House, 18-24 Paradise Road, Richmond, Surrey TW9 1SR

© Michelle Styles 2007

ISBN: 978 0 263 19411 1

Set in Times Roman 15½ on 17½ pt.
42-1107-84996

Printed and bound in Great Britain
by Antony Rowe Ltd, Chippenham, Wiltshire

Although born and raised near San Francisco, California, **Michelle Styles** currently lives a few miles south of Hadrian's Wall, with her husband, three children, two dogs, cats, assorted ducks, hens and beehives. An avid reader, she has always been interested in history, and a historical romance is her idea of the perfect way to relax. Her love of Rome stems from the year of Latin she took in sixth grade. She is particularly interested in how ordinary people lived during ancient times, and in the course of her research she has learnt how to cook Roman food as well as how to use a drop spindle. When she is not writing, reading or doing research, Michelle tends her rather overgrown garden or does needlework, in particular counted cross-stitch. Michelle maintains a website, www.michellestyles.co.uk, and a blog, www.michellestyles.blogspot.com, and would be delighted to hear from you.

Recent novels by the same author:

THE GLADIATOR'S HONOUR
A NOBLE CAPTIVE
SOLD AND SEDUCED

To Donna Alward and Sue Child, who are always there with their help and support whenever the Crows of Doubt attack.

Chapter One

69 BC Baiae, the most luxurious and notorious seaside resort in the late Roman Republic

A little bit further to the harbour wall. That was all. She could hear the sound of the water lapping against it.

Silvana Junia forced her legs to kick. Her gown had started to slip from the belt and the sea-soaked linen curled about her thighs, imprisoning her, dragging her down.

The cries and splashing behind her had stopped a while back. Cotta and his henchmen had given up or decided she was drowned in the bay. She would have dearly loved to have seen his face when she jumped off his yacht. The evening had failed to go as she planned, but neither had it had the ending he intended.

Silvana made a wry face. From now on, she'd remember. Cotta was the enemy.

She gave one last vigorous kick. Her outstretched hand touched the rough concrete, and curled around a tiny handhold. She had made it. The gods were with her tonight. She had done it. Now to get out of the bay and back home.

The harbour wall loomed above her, too high to clamber up. Silvana glanced to her right. A single fishing boat bobbed only a few yards from her; next to it she saw the shadowy outline of a rope ladder. If she could get on the ship, then she could clamber up the ladder on to the wall and reach Baiae's promenade. Carefully she inched her way over. Her belt came loose and the skirts of her gown and undertunic billowed around her.

Silvana reached up and her fingers found a perch on the side of the boat. She allowed herself to hang there, half in and half out of the water, trying to get her breath back. How long had she been in the water? When she first dived in the bay, it had felt like ice, but now it was warmer than the hot pool at the Baths of Mercury.

Her body started to sink back into the bay. She was tired, very tired. The sea called to her exhaustion. She could float for ever in a dreamless sleep.

She stiffened. She would not let Cotta win this way. She forced her body up and out and lay with her face on the wooden decking and her legs dangling. Salty water streamed off her honey blonde hair and dark blue gown. Her legs refused to move, but she tried again and rolled on to the boat with a loud squelch. Her breath stopped.

Was anyone on board? Had they heard her?

Silence except for the quiet lapping of the water against the boat.

The ladder hung tantalisingly close. She'd have to do it. Silvana summoned all her energy, rose and made a dash for it. Her hand closed around the rope. Underneath her, in the hold of the ship, came the sound of muffled voices.

Let them go back to sleep, she prayed. The last thing she needed was another scandal being linked to the name of the already notorious Silvana Junia. She had enough of those, both real and supposed, clinging to her *stola.* Crispus, her younger brother, had begged her in a tablet last Ides, no more scandals until he had secured a place as a junior tribune, and she'd agreed.

After what seemed like an age, the voices became quiet.

Cautiously she began to climb, ignoring the way her gown dragged against her legs, pulling her back down. Her hand touched the top of the harbour wall.

She had done it!

A large scarred hand reached down and grabbed her wrist, held her fast, steadying her.

'You are safe. You have made it to the shore,' a deep voice growled.

Silvana looked up and saw a figure bending over the wall. His legs seem to reach for ever and his tunic skimmed the mid-point of his thighs. His shoulders were broad, but his face was in shadow.

She moved her arm and he released it. With a final burst of energy, she scrambled up the remaining rungs of the ladder and over the harbour wall to the promenade.

'I am on dry land,' she said, looking towards where the pale villas rose with their ghostly white pillars, dark loggias and deep red roofs rather than at the man. 'It is safer than the sea.'

'That depends on who you are. If you are a nymph or maybe with hair like that a sea witch, the sea would be a better place,' the voice continued in its quiet way. Against all reason, the tone made her feel secure, as if her journey across the bay was nothing more than a bad dream.

Silvana pushed a strand of sea-soaked hair away from her face. Nymph? She had no illusions. Her current personal appearance was closer to a drowned water-rat than some mythical beauty. She had had enough insincere flattery to last a lifetime. And neither was she prepared to discuss her reasons for jumping into the bay with a stranger.

'I assure you, I am human.' Silvana used her iciest voice. What she needed now was to get away from here, before the slaves and workmen started moving about, before anyone recognised her. She took a step towards the road.

'Then why were you doing a Venus rising from the sea?' The man blocked her way. 'Not by choice I would imagine. Or are you practising for some new entertainment to titillate the jaded palates of the inhabitants of Baiae?'

'It was the only option left to me,' she said, throwing back her shoulders and standing upright. Even though she was considered a tall woman, her head did not even reach the height of his nose.

'You decided to take a moonlit swim dressed in your finest gown.' The man tapped his fingers together. 'I know Baiae is famed for many things but I had not heard of moonlight-swimming matrons. Tell me—is it current fashion or are you trying to start a new trend?'

'Neither.'

Silvana raised her chin a notch and stared into the angular shadows of his face. It was impossible to discern what sort of man he was. But the sort of man he was made no difference. She had no intention of ever seeing him again. After a warm bath, tonight would cease to be anything but a bad memory.

She squared her shoulders, preparing to push pass. 'If you will excuse me, I need to return home. I have no wish to drip for longer than I absolutely must.'

'It is dangerous to be out at this time of night...alone. I will escort you.' His voice sent a chill down her spine. 'Only thieves, robbers and others intent on harm populate this time.'

'And which are you—a thief or a robber?'

Silvana tried to make her voice sound carefree and unconcerned, but the words came out as a squeak.

The pounding of the surf echoed the pounding of her heart in her ears. To have come all this way only to lose her necklace and ring. It would be a fitting end to a sorry night.

Why had she ever attempted to negotiate with Cotta?

She watched the broad shouldered man to see what he would do next. Would he be satisfied with her jewellery? 'Tell me quickly—what is your intent?'

'Neither.' The man gave a slight bow. 'The name is Fortis and I intend on seeing you safely home. A woman should have a protector at this time of day. You will receive no harm from me.'

Silvana's knees weakened and she stumbled forward. Her hands brushed his woollen cloak and his scent of sandalwood and something indefinably masculine tickled her nose before she righted herself and stood upright. It had been a long time since anyone, in particular a stranger, had been bothered about her safety. Mostly they were concerned with relating the latest juicy morsel about her doings.

'I know my way home. I am safe now that I am back on dry land.'

'An honest man, Pio the fisherman, a client of mine, sleeps on that boat,' the man remarked conversationally but there was a hard edge to his voice, an edge that demanded answers.

Silvana froze, her foot briefly hanging in mid-air before she placed it again on the cold concrete with a loud thump. 'I took nothing.' Silvana turned her palms upwards. 'And only touched those things that I had to. There was no other way. Now let me depart in peace.'

'Will you swear that on the shades of your ancestors?' His hand reached out and caught her elbow.

'Yes, I will swear it.'

She stared down at his long fingers. Warmth travelled up her arms. A slight shiver passed through her body. Would he believe her? He had to believe her.

Slowly, one by one, the fingers released her but he stood still.

Silvana drew a breath in, waiting to see what this man's next move would be. With the weight of her gown, it would be foolish to run. She had to hope that the Fates had not determined on a cruel twist of their spindle—escaping from Cotta, only to be caught in the coils of a much more dangerous man.

'Now we go, sea witch.' There was a hint of laughter in Fortis's voice. 'You might stumble again or cut your feet. Shall I carry you?'

She refused to think what it would feel like to have that man's arms around her, holding her close to his chest. The seawater had affected her brain. She had no business, thinking thoughts like that.

'I can walk perfectly well.' Silvana made her voice sound as haughty as possible. Of all the night's indignities, losing her slippers was the worst. She had been fond of those slippers and they were only a season old. She had to hope that they had remained on board and that Cotta would do the decent thing. It would be a first, but she refused to discount it. 'Farewell, Fortis. Thank you for your concern.'

'You're cold. Sea nymphs should not be cold.'

He took off his cloak and, before she could utter a protest, placed it about her shoulders. The masculine scent of sandalwood and balsam enveloped her and held her. Warm. Intimate.

Silvana swallowed hard. She wanted to stay wrapped in this cloak. She listened to the soft sound of the waves hitting the beach. Her hands gripped the heavy wool. This cloak did not belong to a slave or a working man. In the moonlight his tunic shone a pale white with a dark purple band around the hem, again signalling that her would-be rescuer was no common working man.

But why wear a tunic and not dining clothes so late at night? Where was he travelling to? Or from?

Silvana glanced over her shoulder back to the inky black water. Had she been wrong to trust her instincts? 'I will make the cloak wet.' Numb with cold, her hands fumbled with the clasp.

'Leave the cloak where it is. It will dry.' He gave a sardonic laugh. 'I would hate for you to swim all this way, just to catch a chill.'

'I will be fine.' Silvana gave a series of sneezes, each louder than the last. 'I am quite warm. It is May in Baiae, not December in Rome.'

'Keep the cloak on.'

Lucius Aurelius Fortis, lately a Queastor of Rome, was gratified to see this time the shivering woman obeyed, her fingers drawing the edges of the cloak tighter around her body. By Hercules, this woman was proving more obstinate than he thought possible. Who refused the offer of a cloak?

Fortis considered the woman. She was too old to be in the first flush of youth. Despite her sodden hair and gown, she carried herself as if she was pre-siding over an exclusive dinner party in one of

Baiae's private villas. Her necklace and earrings and the heavy embroidery on her gown proclaimed that her dip in the sea was unplanned. He reached out and tucked the cloak more firmly about her shoulders.

'You are uncomfortable receiving help from strangers.'

'I have discovered help comes with conditions.'

'There are no conditions here.' She saw his teeth flash white in the moonlight. 'Maybe one. I wanted to thank you for the view earlier. It is not often I chance upon a white-limbed lovely rising from the sea.'

His hands, rough with calluses, touched her cheek. Silvana compared them with Cotta's soft hands. She knew whose hands she trusted more. But the time was long past for trust. She had learnt through bitter experience—trust had too high a price.

'I thank you for the loan of your cloak.' Silvana arranged the cloak more securely about her body. 'Let me know where I should return it.'

'I will you see to your villa.' His tone allowed for no refusal.

Silvana blinked. How much did this man know about her? Had Fortis guessed who she was?

'How do you know I live in a villa?'

'The necklace you are wearing could pay the rent on a flat for a year.'

'It was a present from my late husband.' Silvana inwardly made a face. She should never have worn it, not to a meeting with Cotta, her former stepson. What an irony that was. Cotta was five years older than herself. Why she had listened to her uncle and agreed to the meeting, she had no idea. She had known what Cotta was like, that he would offer no practical help.

'Are you ready to go? Standing here discussing jewellery will not get you out of your wet things any quicker.'

Silvana glanced up and saw his dark eyes gazing down at her. Her breath stopped in her throat. He was standing so close and she was wrapped in his cloak. She knew nothing about Fortis, but it no longer mattered.

Silvana turned away and looked out at the darkened bay. Little lights were bobbing about. It was impossible to determine if those lights had anything to do with Cotta. She wondered if at least two of his chins had waggled after she had dived off his yacht. She gave a short laugh.

'Are you going to tell me what is so amusing?'

'I was thinking about my would-be companion for tonight.' Silvana flipped a wet strand of hair back from her face. 'He thought to have me at his mercy, but I escaped.'

'And will he tell the tale around Baiae?' The concern was clearly written on his face. 'Such a thing could ruin a woman's reputation.'

Silvana tilted her head, considering Fortis's statement. What would he say if he knew her reputation was already ruined, ruined beyond repair? The little escapade was nothing compared to some of the stories she had heard whispered in the baths or seen scrawled on the walls. It was the price she paid for independence, and occasionally, at times like this, she wondered if it was worth it.

'No, no, he will come off far worse,' she said with greater conviction than she felt. Who knew what Cotta was capable of? She had to hope that his overly puffed vanity stilled his tongue. 'What sort of man wants to admit that a woman prefers the dark water of the bay to his embrace?'

'I will bow to your superior judgement, but it is time we were gone. Others will come here soon.'

'I must be taking you away from something.'

'I have time to see you home.' He spread his arms out. 'Besides, how else can I ensure I get my cloak back? It is one of my favourites.'

'You sound like you make a habit of rescuing women from the sea.' Silvana peeped up at him from behind her curtain of hair.

'Not lately.'

'Then you have done this sort of thing before.'

'Have you?'

'Of course not!' Silvana brought her head round and stared directly back at him.

'You seem remarkably calm about it all. There are not many women of my acquaintance who would voluntarily jump off a boat, swim across a bay and then not be in a hysterical state afterwards.'

'I am not home yet. No doubt it will hit me then,' Silvana replied. 'But I see no point in tears. I have to do the best with what I am given. And it was my choice to jump off the boat.'

'Indeed—are you going to tell me whose boat?'

A watchfulness returned to his body and Silvana wondered why someone so obviously wealthy would be watching the bay at this time of the night. Another shiver passed through her. She'd think about that later, after she had bathed and slept. Right now the important thing was for her to return home. 'The name of the man makes no difference. I want to put the whole experience behind me. I came through unharmed, if a little damp.'

She started to walk towards the road. Her foot came down awkwardly on a rock and she stumbled. His fingers caught her elbow and held her fast.

'I said I would see you home.' The voice was silken, but she could hear the iron.

She moved her arm and his hand released her. 'I can manage on my own.'

'I made a promise to see you safely home. I keep my promises.'

Silvana pressed her lips together. She would have to let him go with her. Already the faintest rays of sunrise could be seen over the hills. Soon all of Baiae would be up and moving around. It was one thing to face rumours and quite another to be caught in a compromising situation. No one would believe she and this Fortis had met innocently. Her promise to Crispus would be broken before he returned to Baiae from school.

'Shall we go? It appears having you as my protector will be the quickest way to get rid of you.'

'You wish to be rid of me, sea witch?'

'I wish to return home.'

They walked along in silence. Fortis did not attempt to touch her, but Silvana was aware of him all the same, every move he made. She glanced up as the rose light of dawn started to appear on the horizon. His face was angular and set hard. Instead of being black as she had imagined, his eyes were a sleepy green. His black hair curled at his temples, contrasting with the hard planes of his face. Why was he intent on helping her?

'It is here we say goodbye.' Silvana stopped

outside the entrance to her villa. She could see a light flickering under the door. No doubt Dida the porter would still be awake. Possibly even her uncle. Had Cotta appeared and what story had he told?

'Shall I see you again?'

Silvana's hands fumbled with the catch on the cloak. See Fortis again? It wasn't something she had even thought about. There were too many things going on in her mixed-up life. She couldn't risk entangling him in them. This little encounter had been a respite.

'I doubt that will be possible.' She held out the cloak and ignored the sudden chill that swept through her. Her gown seemed to hang heavier than ever.

He took the cloak from her. The pads of her fingers touched his and she withdrew them as if burnt. He lifted an eyebrow. 'Then I will bid you goodbye.'

'Goodbye,' she said and turned to go. The sooner she got into the villa, the sooner she could start assessing the damage. 'I would appreciate you keeping quiet about my swim.'

'I said I would keep you safe.' His hand grabbed her shoulder and turned her around. His eyes in the grey dawn light were a deep green, like the pool in the temple of Mercury. 'This is how I say goodbye.'

He bent his head and his lips brushed hers, gentle but firm, warming her from deep within. Her body trembled, swept away in sensation. His arms came around her and held her against his hard muscular body. Then he lifted his head, stepped away and the kiss was over. Silvana ran her tongue over her lips. They weren't bruised but felt fuller, different.

'Forgive me,' he murmured. 'Your lips bewitched me.'

'I ought to slap your face,' she said, her voice too husky for her liking.

'But you won't.' He touched her cheek with one finger. A shiver ran down her. 'Until the next time you need rescuing, sea witch.'

'I managed quite well on my own. And I am human, not a witch or a nymph.' Silvana held her head high. The next time she chanced upon him, she would not be at such a disadvantage. She would show him that she was not to be mocked, to be kissed as though she was some sea-front daughter of Venus bent on plying her trade.

He paused and turned back. His eyes danced. 'As you wish.'

Chapter Two

'Finally, Lucius, you arrive. My scroll begging you to come to Baiae was sent over twenty days ago. By fast horse.'

'I was unavoidably detained, Aunt Sempronia.' Fortis gazed at his aunt. Despite her grey hair, she retained an air of youth and frivolity. He crossed the loggia of her house in three steps to where she sat, flanked by two slaves, each with an ostrich feather fan. She held out her hand. Ignoring the hand, he brushed his lips against her cheek. 'I have responsibilities in Rome as well as to members of my family.'

'I suppose there was business at the Senate, but really, Lucius, it was too bad.' Sempronia made a little moue with her mouth. 'I need you here. You must help me. Matters have only become worse, much worse. The very reputation of our family is at stake.'

'You have Eutychus with you now. He arrived

back from North Africa over a month and a half ago.' Fortis accepted a cup of honey water from a servant. 'By next Ides, he will have turned twenty-one and will have come into his inheritance. He will be taking care of all your business affairs then.'

'It is my son I wish to speak to you about. He is positively insupportable!'

Fortis raised his eyebrows. What had Eutychus done to deserve such indignation? Normally, his aunt was protective of her only child, clinging to him like a tigress. It had only been as a result of his inter-ference that she had finally consented to Eutychus's request to become a junior tribune, an essential first step if he wanted to serve in the Senate.

'What is so dire you did not even dare write about it? What does Eutychus want this time? We agreed a new chariot and horses were safer than borrow-ing his friend's.'

'It's that woman.' Sempronia gave a long drawn-out sigh and fanned herself more vigorously. 'She has her talons into him. He's besotted with her and he refuses to listen to his mother. You must help me, Lucius. I am at my wits' end. Say you will help me.'

'You sent several urgent scrolls, begging me to drop everything and come to Baiae with all speed because my cousin is head over heels about some woman?' Fortis stared at his aunt who gave a barely imperceptible nod. 'Rest assured my dearest aunt, your only son will get over it. It is calf-love. He will outgrow the woman before the season is out. It is one of the hazards of living in Baiae.'

'He is headstrong like his father. And less than two months away from his inheritance.' His aunt's curls quivered. 'My baby lamb—innocent, easily led. Once that woman has her claws into him, she won't let go. I know she won't. She will hang on to him for dear life. My nerves cannot take it.'

Fortis pressed his lips together into a firm line. When Sempronia was like this, he had to ride out the storm. As the eldest male in the family, he was responsible for her and Eutychus until he came of age. Eventually she would see that to do nothing was the best course of action. Eutychus was a good sort, if a little overindulged. 'And?'

'He is determined to marry her. He has told me so. You are his guardian. You must do something. The family is not worthy. And when I think of what she did to Drusus Cotta!'

The name of his old adversary caused Fortis to start. He had never heard of any woman besting the man.

'What did she do to Cotta?' he asked.

'She married him.' Sempronia sat bolt upright, her eyes blazing. 'She married him and twisted him around her little finger.'

Fortis's eyes narrowed. 'Drusus Cotta is no fool, Aunt Sempronia. When he tried to cheat you out of that pottery last September, you rained curses down on his head. Why change your mind?'

Sempronia made an irritated noise in the back of her throat.

'I speak not of Drusus Cotta the Younger, but of his adopted father.'

'Why should Eutychus be interested in a woman three times older than he is? Cotta the Younger is my age.'

'I despair of men, I really do.' Sempronia shook her head. 'Are you asking me to believe you are ignorant of one of the biggest scandals of the last decade? Cotta the Elder married a girl barely old enough to put her hair up. All Rome, the entire Republic, buzzed about it for months. Of course, she never provided him with a son or any sort of child and Cotta the elder had to adopt, but there you have it.'

'I can see where such an ill-advised marriage might reflect on the parents, but hardly the woman. Surely she must have a guardian.'

'That was only the start of it.' Sempronia leant forward, her eyes eager and her tongue licking her lips as she imparted the latest juicy morsels of gossip. 'Hardly a month goes by without either the woman or her uncle, Junius Maius, being embroiled in some scandal. I can't stand it. I won't. Eutychus can't marry the woman. It is insupportable. Her veil reveals more than it conceals. Even that wretch Cotta the Younger agrees with me.'

Fortis shook his head. He hated to think what outrage his aunt would feel at the sight of the woman he had encountered this morning. Dripping wet, alone on the seafront, his sea witch would be torn to pieces by the ravening pack of scandal-mongers. And yet she had done nothing to deserve it. Had this woman?

'I have never cared for Cotta the Younger. He served as a junior tribune in Bithynia at the same time I did. He can be a nasty piece of work when he wants to be.'

'Precisely. I knew you'd agree in the end.' Sempronia signalled to one of the servants. 'You will join me in a glass of honeyed water to seal our pact.'

'What pact are you talking about?'

'You are going to help me get rid of this harpy.' She gave a great sigh. 'I don't have anyone else I can turn to, Lucius. I need your help. He swears he will marry her or die in the attempt.'

'And the woman?'

'I shudder to think how much she will want. We can't have the most notorious woman in Baiae in the family. It would be insupportable.'

Fortis regarded his aunt. Her curls shook and the beginnings of a double chin trembled. And he knew in the end he'd agree Eutychus was not safe on his own amongst the harpies of Baiae. The boy had just finished his first rather undistinguished tour as a junior tribune in Spain. In a few months time, he'd inherit a fortune from his father. He was the right age to fall in calf-love, and learn what women were really about. The last thing Eutychus needed was some well-experienced woman getting her claws in him. He knew from bitter experience what it could be like, how such things always ended when you were young and naïve. And, if he was being honest, he wanted a reason to stay in Baiae.

'I had planned to stay in the area until the next Ides. There are things I need to attend to.'

'It will be horses.' Sempronia's eyes gleamed. 'Cotta has a new pair. He is willing to bet against all comers that they are the swiftest.'

'I hadn't heard.'

'You and your horses. You do not fool me one little bit.' Sempronia clapped her hands, summoning a servant and indicating she wanted another cup of honey water. She took a long sip and smacked her lips. 'You are just like my brother, your late father. If it wasn't racing horses, it was racing his yacht.'

'I no longer race. I haven't done for years, not

since the crash that killed Murcia. I save my energies for the Senate.'

Sempronia toyed with her fan. 'I had forgotten that. Your devotion to your late wife ensures you are held in great esteem in some quarters no doubt.'

'No doubt.' Fortis gave a casual shrug of his shoulders. His devotion to Murcia had vanished when he found her private tablets. But he saw no need to inform his aunt of the mistake. Such things needed to remain in the past. 'But what does my current mode of living have to do with anything?'

'Eutychus worships the ground you walk upon. I knew I was correct in summoning you. What would there be to do in Rome but lawsuits and dreary Senate work?'

'I never said I would do anything.' Fortis looked hard at his aunt, trying to control his irritation.

'But you will.' Sempronia concentrated on rearranging the folds of her gown, but there was a superior expression on her face. 'I can feel it in my bones. And the soothsayer said the omens were good. In any case, here you are. You have to do something. I am depending on you.'

Fortis resisted the temptation to point out once again that he had not agreed to her proposition. He restricted himself to giving a slight nod.

'Eutychus is dining with her and her uncle tonight.

Every night she and that reprobate uncle of hers entertain. There's gambling and conversation. Imagine what that would do to Eutychus's reputation if it got out.' Sempronia looked over both her shoulders, beckoned Fortis forward and then said in a hoarse whisper. 'How fond he is of dancing.'

'You do say.' Fortis could all too easily imagine the scene and Sempronia's worry now made sense. A reputation for dancing was not considered suitable for any who wanted to become a Senator. That was unless they wanted to be for ever tarred with the term 'loose belt'. Equally many of the best families would lock up their daughters before they would allow them to be associated with such a person.

'You will save poor Eutychus for me.' Sempronia reached out and clutched Fortis's hand. 'I have such high hopes for his career in the Senate. It can't be over before it has begun.'

'I will do what I can.'

She'd play her part to perfection tonight. Then she'd convince her uncle there was another way to find the money for Crispus to become a junior tribune. A favour from a friend of a friend, perhaps—something that did not require coin.

The only thing Baiae did was to suck money from them and make them fodder for jealous gossip.

Maybe it was time for them to return to Rome and begin again. Silvana touched the tiny statue in her make-up cupboard for luck. The sea water must have addled her head more than she thought. Her uncle would never return to Rome. He enjoyed his soirées too much.

She arranged her *stola* so that the V of the neckline was more pronounced. She was the female attraction, the bait. Witty and charming, she told herself, not exhausted and overwrought. She had slept for about an hour since she returned home; even then her dreams had been filled with tall dark men who had sleepy green eyes.

Thankfully, Lyde, her tire-woman, had only raised an eyebrow when she saw the state of Silvana's gown, saying that the fuller would probably be able to get the worst of the stains out. Now, with her hair pinned into a tumble of tight curls and her violet gown immaculately draped about her body, Silvana was barely recognisable from this morning's sea witch.

Soon the dining room would be full of men and one or two women who no longer had a reputation to lose, seeking relief from the day's cares and ways to lighten their purse. This was Baiae and not censorious Rome. Here, people came to play, to laugh and to live a little. To escape from the worries and constrictions of everyday life. And who was she to pass judgement?

After supper, the dice and the boards for twelve lines, a popular game of counters and dice, would come out, more people would arrive and the real business of the evening would begin—gaming. Officially it was banned in Baiae, the same as in Rome, but if you knew the right people and were prepared to pay, the *aediles* would turn a blind eye. After the money had changed hands, and the wine had been drunk, the dancing would begin and she'd gracefully retire. Of course, the gossips and those jealous about not receiving an invitation would have it that she stayed.

As she turned from the makeup cupboard, her veil caught the statue and sent it crashing to the ground. Silvana ran a finger down the girl's face before she placed the figurine back on its stand next to the gladiator figurine Crispus had sent for a saturnalia present. How far she had come from the innocent girl depicted here and how much they were still alike. She straightened her shoulders and started towards the reception rooms.

'Silvana Junia, come. Our guests arrive,' her uncle called out in his most jovial host voice. 'See, here is Pius Eutychus and his cousin. If you do not attend him, I fear your swain will slip through your fingers. I feel certain he has had six or seven dinner invitations.'

'Your uncle jokes, Silvana,' Eutychus said, as she entered the room. 'You know my heart belongs to you and you alone.'

Silvana turned towards her would-be admirer. Today he was dressed in dining clothes of the purest apricot. He had grown a goatee beard that was at odds with his black curly hair. The very picture of a 'loose belt', one of the elite of Baiae. He had a pleasing manner and would make some girl a good husband, but not her. She had the same sort of fondness for him as she did for her brother.

'Eutychus, I did not think to see you tonight.' Silvana forced her voice to be light as she held out her hand to be kissed.

'Silvana Junia, you are a joy to behold, a veritable goddess, but you do tease me. You knew I would be here.' Eutychus raised her hands to his mouth with an exaggerated sigh. He gestured behind him. 'Permit me to introduce my cousin, Lucius Aurelius Fortis. Fortis, this is the goddess I have been filling your ears with. See what light she brings to the room.'

From the shadows stepped her rescuer. Silvana pressed her hand to her mouth. How could she ever have thought the man safe? Even the way he moved was dangerous and untamed.

Dressed in diaphanous dining clothes of a light violet, a colour she had always considered a woman's colour, he ought to look effeminate, but somehow the colour underscored his raw masculinity, contrasting with the bronze of his arms and face. The lightness of the cloth meant the hard contours of his body were clearly visible—even his muscular thighs were hinted at. Definitely not safe.

Silvana swallowed hard and realised that Eutychus was saying something to her and would expect her to respond. She had to say something, but nothing that would reveal her earlier encounter with Fortis.

'We have not yet had the pleasure of your company at our dining table, Aurelius Fortis.' Silvana made sure her smile included both Fortis and Eutychus.

'A matter I am hoping to remedy, *Silvana Junia.*' Fortis captured her hand and brought it to his lips. A wild tremor ran up her arm. 'Eutychus has been extolling its delights.'

'My cousin just arrived in Baiae,' Eutychus said in his bouncing, puppyish way. 'But he will be here for the rest of the season.'

The rest of the season? Silvana blinked. She had expected to put the whole experience in a tightly sealed chest. Now she would be encountering Fortis again, hearing about him.

'And are you enjoying your visit to our pleasant town so far?' she asked cautiously.

'I have found it…enchanting. So many new experiences,' Fortis murmured, his dark gaze firmly on her mouth.

Silvana choked back the words asking what those experiences were. She forced a tinkling laugh. 'Baiae is famed for its new experiences as well as its purple-skinned oysters.'

A green light flashed in his eyes. 'And nymphs. I heard Baiae is quite famous for them.'

'Stories told around a brazier, I am afraid.' Silvana shrugged a shoulder. 'Tell me why Baiae should be interested in you?'

'Fortis has just finished his year as *Queastor* in Rome. He was elected the very first year he was eligible. They say he may even become a consul one day,' Eutychus chimed in eagerly.

'The pole of Roman politics is very greasy indeed, young Eutychus. It is not good to tempt the Fates in that manner,' Fortis said. 'One false move, one scandal, and a career could lie in ruins.'

'A single scandal?' Silvana pretended to scan the rapidly growing crowd. She tapped a finger against her mouth. 'How many careers will be ruined tonight? I see four senators have arrived already.'

'That will all depend on what you have planned for the evening's entertainment.' Fortis lifted an eyebrow. 'Eutychus and I are safe for now. But scandals are a serious business to a young man beginning his career.'

'Tell me, Aurelius Fortis, how many paragons does that snake pit of a Senate boast?' Silvana gave a light laugh. 'I can think of nary a one…except maybe Cato the Younger, and even he has Servilia as a half-sister—and you know what they say about her. Everyone knows Roman politics is a nasty business.'

'I would be a fool to deny the rough and tumble of Roman politics.' Fortis's eyes assessed her and Silvana wished she had worn something more modest. 'Maybe I have seen far too many would-be senators' careers cut short through an ill-advised alliance. I merely sought to warn my cousin. According to the augurs at his birth, his destiny is to reach far.'

'Fortis is much too modest,' Eutychus said. 'His queastorship was a model, or at least I heard one of the consuls say that to Mother. He is the best hope for reaching the consulship that the Aurelii have had in three generations. Some day his wax mask will hang proudly in the atrium and be paraded at all the funerals.'

'I hope it will be a long time before that happens.' Fortis gave a mocking bow. 'Do not seek to write my eulogy yet, cousin. I remain on this side of the River Styx.'

Eutychus coloured. 'That is not what I meant… Oh, Silvana, do say that you understand. I meant to compliment him.'

Silvana gave a laugh. Eutychus looked so downcast, worried that he had offended his idol. She hoped that Fortis encouraged the boy in the right way. 'It is all right, Eutychus, I understood what you meant. I will agree that it will take more than one scandal to cause Fortis to slip from his position on the pole.'

'Silvana, I knew you would understand. Isn't she enchanting, Fortis? Just like I told you she would be.'

Fortis tilted his head to one side, assessing her. Silvana stared straight back at him, her gaze caught by his full lips. The memory of how they had tasted flooded through her—she wanted to taste them again. Silvana looked away, but not before a knowing smile had crossed Fortis's face.

'Tell me, Silvana Junia, do people swim much in the bay?'

'It would depend on the circumstance. It has been known to happen.' A tingle ran down her spine. 'I should imagine it would be very cold indeed in those waters.'

Eutychus looked aghast. 'Fortis, Silvana teases. I have never seen anyone swim in the bay. Can you imagine the scandal?'

'I can, indeed, and I was not suggesting Silvana Junia had ever swum in the bay...voluntarily.' Fortis's green gaze held hers firmly in its grip.

'Only if I was forced,' Silvana replied and watched the muscles in Fortis's neck relax.

'I expected no less.' He gave a slight nod.

'It is my intention to make a marriage offer for Silvana Junia,' Eutychus broke in. 'You must not insult her by making such an infamous suggestion. You will have to answer to me soon.'

'I was not insulted,' Silvana replied. She pressed her fingertips together. She had become used to Eutychus's declarations of undying love and offers of marriage. He had chosen to ignore her refusal and she chose to ignore his repeated offerings. She felt sure it was a habit that would vanish in due course. But neither did she want him making any claim he was not entitled to. 'My honour is safe.'

'I am pleased to hear that.' Fortis bent over her hand and raised the tips of her fingers to his lips. 'I would hate to insult you *unintentionally.*'

'May you pass a pleasant time in our fair town, with or without swimming.' Silvana leant forward. 'But in case Eutychus has not told you, the Temple of Mercury boasts an indoor bathing pool, heated from the thermal water. Many people find it pleasant to swim there, much warmer than the bay.'

'And do you swim there regularly?' His green eyes twinkled with hidden lights.

'Only with women.'

'What a pity Baiae does not yet condone mixed bathing.'

'There are some things even Baiae does not dare.'

'And you, Silvana, do you dare?' Fortis's voice dropped to a whisper. 'Is it something you long to do?'

Silvana straightened her back. She was not going to think about what it might be like to bathe with Fortis. The kiss they had shared was bad enough. Her life had no room for such attractions. She had to keep her wits about her and remember why she was here: and her duty towards her uncle and, more importantly, Crispus's career prospects. She'd go now. 'If you will excuse me, Aurelius Fortis and Eutychus, there are other guests I must attend.'

Fortis watched the back of Silvana, her skirts gently swaying. He heard her laughter as she stopped to greet her uncle's guests. Her hair, which had fallen in wild tendrils this morning, was now tame and piled on the top of her head. Her face was painted with wine dregs and shimmering powder. Her gap-sleeve gown hugged her figure. The perfectly poised woman, the height of Baiae society, smiling and greeting the more recent arrivals. Save for her storm-tossed eyes, there was no hint of the sea witch he had pulled out of the bay this morning.

He allowed his gaze to wander around the atrium. Silvana and her uncle had an odd assortment of guests—senators mingled freely with freedmen and those on the make. In the corners of the room, several were already gambling, playing *micatio,* the game of odds and evens where the players had to guess the number of fingers that their opponent held out. No doubt the dice and the gaming boards would appear later and continue throughout the evening, even when the dancing began.

'Junius Maius appears to have captured the attention of the early season visitors to Baiae.'

'More than captured.' Eutychus leant forward. 'It is all the rage. Silvana's beauty is renowned and her uncle is judged to keep a good table. Plus the entertainment is unparalleled—musicians every night. Invitations to dine are highly prized. You have no idea the trouble I went to, to get you an invitation. Most have to arrive later when the gaming starts.'

'Interesting.' Fortis heard the light chimes of Silvana's laughter over the latest crowd of people to surge through the door. 'And Silvana Junia presides over it all?'

'Silvana Junia is a goddess. The reigning queen of Baiae.' Eutychus gave a lovelorn sigh. 'Now do you understand, Fortis? You must help me persuade Mother. Silvana Junia is simply divine. I worship the ground she walks on.'

'In my experience, worship is not a good place to start a marriage.' Fortis picked up a goblet of wine from a tray offered by a servant. He took a cautious sip. While not Falerian, the honey wine was of a good vintage and had not been overly mixed with water. Was it any wonder establishments such as these rarely showed a profit?

'Mother has already spoken to you.' Eutychus's mouth twisted. 'I tell you, I will marry Silvana Junia and no other. Once you get to know her, you will see what she is really like. No woman would be good enough for me in Mother's eyes, you know that.'

Fortis swirled his wine. There was some truth in Eutychus's statement. Aunt Sempronia had already rejected two possible candidates on the grounds that they wouldn't understand her son. However, he knew the sort of woman Silvana Junia was and there was no way he intended to let his young cousin marry a notorious widow of Baiae.

'You remind me of another young man. He made statements like that,' Fortis said quietly. 'Has she agreed to marry you, then? Have the betrothal agreements been signed?'

'She no longer laughs at me when I propose.'

Eutychus made an earnest face. 'I have great hopes. She accepted a poem from me. I took it as a sign. She will come around. If only that awful Drusus Cotta would stop sniffing around. She doesn't like him. I know that. And then there is Leoparda, Bato and a number of other tribunes who are nearly always here, but she has singled me out for special attention.'

Fortis laid a hand on Eutychus's shoulder. 'You have much to learn about women, Eutychus.'

Eutychus shook the hand off. His bottom lip stuck out. 'And what do you know? Your marriage did not last even six months, and you have never remarried. How many years has it been—five?'

'It has been seven years since she died.' Fortis closed his eyes, and willed himself to keep his temper. His cousin was as hot tempered as he had been at that age.

'Silvana isn't one of those Baiae women Mother gossips about, Fortis. She is a very nice person. Yes, I know that her uncle is rather effusive, but she is different, real character. You should talk to her, get to know her. She had a hard life. I can tell from her eyes. Did you know she supports her younger brother?'

'I will make my own judgement in due course.'

'I knew you would be on my side.' Eutychus clapped Fortis on the shoulder. 'Mother is far too concerned about appearances. She looks down on these dinner parties that Silvana's uncle gives. She doesn't approve of the mix of people.'

'Aunt Sempronia always did like preserving the niceties of society.'

'Exactly.' Eutychus gave a wide grin. 'She never goes to such places, but you do.'

'I may frequent these sorts of places on occasion, but I have never wanted to marry anyone from them.'

'Give her a chance. Once you get to know her, you will see Silvana Junia is different.'

Fortis regarded Silvana as she plucked a hair from a senator's cloak, her eyes shining with hidden mischief and her light silk gown revealing a little more of her curves than strictly necessary. She was not the right woman for his cousin. Every fibre of his body told him that.

Chapter Three

'Have the musicians arrived yet? They're late and we can't have a dinner party without musicians. Our guests expect dancing.' Silvana heard her uncle call out from where she stood on the second floor's loggia, gazing out at the white-capped water. She had retreated here after her encounter with Fortis to repair something of her tattered nerves. She had thought herself prepared for everything, but she found it difficult not to remember the feel of his lips against hers.

She didn't need the complication of a love affair now. Not when she was trying to secure Crispus his position. He would be arriving back from his school in a few days' time and his latest letter spoke of his anticipation and nervous excitement at becoming a junior tribune.

How could she tell him that, no, Uncle Aulus had lost the money?

The pounding of Silvana's head increased. Eventually she would sleep, but first she had this dinner party to get through. She had thought it would be an easy matter, but then Fortis had appeared, and she knew she was far more on edge than she had imagined.

Should she simply plead a headache or would Fortis correctly guess that she was running away? She fingered her amber necklace and gazed once more at the sunset-lit sea.

'Silvana, the musicians! I swear today you are away with the nymphs and dryads.' Her uncle appeared in the doorway of the loggia, dressed in his second set of dining clothes of the evening, this time a vibrant yellow in a fine linen. His belt was loosely draped around his middle, proudly proclaiming his allegiance to the fashionable set. Silvana dreaded to think what the bill would be. 'I can't give a dinner party without musicians. It was bad enough not to have them here for when our first guests arrived, but the meal is about to begin. I will be the laughing stock of Baiae, I tell you!'

The gods had decided for her. She would have to return and manage the musicians, soothe any ruffled guests. Their future prosperity depended on the guests returning night after night.

'The musicians have arrived,' she said, 'You can hear one tuning up his lyre if you listen.'

Uncle Aulus tilted his head and gave a grunt. 'Their performance had best be more accomplished than the last time. To think the amount of money I pay them. The last lot couldn't even keep a decent tune.'

'I know we can't afford to buy any musicians but, Uncle Aulus, would it do any harm if we occasionally hired a Greek poet to recite? I have heard of one or two who have excellent reputations.'

'To have to listen to dreary reciting would put me off my meal.' Her uncle gave a shudder. 'This is what people expect of a meal at Junius Maius's house: a pleasant time, a bit of gambling, perhaps some dancing. A Greek intoning his philosophies, never!'

'Uncle, is it time to think about economies?'

'Economies, my darling niece? You are asking me to economise? People will talk if I start to economise. They will find another place to go for their after-dinner entertainment. Need I remind you how much I earn off the gambling and the little tips about shipments…'

Silvana rubbed her temple. One of those little tips had led to her trip out on the Bay of Naples with Cotta the Younger.

'They would come.'

'Humph. You may be an acclaimed wit, Silvana, but you don't know anything about the fickleness of men.' Uncle Aulus stroked his chin. 'No, Silvana, we carry on as we have done for the past year and a half. I provide the hospitality and the decoration that loosens men's tongues. We make a good team, you and I.'

Silvana gave a small smile. Her uncle tried so hard for all of them—herself and Crispus. It was not his fault that several of his business ventures hadn't worked out. She'd always be grateful to him for offering her a home after her husband died. He had been the only one of her relatives to understand when she refused to remarry. 'Yes, Uncle.'

'Silvana, don't look at me like that.' He put a hand on her shoulder. 'My luck will turn, you'll see, and these last few months will become but a distant memory.'

'Yes, Uncle.'

'There was no joy, I suppose, with young Cotta, your erstwhile stepson.'

'I believe he prefers to forget that he was ever related to me.' Silvana laid a hand on her uncle's arm. 'Please remember the adoption was only made formal on my husband's deathbed.'

'I had thought perhaps... He had seemed so interested the other night.'

Interested in what? Silvana bit back the words. Flinging accusations was not going to make her error of judgement go away. She should have foreseen the potential problem on the yacht. She should never have stepped foot on the yacht.

'I will do many things for you, Uncle Aulus, you know that, but I will not play a daughter of Venus. Not for you, not for anyone and particularly not with Cotta the Younger.'

Her uncle stared open-mouthed at her.

'Is that what the young cub wanted? I should take a horse whip to him.'

'Nothing happened. And remember—he still holds the scroll to this villa.'

Her uncle crumpled slightly before her eyes. 'I will find a way, Silvana. I would never have taken a loan against the house if I had thought there was the slightest chance of losing it.'

'There has to be a way, though...' Silvana tapped her finger against her mouth. 'We were doing so well...'

'There is no chance of you marrying young Eutychus, I suppose? Rumour has it that he will gain control of his fortune in a few months time. I saw him making sheep's eyes at you just now.'

Silvana lowered her gaze to the chipped black-and-white mosaic floor, the picture of demure womanhood. Uncle Aulus was her guardian. He could force her to marry whomever he wanted. And she had no intention of returning to that state of unbliss any sooner than she could possibly help.

'Eutychus is young, Uncle.'

'You have had an ancient husband. The gods only know what your father intended, agreeing to marry you to that old reprobate. Why not live a little? Eutychus is far from repulsive.'

But she wasn't attracted to him. Silvana bit back the protest and refused to think about the cousin she was attracted to. That attraction had to end before it had even begun. 'I think I hear the musicians.'

'You are trying to change the subject away from your marriage, Silvana.' Her uncle shook his finger at her. 'You and your brother are the only family I have got. Why wouldn't I want to see you well provided for?'

'We couldn't afford the dowry,' Silvana said, plucking a stray piece of lint off his dining clothes. 'Not with Crispus's junior tribuneship unsettled. Please let me handle this my way. We will find a solution, but not by marrying someone I have no desire for.'

Her uncle's eyes twinkled. 'Only if you will continue to let me have the musicians.'

Silvana put a hand to her face and, laughing, shook her head. 'You are incorrigible, Uncle. More of our guests will be arriving.'

'And I have not inspected the wine.' Her uncle gave a huge sigh. 'The sacrifices I make for you, but families stick together. I mean that, Silvana. My family means the world to me. Now, back to our guests before they begin to mutter about economies.'

Silvana returned to find the courtyard more crowded than ever. The brittle voices were discussing the latest indiscretion. Something about a gladiator, thankfully, and not her swim. The more time that passed, the less likely that it would be seen to be a major scandal. A minor indiscretion, but these things were expected from the notorious Silvana Junia.

'You have returned.' Fortis's voice flowed over her. He was standing by the doorway, a goblet of wine in his hand. The light from the oil lamps caught the folds of his tunic, highlighting his muscular legs.

'There were a few things I had to see to. The house doesn't run itself.' Silvana resisted the temptation to pat her hair and smooth her gown. Fortis had tracked her movements. The thought gave her a tiny glow of pleasure.

'You relieve me. I had worried that it was something I did or said.' The twinkle in his eyes increased.

He was flirting with her. She had flirted a thousand times before, but for some reason he made her feel awkward, as if she had barely crossed the threshold of the schoolroom or sacrificed her dolls to Venus.

'You have behaved perfectly properly…tonight.' She inclined her head.

'And are you saying I didn't behave properly this morning?' He reached out and touched her elbow, holding her there. 'I behaved, I thought, in a gentle-manly fashion. Of course, if you would have preferred me to leave you stranded for any passer-by to see…'

'I would prefer my doings were not common currency for gossip.' Silvana prepared to sweep past. The way this conversation was going was a mistake. In another sentence or two, he would make a remark about the kiss.

'I have offended you.' A furrow appeared between his eyebrows.

'I believe that was your intent.' Silvana glared him. 'You have deliberately sought to provoke me.'

'If I sought to deliberately insult you, you would know.' His eyes searched her face. He captured her fingers and raised them to his lips. 'If I have given some offence, I humbly apologise, beautiful lady.'

Silvana withdrew her hand. 'A pretty speech. No doubt you are practised in them. Your cousin is also given to pretty speeches.'

He lifted an eyebrow. 'And you are not fond of them.'

'One pretty speech is much like another.' Silvana drew a deep breath. She was back in control now. She knew the rules of the game. Fortis was like a hundred other men who attended her uncle's parties. After one thing and one thing only. She had to remember that. 'Flirtation is one of the games people play on the sands of Baiae.'

'And you know about playing games.' His eyes hardened.

'After two years in Baiae, I have become adept.' Her mind swept back to the girl she was before her marriage. 'I have to be.'

'Tell me, Silvana Junia, do you enjoy them?'

'It depends on the game.' She turned on her heel and walked away before she revealed any more of herself to the man.

Silvana threw herself into the dinner party, trying to forget Fortis was standing there, watching her every move. Between the new arrivals and smoothing over the minor mishaps, she barely had any time to think, but her whole being seemed to be aware of him.

After the food had been served, she noticed the once-pristine tunics the guests wore had become splattered with food and wine, the jokes more feeble and the laughter louder. She gave a prearranged signal to the musicians, who started playing a livelier tune. Soon the cloaks would be discarded and the dancing would begin. She would make her excuses and depart as she always did before the entire evening descended into its customary chaos.

She glanced over to where Fortis reclined, and saw to her surprise that he, for one, had no splatters on his dining clothes. He raised his goblet to her and she glanced away. An acquaintance of her uncle's, a self-made man, noticed where her gaze had fallen and leant over, speculating how much Aurelius Fortis's dining clothes must have cost.

Silvana's pleasantry died on her lips. In the doorway, looking like a giant black spider, was her adopted stepson. In the whirl that was the dinner party, she had forgotten about him. But he had appeared at the very time guaranteed to give the most publicity. There was no hope for it. She would have to greet him, and hope that he'd realise he could do far more damage to his own reputation than to her already tarnished one.

Silvana rose from her wicker chair. She forced her feet to glide in an unhurried pace. She was the hostess, greeting a tardy guest—that was all.

'Cotta, what a pleasant surprise.' She put on her best hostess voice. 'I had no idea you were coming to dine. We have already started on the final course, but I am sure space can be found at one of the couches for you.'

'Ah, Silvana Junia, I had wondered if you might be here.'

'Why wouldn't I be here?' Silvana asked. She refused to panic. She had to be right on her first assessment—Cotta would not want the news broadcasted that he had made his stepmother an offer and she had chosen to brave the waters of the Bay of Naples rather than sleep with him.

'I heard you were indisposed.' Cotta frowned. 'You looked a bit peaked last evening when we dined. I feared you might have a chill.'

'I fear you were misinformed. I am in the best of health.' Silvana tilted her head to one side and decided to go on the attack. "Why are you here, Cotta?"

'Your slippers have been delivered to your room.' Cotta made a bow. 'I remembered how fond you are of pretty things. A gift from my late father, I believe. I thought only to return to you something of value, as I know what a great store you put on objects,' he said, between gritted teeth. 'And my offer of last night still stands.'

'Once again, I must decline.' Silvana lowered her lashes and prayed it would be the last time. 'I can only hope we remain friends.'

'Drusus Cotta the Younger, how good it is to see

you again,' Fortis said, coming to stand by Silvana's shoulder. 'How long has it been since Bithynia?'

'Aurelius Fortis, I had heard rumours you had arrived. I trust all is well with Rome.'

'When I left, the Forum stood.'

'Your presence here is intriguing.' Cotta gestured about him. 'It is not your type of haunt. A bit down-market for you.'

'My cousin is enamoured of the company.' Fortis brushed a speck of dust off his tunic. 'And I find it very charming.'

Cotta pursed his lips and Silvana waited for an outburst, but he appeared to control his temper.

'Having done my duty, I will now depart for more congenial surroundings,' Cotta said, making a sweeping bow.

Silvana released a breath. He had gone and without incident. She heard the rattle of dice and clank of goblets being refilled with wine as the noise in the dining room started to swell again.

'No one noticed your encounter, and Cotta has left. Relax and you will be fine,' Fortis said in an undertone.

'Am I that transparent?' Silvana resisted the impulse to draw her veil across her face.

'Your cheeks are flushed and your eyes hold a determined glint.'

'Are you well acquainted with my former stepson?' It would be her misfortune to have been rescued by one of Cotta's associates.

'We served as junior tribunes together, much to both our regrets.' There was no mistaking the steely determination in Fortis's voice. 'He can be unpleasant when the mood strikes.'

Silvana bit her lip. It was bad enough having his help earlier. One lesson she had learnt was nothing ever came free. 'It was a little family misunderstanding. Everything is solved.'

'Now that he has returned your slippers.' Fortis's eyes became colder. 'I could not help overhearing.'

Silvana fought the impulse to laugh wildly. The slippers had nothing to do with the problem. Cotta was merely renewing his offer. The next time he would make sure she could not escape until she bowed to his wishes.

'It is something I do not like to talk about.' Silvana kept her eyes trained on the mosaic tiles. 'If you will forgive me, I shall retire. This evening has been rather fraught.'

'But I thought you led the dancing.'

'There are some things that the gossips exaggerate, Aurelius Fortis.' Silvana drew herself up. 'I fear my dancing is one of them. I rarely dance and only occasionally play the lyre.'

'Unless you have no other alternative.'

'There are things one does to survive.'

Silvana felt his eyes assess her.

'Stay. Play a game of twelve lines with me,' Fortis said. 'I noticed there are several boards set up. The evening is still young.'

Silvana started. Her gaze flew upwards to his piercing green eyes. 'Is there any particular reason?'

'My cousin has spoken very highly of you. I wish to spend some time in your company, getting better acquainted. I understand you are a keen player.'

'Eutychus is a very pleasant young man. His tongue is overly given to flattery.' Silvana gave a strangled laugh.

The true reason for Fortis's appearance here was obvious. She had been wishing on Venus's sparrows to think he was here because he wanted to see her again, that somehow he had appointed himself her official protector. But he was here because of his outspoken cousin. No doubt his repeated claims of betrothal had reached his relatives' ears. If anyone approached her, she'd be quite happy to explain— she found him amusing, but she had no intention of ever marrying him. In due course, his infatuation would vanish and he'd find a more appropriate bride.

She had seen it happen before. Many times.

She liked the young man and wanted to keep him

out of the clutches of the harpies who inhabited some of the villas. They would not see his shy smile, or his good nature. All they would see was his inheritance and how they could help him spend it.

'You do not appear to take him seriously.'

'If I took every young junior tribune who passed through my uncle's dining room seriously, my head would be too big to fit through a door.' Silvana gave a small laugh and signalled for a twelve-lines board. 'No, Aurelius Fortis, I do not believe compliments as they are too easily given. Do we play this game for money or for pleasure?'

'For both. Isn't that how things are done in Baiae?'

'Baiae, like Rome, welcomes profit.' Silvana took a sip of her wine. 'There is nothing wrong with it.'

'And do all things have a price?'

'You are a cynic, Aurelius Fortis.'

'I prefer—a realist.'

'Shall we play?' Silvana reached for her counters. 'And it will be for money.'

'I understand from my unreliable cousin that you are a very accomplished player. It has been a long time since I have seen such beauty and skill combined.' His eyes were fixed firmly on her lips. 'But I forget, you have no liking for compliments. Forget I said the last.'

'I am fond of them. What woman wouldn't be? I

simply choose to believe other things.' Silvana shrugged a shoulder. 'We shall see if your skill matches mine.'

'I think it will prove more than adequate.' Fortis reached for the dice and placed them in a shaker. His long narrow fingers held the shaker out to her. 'Unless you have changed your mind and don't wish to face me.'

'I am not afraid of you.'

'Good.' He turned his hand and she could see a faint white scar on the palm.

The memory of his hand holding hers, hauling her up on to the harbour wall, assaulted her and she nearly dropped the shaker. Silvana bit her lip. If she wanted to win, she would have to pay attention and stop looking at his hands. Twelve lines was one of the most popular games in Baiae because it required skill, luck and utmost concentration. She had to trust the goddess Fortunata would not desert her.

'You will find your purse lighter at the end of the match.' Silvana sank down on a stool opposite Fortis and reached for her stack of counters and another dice shaker. She rolled one of her dice. A six. 'It would appear my luck is in tonight.'

'Two hundred *denarii* is the usual opening stake in this house, or so my cousin informs me.'

'Your cousin is correct. The games here are for the

serious gambler.' Silvana gave a light laugh, but her body was alert to what he might do next.

Fortis reached into his arm purse and placed a stack of coins on the table. 'Do you have coins or do you play with a tablet?'

'You are a welcome guest. Here we play with a tablet and you can settle the debt at the end of the evening or the next morning. The system makes it easier to concentrate on the game.'

Fortis gave a nod and scooped the coins back into his purse. He threw the dice. A two. 'Your move, Silvana Junia.'

Silvana's hand trembled as she started to place the first of her fifteen counters on the centre word. The game board's message spelt out: Hunting, Bathing, Playing Games, This is the Life. Not a bad omen, but she would have preferred another.

'Shall we increase the stakes?' Fortis asked after she had easily won the first match. 'Make this game more intriguing?'

'I thought it was only one game you wanted.'

'It is not often I encounter a player of your skill and talent.' Fortis swept his hand through his hair, making it stand upright. 'I fear I may have taken too much to drink at dinner. Allow me the chance to get even, unless of course you are worried that your winning was a fluke.'

Silvana looked down at her counters. Her skill won the game. She was certain of that. 'I do play the game nearly every night.'

'Then, where is your hurry to leave?' Fortis reached out and covered her hand with his.

Silvana allowed her hand to stay there, briefly. She knew what this game was about now. He wanted to get to know her better. She had encountered men like him before, and yet this time she wanted Fortis to be different, to want her for herself, rather than the thrill of being linked with one of Baiae's hostesses. She busied her fingers with moving the counters about. 'It is your money. Shall we say three hundred and fifty *denarii* for the winner of this match?'

'Four hundred.'

'Four hundred it is, then.' Silvana made a note and then rolled the dice—a five and a six. Fortunata was indeed with her tonight. She wanted to laugh out loud. Her sense of jubilation increased as this game too went her way. She couldn't lose. She had been in this position too many times before. Fortis had made several simple errors. 'Shall we increase the size of the bet to five hundred?'

'If you wish...' A small smile crossed Fortis's face as he considered the offer. 'You like to take a risk.'

'A calculated risk.'

Silvana took another look at the game board. Was there any way he could win? She drew her eyebrows together. One way, but the possibility was so remote she had overlooked it. She glanced up into Fortis's deep green eyes. She had to hope he had not seen the chance either.

'Consider the stake raised.'

Silvana concentrated, shook the dice but one rolled off the table. Fortis bent to retrieve it. His warm fingertips touched hers. A tingling sensation went up Silvana's arm. She jerked it back as if she were burnt.

'Are you sure you can afford to lose the money?' he asked quietly. 'It is rather a large sum and I'd hate to think I was responsible for you jumping into the sea again.'

'I have not lost yet. Nor do I intend to.'

However, her hands shook slightly as she rolled the dice. Two dogs. Not what she wanted. It gave Fortis a slight advantage, one that he took readily.

After that, the game seemed to get away from her. Fortis played with a lazy skill, but took every point. Where she had been ahead, now she was behind. She threw again and went ahead. In her next turn, she'd win unless Fortis threw a double six.

He shook the dice. With a sickening thud of her

heart, Silvana watched first one six and then the other appear. She blinked rapidly.

'My game, I believe,' Fortis said, removing his last counter. 'You owe me five hundred *denarii.*'

Silvana stared at the board uncomprehendingly. She had lost. For the first time in months, years, she had lost at twelve lines.

'How? How did that happen?'

'A game is never won until the last roll, Silvana. My father told me that and it is something I live by.'

Silvana wanted to weep. She had been over-confident. She hated to think what it would do to the household expenses. Then there was Crispus to think of. She should never have taken the chance, upped the bet to that level. Her throat closed. 'Yes, of course. Silly of me, really. I will go and get you the money.'

His hand reached out and forced her to sit back down. His eyes assessed her. A faint gleam of something appeared in them.

'I will consider the debt paid, if you will come for a walk with me tomorrow morning. I wish to speak with you about something in private.'

Silvana tilted her head and regarded him through her lashes. His face was bland, but she saw a muscle jump in his jaw. What did he want?

'That is a large purse of coins for a walk.'

'Maybe, but it is my money.'

'You need not be kind to me. We have the money.'

'Kindness has nothing to do with it, Silvana.' Fortis expertly replaced the counters in the container.

'You know how to play twelve lines.'

Fortis gave a deep husky laugh. 'It is played in other places besides Baiae. Eutychus will tell you that I made quite a name for myself with the game.'

'You tricked me!'

'A little,' he admitted, his eyes crinkling at the corners. 'Will you come for the walk with me…unless you are frightened of being seen with me?'

'Alone? Are your intentions honourable?' Silvana gave a laugh and tried to keep her mind from returning to this morning. That too had only been a walk and it had ended in a soul-searing kiss.

Silvana reached for a wax tablet. She couldn't afford the *denarii,* but she was not that easily bought. Exactly what were Fortis's intentions?

'I do not seek to ruin your reputation.' Fortis's hand covered hers, preventing her from writing. The touch was but an instant, but it was enough to send a tingle through her body. 'Only to speak with you. Which will it be, the coins that you can ill afford or a short stroll with a man who promises to behave impeccably?'

Silvana ran her tongue over her suddenly dry lips.

These were much higher stakes than money, she was certain of it. A green flame glowed in his eyes. She scooped up her counters, put them back in the box. 'You leave me very little option.'

Chapter Four

A single olive-oil lamp shone in the *tablinum* of Fortis's villa. Like the rest of the house, the furnishings of the main living room wore a disused air. It had been seven years at least since he had last lived here for any length of time. If he intended on staying, the leak in the hanging bath would have to be fixed, the shutters in the dining room needed renewing but, most of all, the entire house was in urgent need of redecoration. It was difficult to believe that once his taste had run to dancing-girl frescoes and statues of nymphs. Those items would not have looked out of place at the Junia compound, but here they were an unwelcome reminder of ages past.

He could clearly recall Murcia's pleasure in the room when it was finally finished. It was only later, after her death, that he discovered exactly why.

Fortis handed his dining cloak to Merlus, his

manservant. Merlus bowed low, the golden glow from the oil lamp glinting off his bald head.

'Enjoyable evening?' Merlus asked as he busied himself with ostentatiously folding the cloak. His desire to be the ultimate manservant surprised Fortis, as he had discovered Merlus half-dead after a gladiatorial bout. Merlus's days in the ring might be over, but he served as a useful bodyguard. His only fault was his belief that his opinion on all things should be heard.

'I have had worse.' Fortis picked a tablet off the table, scanned it. 'When did this arrive?'

'Shortly after you left, master. Is it important?'

Fortis tapped the small piece of wood against the carved table. 'It could be, but there again, it is all too convenient. I arrive in Baiae and suddenly a good-spirited citizen decides to inform me of pirate activity to the south of here in Surrentum. I think not.'

Merlus pursed his lips. 'It is up to you, sir. Did you discover that devotee to the arts of Venus that Pius Eutychus is enamoured of? No good ever comes of such women.'

'And what would you know about society women, Merlus?' Fortis raised an eyebrow. 'While I am well aware of your extensive experience with barmaids and hairdressers, I was unaware of your expertise in the more gently bred members of the fairer sex.'

'You'd be surprised.' Merlus brought a glass of muslum wine and several wheat-and-honey cakes on a tray. 'Society women are gladiator-mad. We used to have to beat them away with a stick. Fancied a bit of the rough, some of them, and I was only too happy to oblige.'

'Even you?' Fortis did not bother to hide his surprise. Merlus had suffered several broken noses and his nose was now more crooked than straight, and a jagged scar ran down half the side of his face. 'I would have hardly said you were a Greek statue.'

'Even me, sir. It's the widows who are the worst. There was one time when three of them came at me—'

Fortis held up a hand. 'That is enough, Merlus. Even my limited imagination can supply the details.'

'Very good, sir.' Merlus was silent for a breath. 'Are you sure you don't want to hear about the widow who hid in the changing rooms?'

'Quite sure.' Fortis drained the cup, his eye drawn to one particular fresco. The woman held a garland out, her head tilted to one side, and her upturned lips reminded Fortis in no small measure of Silvana as she had been on the quayside. Innocent, untouched. Very different from the poised society hostess who had greeted him this evening and who had unashamedly indulged in flirtation—a woman from the same mould as his late wife.

'But tell me in your new guise as expert on the female sex, Merlus, what would you think of a woman who accepted a stroll with a man she had just met in lieu of paying a debt of five hundred *denarii?*'

'I would say whoever offered her the choice was a fool, a weak-minded fool. If you will pardon me saying so, sir.' Merlus shook his head gloomily. 'She won't show or she'll send her maid with an excuse and then the poor unfortunate will be left with his purse considerably lighter.'

'It is a possibility, Merlus.'

'I would wager a *denarius* that will be the case.' The manservant displayed a row of crooked teeth. 'And you know how I hate to part with a *denarius.*'

'Done.' Fortis gave a sweeping glance around the room. Something would really have to be done about this room, but not on this trip. There were enough echoes here to remind him of his youthful folly, and to prevent him from making the same mistake twice. 'Pack my bag and inform Pio that we are going on a small trip… Surrentum.'

'And the widow in question?'

'Will not be joining me.'

Merlus gave a low bow. 'Very good, sir.'

* * *

Fortis adjusted his travelling cloak as he waited outside the Junia villa. Despite the earliness of the hour, the cloudless sky gave a certainty of searing heat later. The clear sunlight lit the Junia villa, bathing it in golden brilliance. But the doorway remained empty with no sign of life stirring within.

An indication of the way Silvana intended to treat her promise?

Last night's performance with her quick turn of phrase and flashing eyes confirmed his suspicion his aunt was correct. Silvana Junia was definitely not the right woman for Eutychus.

The youth was a danger to himself. His open admiration of Silvana was leading to comment and speculation. No less than three senators had approached Fortis and asked if he looked forward to welcoming Silvana and her grasping uncle into the family.

Fortis tapped his fingers against the cold stone. The situation had to be delicately handled. All Sempronia had done so far was to drive Eutychus further into Silvana's circle. Eutychus was in the throes of calf-love. It would pass, but Fortis wanted to make sure it would pass with the least harm done. He knew all too well how an *adulescens* folly could blight a life.

No, the way to approach the matter was through the woman in question. Silvana Junia was a woman of the world in much the same manner as his late wife had been. He knew what motivated such creatures—money or trinkets. If approached in the right manner, he had no doubt he and Silvana could come to a convenient arrangement.

The door creaked and a figure wrapped from head to foot appeared, but the shawls and *stola* only accentuated Silvana's figure. In her hand she held a parasol to shield her face from the sun. Fortis frowned. He preferred the sea witch—at least she was free of artifice. He had not needed the dark mutterings of his manservant as he had dressed to remind him what such women were capable of. And here was one of the queens of Baiae. She extended her hand in a regal manner.

'Forgive my tardiness. My maid allowed me to oversleep.'

'When one is confronted with a vision, it makes the wait worth while.'

She raised an eyebrow. 'Another pretty compliment, Aurelius Fortis. How easily they come to you. Shall we go for the stroll you won from me?'

'It appears Merlus will owe me a *denarius* after all.'

'Who is this Merlus?' Silvana asked, tilting her head to one side and peeping at him from under her lashes. Her stormy eyes danced with hidden lights and a dimple appeared in the corner of her mouth. 'And why does he have such a low opinion of me? What have I done to offend?'

A studied move, Fortis reminded himself, designed to show her neck to its best advantage and entice the observer into a flirtation. He was no untried youth, but a veteran of many campaigns.

'My manservant.' Fortis inclined his head. 'He has a very low opinion of women. He said you would send your maid instead. I was being more generous. I thought you would come yourself with an excuse as to why today would not suit.'

'I have proved you both wrong.'

'You have indeed.'

'If I had done as your manservant or you suggest, the news of my deception would have spread through Baiae faster than a fire through Subura on a summer's day.' The flirtatious light vanished from Silvana's eyes. Her nostrils flared slightly, before she regained control of herself and her face became a smooth and bland mask of perfection. 'Who would come to my uncle's parties if it was known we did not honour our bets or pay our debts?'

'Faultless logic.' Fortis held out his arm. 'I will try not to detain you any longer than absolutely necessary. A simple stroll is all I require, but please listen to my words before rejecting them.'

Silvana tossed the end of her shawl over her shoulder. She hated having her motives easily dissected. It was better than Fortis guessing the truth—that she was attracted to him and intrigued to find out why he wanted to meet her. Intrigued enough that she was willing to bend her own private rules and meet him outside her uncle's villa.

She had expected him to be dressed in the conventional toga with a purple stripe as befitted his status as a senator; instead he wore a simple but elegant tunic and a travelling cloak that revealed his muscular calves. Silvana went back over their conversation last night. She winced. She had agreed on the walk, but not the duration of it.

Where exactly was he planning on taking her? And why were travelling clothes necessary?

She had behaved like a girl who had not sacrificed her dolls. Make sure of all the conditions. She should have been more specific. He had fooled her over his skill at twelve lines, lulled her into a false expectation. She was determined that this was not going to happen again to her. Already she had experienced near disaster with Cotta.

Exactly what did Fortis want from her? Five hundred *denarii* was too much to pay for a stroll of less than an hour. If he thought she would be accompanying him for the day, to continue their stroll along the beach, he could think again. She was wise to that sort of behaviour.

'My maid will accompany us.' Silvana nodded towards Lyde, who waited just inside the doorway. 'Where do you anticipate this journey will take us? You failed to mention the need for travelling clothes last evening.'

'To the seafront.' Fortis gave a nod towards the promenade. 'Eutychus assures me it is the fashionable thing to do.'

Silvana winced as she heard the excited voices on the breeze, digesting and spitting the latest morsel of gossip. Already the fashionable and those who wanted to be had begun to gather. Her appearance with Fortis would be sure to cause a few heads to turn. No doubt more than one matron would already know the precise reason he was escorting her, or would at least pretend to know. Silvana wondered what the gossips would ultimately decide.

Who had seduced whom? She doubted any would guess the truth, but it would be yet another minor scandal and she was strangely reluctant to expose Fortis to it.

'I thought you didn't care for fashion.'

'When in Baiae…' He made a little flourish with

his hand. 'It does my heart good to see that certain things about this place never change, that the world goes on much as it has always done.'

'You have passed time in Baiae.' Silvana tilted her head to one side, trying to assess him. Fortis's face was a bland mask, polite and a bit distant. The intensity of yesterday morning had vanished.

'In my misspent youth, I was well acquainted with this town and its many dubious pleasures.'

'Pleasure is what I like about this town.' Silvana gave a little twirl of her parasol. The word 'dubious' stung. She knew there were parts of the town, parts of the lifestyle, she detested, but here she was allowed to be free. 'Such a change from the dreariness of Rome. No one comments if a woman decides to join in discussions or even dances a few steps at a party.'

'The pursuit of pleasure is like honey cakes. One or two excite the palate but then they become sickly sweet. I need something more to my life.'

'You are not planning on staying in Baiae long.' Silvana tapped a finger against the handle of the parasol. The sooner she was through with this man the better. He had swept into town, passing a critical eye over the whole enterprise. No doubt when he returned to Rome, he would make a speech on the evils of Baiae and how depraved all its occupants were, particularly when they swam in the bay at night. 'And yet you have already passed judgement. Tell me, is it a difficult burden always being so stern?'

'I regret my duty calls me elsewhere. There are some properties in Surrentum I need to check. I am due to sail on the next tide.'

'I hope you are not proposing that this walk continue in Surrentum.' Silvana gave a short laugh but the knots in her stomach grew. 'Like you, I have my own duties to attend to.'

'I am travelling to Surrentum on my own. Our walk should be a pleasant way to pass the time before I depart. The tide needs to turn in my favour.' He smiled down at her. 'I regret I could not say anything earlier, but the news I am required elsewhere only reached me when I returned to my villa, far too late to cancel our stroll.'

Silvana released a breath, but a vague sense of disappointment ran through her. The sense of an opportunity missed. Not what she had expected at all. Men postponed journeys for her. They sent long regretful poems in her honour when they had to go away. It was rather disquieting when this one did not.

'Shall we fulfil the terms of our bargain, then?' she asked as brightly as she could. 'I have no wish for you to miss the tide.'

'If that is your desire....'

'It is what I agreed to do.'

He offered his arm and she rested her fingers lightly on his forearm. Her whole body tingled from the contact. She allowed her glance to sweep upwards and rest on his face. He was not immune to her. She could tell from the slight flaring of his nostrils. Perhaps she should stop wondering what he wanted. He was no different from the other men who inhabited her uncle's dining room. Interested in only one thing.

'Tell me, Silvana, do you always do things you agree to?' Fortis asked after they had strolled down to the end of the walkway and stood looking at the many boats bobbing up and down on the bay— military triremes, yachts and the humbler fishing boats—jostling for space. Above the gulls circled, calling to each other as they attempted to steal fish.

'Promises are very important to me. I dislike breaking my promises. It is how one can earn a bad reputation.'

'There are other ways to earn a bad reputation.'

Silvana ran her tongue over her suddenly dry lips. Fortis might be many things, but he was definitely not husband material. She had learnt a bit of his background last night from Lyde—married young, wife tragically killed in an accident, had managed to avoid a second marriage through a series of adroit moves. They said he kept the house as a shrine to her. No doubt when he married it would be for prestige and to further his career in the Senate.

The sea breeze ruffled her hair as a tern swooped down to the sun-sparkled water to catch a fish. The little boat she had clambered up yesterday had a swarm of activity surrounding it. Was this the boat Fortis was going to use on his journey?

Even though it was early the promenade was becoming more and more crowded with ladies taking the morning air, children playing with hoops and porters carrying all manner of amphorae.

Silvana took a half-step and stumbled, nearly falling head first towards the bay. She felt Fortis's hands catch her waist, hold her back. Her breath came faster. He should let go. Propriety demanded he let go. But he kept his hands about her waist, becoming more possessive. Silvana knew if she turned, she'd see his lips and want to claim them. She wanted to experience the soul-scorching heat of them. She remained still. To do so here, in such a public place, would ruin her mystique. Silvana pointedly removed his hands. 'I am not your mistress.'

'Not yet.' His mocking eyes assessed her. 'Is it a matter for discussion?'

Silvana ran her tongue over her lips. They were too close even now. Their bodies nearly touched.

The memory of yesterday morning swamped her, of how they had stood almost in this very spot. What would it be like to be his mistress?

'Not ever.' She gave her head a decisive shake, banishing the thought. 'I find it best to keep all my counters on the table where I can see them.'

'Generally women wait until they are asked before making provocative statements like that.' His eyes became hooded, but he made no attempt to re-capture her waist. 'I had no plans on making you my mistress. There again, I do enjoy a challenge.'

'It is what the women will be whispering in the bathhouses if I permit you to put your arm about my waist.'

'I must protest my sole intent was to keep you from falling and since when does a woman as noto-rious as yourself worry about the gossips? Whether you do or don't, the gossips will say what they like.'

'I worry when the gossip harms me or my family.'

'It appeared differently to me from where I stood.' A dimple shone in the corner of his cheek. 'A little light flirtation never harmed anyone. Not in the Baiae I know.'

'But you want more than a flirtation before you depart for shores unknown. You paid a great deal of money for the pleasure of my company.' Silvana placed her hands on her hips and stared him directly in his eyes. 'If you have no desire for me to become your mistress, to stake your claim, what was your purpose? You do not look to be a man who throws away *denarii* lightly. My uncle says that only Crassus has more money than you.'

A forthright woman. Fortis could respect her. Perhaps this problem was going to be easier to deal with than he had imagined. Fortis smiled. 'You wish me to lay the game pieces on the table. Very well, the reason I asked you out was to speak to you about your growing relationship with Eutychus. I want to get certain things resolved before I go off to Surrentum. I want my aunt's head to rest easy on her pillow at night.'

He saw her eyebrows draw together in a straight line as she twirled her parasol. Then suddenly, like the sun peeping out from behind a rain cloud, her eyes twinkled with mischief. 'Ah, dear sweet Eutychus. He has become quite the fixture in my uncle's house. He has a pleasant wit and is quite a keen dancer.'

'His mother also is aware of his dancing.'

Silvana laughed. 'When you were a junior tribune did you not do things that made your mother despair? I dare say it is good for Eutychus to break free from the bonds that hold him. I gather she would love to wrap him in linen bandages and keep him from all harm.'

'I concede the point.' Fortis inclined his head. 'He is her only child.'

'It would be good for Eutychus if she loosened the strings. He no longer wears a *bulla* about his neck,' Silvana said, naming the gold amulets that Roman boys wore until they had achieved their manhood. 'He needs to learn what it is like to become a man.'

Fortis knew he agreed with her. Sempronia was stifling Eutychus, but what could he do, except try to prevent his cousin from compounding his mistakes. 'Nevertheless, it would be a good idea if you looked elsewhere for a husband.'

Then he waited, with an arched brow, to see what she would do. How would she respond?

'Who gives you the right to say such things?' Silvana's voice rose an octave. 'To presume such things!'

'Do you deny Eutychus has asked you?'

She lowered her parasol so her face was hidden. 'As you were standing next to him when he made his latest declaration, I can hardly deny it.'

'Such an alliance would do him no good.' Fortis paused for deliberate effect. Silvana had to understand he was serious and see reason. He had no doubt that underneath the bluster lay a hard-hearted pragmatist. 'Nor you, come to think of it.'

'He has made an offer and has repeated it several times. I fail to see why you should be concerned.'

Silvana gave the parasol another twirl. Exactly what was Fortis's game here? What was he asking her? Before the walk had begun she had resolved to tell him of her non-interest in Eutychus and ask for his help in steering Eutychus towards a woman who might be better able to appreciate his qualities. She had no doubt he would make a fine husband in due course. Then Fortis had made the remark about becoming his mistress, and she knew he no longer saw them on the same social scale. Therefore, she saw no reason to enlighten him. He deserved to sweat more than if he were in the hot room in the baths of Mercury.

'Surely you must know that his guardian must give his approval?'

'Who is you,' Silvana stated. Her words tasted bitter in her mouth. To think she had been looking forward to seeing Fortis again. He was like the others, judging on the basis of appearance and that was all.

'Who is me.' Fortis gave an arrogant nod. 'From what I have seen over the last day, you two would not suit. Within a month or two, you would be yawning with boredom.'

'Arranging other's people's lives—is this a talent you were born with or something you acquired?'

Silvana tapped her sandaled foot, a gesture that Uncle Aulus always watched for and then took cover, knowing an explosion to be on the horizon. Fortis, however, looked vaguely amused.

'Someone has to. Someone has to hold back the folly of youth.' He gave a shrug and raised his hand to his mouth. His eyes had become two points of green glass. 'Silvana Junia, you are an intelligent woman—surely you must see the folly. You will thank me in a year's time. He is not the man for you.'

Silvana gave the parasol another slow twirl as she permitted a small smile to appear on her lips.

'Within two months, Eutychus will have attained his majority.'

'Is that a threat?' He put his face close to hers. 'I dislike threats.'

'As do I. It was a statement of fact.' Silvana paused, ignoring her pounding heart. Why had she ever thought him kind? The man was arrogant, as arrogant as they came. She would make him sweat. 'Eutychus has mentioned it several times. He has obliquely hinted I should throw him a birthday party with plenty of dancing.'

She had the satisfaction of seeing Fortis's face grow red and his fists clench. But only for an instant, then he regained control.

'You must know an alliance with your family would cause his mother, my aunt, a great deal of distress.'

'I was under the impression that an alliance with any young woman would immediately send his mother to bed for the remainder of the season.'

The corner of Fortis's mouth twitched and Silvana knew he had silently acknowledged the reality of Eutychus's mother. But it rankled that he should deem her family unfit. Why? Because he had stolen a kiss? Because her uncle ran a private establishment for the wealthy? She might be notorious, but Crispus was the model of propriety and she had high hopes for his future.

'It is not just his mother who has concerns. Eutychus has a glittering career ahead of him.'

'The prospect of a glittering career.' Silvana permitted a smile to play on her lips and she laid a hand on Fortis's forearm. Her years of being a society hostess, first for Cotta and then her uncle, had taught her many things, among them the value of the well-timed barb and the necessity of not showing one's true emotions. 'Let us not be under any illusions. The same could be said for most of the young tribunes who pass through Baiae, but very few will grasp the opportunity.'

He drew away from her, and his face grew hard. 'As his guardian, I for one do not intend to let him jeopardise his future career by marrying a notorious woman. I have seen far too many men sacrificed on that particular altar.'

'I would say then that it is their own fault.' Silvana made a clucking noise in the back of her throat. She knew the type of woman Fortis was referring to, but she was not one of them, could never be. 'They blame the woman rather than admit to their own failings. Believe me, I have seen it happen many times. Far easier to blame the defenceless woman than to take the responsibility themselves.'

A certain wild exhilaration filled her. She was at last saying things that she had held inside her for a long time. Several matrons paused, drew their *stolas* slightly back, as if afraid of the contagion, and then hurried on.

Fortis's eyes bored into hers, fury blazing. Silvana took a step backwards. What had she done? Somehow she had stirred up demons.

'How much?' he asked between gritted teeth. 'How much do you want? What is your price? Everyone has a price in Baiae.'

Silvana forced herself to return the stare measure for measure, not to flinch. 'What exactly are you offering?'

'You are in need of funds. That much is obvious from your villa. Your uncle spends money as if it were water. I propose to give you one thousand gold pieces, if you release Eutychus. In short, I am so convinced of the unsuitability of this relationship that I am prepared to pay you to end it before you do him harm.'

Silvana's mouth dropped open. She blinked twice and shook her head to clear it. But the words echoed and re-echoed through her brain. One thousand gold pieces. Surely she must have heard wrong. He had offered her money! A small fortune. He had assumed that her sole motivation was money. He thought her a mercenary harpy like the other Baiae harpies who would sell their bodies for the merest hint of a gold piece. Her shawl quivered as she fought to control her temper.

Out of the corner of her eye she saw two gaudily dressed women pass by and give her a curious look. She paused and forced her fingers to uncurl. She nodded to them and they moved on, gossiping behind their hands.

To think she had thought Fortis was a potential friend and she had been about to confide in him, to ask him for help with Eutychus. She had wanted to let Eutychus down gently, but now everything had changed. Fortis deserved to feel uncomfortable. Things came far too easily for him. He needed to be taught a lesson.

'You are offering me money to give up Eutychus,' she said, giving the parasol a twirl and making sure a simpering smile was on her face. She had to give the impression that she was seriously considering the offer.

Something akin to pain crossed Fortis's face, but vanished before Silvana could properly register what it was. In the blink of an eye, his eyes became hard points of glass and his lips a thin white line. His eyes raked her form and Silvana felt as if she were a horse at auction or, worse, a slave with all her wares being weighed up. A complete change from her rescuer of the other night. Then he had not asked her how much, but had offered her his cloak. Silvana refused to feel any regret. He had made the original suggestion. Now he had to live with the consequences.

'Then you will consider it?'

She tilted her chin and stared directly at him. 'Yes, but it will not be easily done. There are feelings to be considered.'

'One thousand gold pieces will compensate you for any hurt feelings,' he said with an arrogant curl of his lip. 'But I want the break painless and done quickly. Today, if possible; if not, by the Ides. I will instruct my man to pay you once Eutychus has returned to his proper senses.'

Chapter Five

One thousand gold pieces.

Silvana stared at Fortis. A sea breeze ruffled his short dark hair, making it stand upright, like a boy's but there was nothing boyish about his face. The amount would pay off her uncle's debt and there would be some left over for Crispus's junior tribune-ship. Silvana closed her eyes and firmly pushed the thought aside. Tempting, but what would it make her? She gave the parasol a twirl and batted her lashes.

'Too little.'

'Two thousand five hundred, then.' Fortis brushed a speck of dirt from his cloak. 'But I want it done subtly. I take it you do understand what I mean? I have no wish to see Eutychus hurt—merely for him to emerge a little sooner from his fantasy than he would have done.'

He stood, with a mocking expression on his face.

Silvana forced the breath to hiss through her lips. She wanted to scream that no amount of money would make her forget her principles. She was not easily bought or sold! But she paused. There had to be a more subtle way, something to send a forceful message. And she intended to teach this arrogant senator a lesson he would not soon forget. She lowered her parasol and crossed her arms.

'I have changed my mind.'

'You have done what?' Fortis's mouth fell open as his eyes became wide. He ran his hand through his hair and then a thin smile twisted his lips. He gave a small nod as if to say he understood her game. 'Silvana Junia, two thousand five hundred is my final offer. You will not squeeze another *as* out of me or my family.'

'I have no intention of taking your money. Not a single copper *as* of it.' Silvana gave a light laugh, the one Eutychus always described as charming, but she thought sounded like a nightingale practising her scales.

The shock and amazement were clearly visible on his face. She could see the muscle in his jaw as he worked out how best to answer. She should be grateful to discover what he was really like—she had thought him different from the others. He wasn't. He was exactly the same, except possibly more arrogant. She was used to such men. She hadn't survived in Baiae for two years without being able to handle herself.

Time to give the knife that added little twist. Silvana leant forward and allowed her shawl to slip, framing her face to perfection, her lips parted as if she expected a kiss.

'I should be grateful to you, for you have shown me what a rich prize Eutychus is. Why should I take such a measly payment when Eutychus's purse will soon be open to me? And you know how he adores me.'

'You intend to marry him?' Fortis blinked rapidly as he brought his chin into his neck. 'You intend to be his bride?'

Silvana fluttered her eyelashes and lowered her voice. 'Now that you have shown me how much he is worth, how could I contemplate doing anything else? Particularly as I am one of those notorious women from Baiae?'

Fortis winced and she knew her barb had struck home. Good. He deserved to be crossed. She would feel no pity for him. Let him think she set the standard for disgraceful behaviour among the Baiae hostesses.

'Is your brain only filled with thoughts of gold?'

'You say it is.' Silvana flipped the end of her shawl over her shoulder. 'And I would keep your voice

down, unless you want to cause a scandal that re-
verberates from here to Pompeii.'

He swallowed hard and started to say things several
times. All the while his eyes blazed. Silvana knew
she was playing with fire, but she had no choice.

'Have you no consideration for the distress it will
cause his family?' he asked with growing disbelief
in his voice. 'That he will be shamed? And you will
be looked down upon? Everyone will call you a
mercenary widow.'

'These are risks I am prepared to take. After all,
my Eutychus and his considerable fortune are close
to my heart. I care about what might happen to him.'

'If you truly cared about his welfare—' Fortis began.

'If *you* truly cared about his welfare, you would
want him to be happy and contented in his choice
of marriage partner.' Silvana crossed her arms and
dared Fortis to find a counter-argument. She
enjoyed the slight flush on his cheeks.

He lowered his gaze and continued in a quieter tone.

'If I thought he'd be happy, I would aid him and
his choice. I would do everything in my power to
bring about the marriage he desired, but I have to
look beyond the present and think what he will be
like in a few years' time. Where will his heart's
desire be then? My aunt and I want what is best for
my cousin.'

'How can you even know what he wants when you spend your time in Rome and he in Baiae?' She gave a little flutter with her hand and then her eyes narrowed as she allowed her indignation full reign. 'You breeze in here, order people around, throw a money bag or two and then leave. You do not even know your cousin. He has returned from Cyrene a changed man.'

His eyes raked her form up and down in a lazy manner. An insolent smile spread across his face. 'I have seen enough to know an alliance between you and my cousin would only lead to disappointment, disillusion and disaster.'

Silvana kept her head high, refusing to flinch. 'If you truly believe that, you are running away from your responsibilities.'

'I never run.'

'Aurelius Fortis, no doubt you always believe you have an excellent reason for arranging things exactly as you wish.' She paused, crossed her arms and shook her head. 'What a shame it must be when people refuse to fall in line with your dcsires.'

To her surprise he lifted an eyebrow and a small smile played on his lips. 'Perhaps you are right. Perhaps I have been too hasty. But it will take some convincing to show me that my initial impression is wrong. A few days here in Baiae will be a pleasant way to pass the time. My business in Surrentum can wait.'

'This is where our stroll ends,' she said, motioning to Lyde, who was following several steps behind.

He shrugged a lazy shoulder as if to say her reaction was expected. 'The offer stands. Any time you wish it. Take your time. Think about it. Send me a scroll when you decide to work your mischief on a man instead of an *adulescens.*'

Silvana blinked. The world seemed to tilt slightly to the right. She ran her tongue over her lips. Perhaps he was more dangerous than she had previously thought.

Not more dangerous. She had to trust her instincts. His being here changed nothing. She refused to be attracted to him.

'You have made your offer. I utterly refuse. Like you, I rarely change my mind.'

'You are taking quite a risk.'

'You forget I am a woman who likes to take risks.' Silvana snapped her fingers in the air. 'I have done my calculations.'

'He may yet meet someone else. People are arriving all the time. The season has barely started.' Fortis nodded towards two carts filled with one family's belongings. The plump matron berated a servant for going in the wrong direction. Three women bearing a distinct resemblance to the matron peeped out from the last cart. 'If he finds another and marries her, then you will be left with nothing. Men can be fickle creatures.'

Silvana struggled to hold on to her temper. She had no wish to be goaded into saying anything rash. She wanted to give him no indication of her real intentions. And she knew she had overplayed her counters in their game of twelve lines.

'You would hardly be offering me such a large sum of money if you felt it was anything but a remote possibility.' She batted her eyes innocently, the very picture of Baiae womanhood—a woman with her eye on the size of the purse. She dropped her voice to a low purr. 'Once I marry Eutychus, I plan to have gambling and dancing every night— the way he likes it.'

A little voice nagged at the back of her mind—had she overdone it? Fortis's eyes had become hard points of emerald glass, his mouth a tight white line.

'You wouldn't dare! You would ruin him and destroy any hopes he had of a senatorial career.'

'Do you even know that he wants to become a senator?' Silvana crossed her arms in front of her chest and tapped her sandal. 'I suppose I should thank you for telling me how deeply Eutychus's feelings run. Without you and your offer, I might have done something foolish like throwing him over for a seemingly better prospect, but now I know.'

She enjoyed watching the parade of emotions cross Fortis's face. He started to say something, changed his mind and stood glaring at her.

'Until the next time we encounter each other—' Silvana made a flourish with her hand '—who knows, perhaps then I shall call you cousin!'

Fortis appeared to grow several inches taller. Silvana wanted to pick up her skirts and run from the explosion she knew must be coming, but she forced her feet to stay still. She had to appear serene. He must not know the extent of her anger or her true intentions.

'We are not finished!'

'And I say we are! Pray do not make a scene, Aurelius Fortis or otherwise you will gain a notorious reputation. Something I feel certain you have worked hard to avoid.'

Silvana turned on her heel and walked away.

Fortis stood rigid, watching the twitch of her skirt, torn between the desire to throttle her and to kiss her senseless. He had expected a few mock tears, maybe a stamping of the foot, but definite signs of greed. Instead, he had been confronted with righteous indignation.

For the first time in a long time he had completely mishandled a situation. And it bothered him. She had no real devotion to Eutychus, he was certain of that. Her response to the kiss they had shared the other morning and her reaction to him last night convinced him of that. And yet she refused to give Eutychus up? For a small fortune? What exactly was the sea witch's plan?

His mouth twisted. He had left himself vulnerable to attack as well. All she had to do was to inform Eutychus of his offer and any influence he had over the youth would vanish. An elementary mistake, one he fully expected to have to pay for. He should have thrown her back in the water when he first met her and saved himself. The Fates were against him that night.

Fortis tapped his fingers against his thigh. He had to salvage something from this. His pride demanded it. No hostess from Baiae would best him. He refused to stand for it. Silvana Junia and he were far from finished. There were other avenues to be explored. They were not finished until he decided they were.

He walked over to Pio's boat and called down to Merlus, who was supervising the loading of his personal belongings. 'Unload my trunk. It appears I owe you some money after all.'

'What do you mean, master?' Merlus appeared with a trunk in his arms. 'I saw you with the lady in question. You were together, walking along the promenade. Always before, the goodbyes are short.'

'She refused my offer. She prefers to take a chance on Eutychus marrying her rather than accepting a sack of gold.'

He watched the manservant's face grow incredulous. 'She is after more money, that one,' Merlus muttered.

'I don't think it is money that motivates her.' Fortis regarded the promenade. Silvana had long since vanished, but the sight of her gown twitching as she strode away was vivid in his memory. 'The indignation in her voice was too genuine. There is something else. Another piece to the mosaic that I have missed.'

'What are you going to do next? What about Surrentum? It will be a long time before you get a lead like that again.'

'I am sending you in my stead.' Fortis watched Merlus straighten. 'The information I was originally given by Livius Tullio was that the pirates' contact resided in Baiae. All activity was around Baiae. Draco has friends who protect him here. No, trust me. Surrentum has all the hallmarks of being a false trail laid for the hounds but it needs to be checked out, if only to lull our quarry into making a mistake. You and Pio may investigate and I expect your report within the next seven days.'

'Very good, master. I won't let you down.'

Fortis watched the small fishing boat pull away from the docks. A grim smile appeared on his face. 'It is between you and me now, Silvana Junia. May the best man win.'

Silvana slammed the door to the compound with a reassuring thud. Her uncle's greyhound covered his nose with his paws as she stamped towards the atrium where her uncle sat.

'Had a good morning, dear?' her uncle asked, looking up from the scroll he was reading.

'I had an interesting morning, Uncle.'

'That was why you felt the need to slam the door with the strength of a harpy bent on capturing her prey.' He patted the stone bench. 'Care to talk about it?'

'Aurelius Fortis is an arrogant sea turtle.'

Her uncle stroked his chin. 'But an extremely wealthy one. Breeding, wealth and position—what did you expect? Tell me, what did he do—offer to set you up as his mistress? I saw the way he looked at you last night. There are many women in Baiae who would jump at the chance.'

'No!' Silvana started to pace around the garden, making a line for the statue of Mercury and then circling back to her uncle, clasping and unclasping her hands together. She had not considered her interest in Fortis had been so blatant the night before. How many others had noticed? Then she saw the mischievous look in her uncle's eye and continued in a quieter voice. 'He did nothing of the sort. Uncle, you had me worried.'

'Silvana, you are making me dizzy just watching you. Stand still.' Her uncle placed the scroll down. 'What has he done then? Or are you upset that he didn't offer?'

She wanted to put her head in her hands and weep, but managed a weak smile instead. 'He offered me money to give up Eutychus and return him to the family's bosom.'

'Our coffers could use a fresh injection of coins. How much?' Uncle Aulus picked up a stylus. 'Let me make a reckoning of our accounts. You could make some merchants very happy indeed. The fuller has been demanding payment for my new toga since last Kalendis so we can start with him. Then there are the wine bills, the olive oil, the fish sauce…'

'Uncle Aulus!'

Silvana put her hands on her hips and her uncle had the grace to look chagrined. It bothered her that even her uncle thought she would take the money. What had she done to make everyone think she had abandoned her principles, and had no finer sense of right and wrong?

She stared hard at her uncle. Eventually he looked down and fiddled with his sandal strap.

'You have no intention of marrying the lad.' The words burst from her uncle. 'You made that perfectly clear to me at last month's Festival of Flora. Why not profit from it just a little? Think about it, Silvana. You would be paid for doing exactly the thing you intended doing all along.'

'It is the principle of the thing. Without my principles, I am nothing.' Silvana clasped her hands together and fought to keep her voice from trembling. Surely Uncle Aulus knew what she believed in. To have him doubt her was almost worse than having Fortis offer her the gold. 'We may not have much money, but I have never taken money, would never take money, for such an infamous reason.'

'Ah well.' Uncle Aulus put down his stylus and pushed the parchment away. 'The fuller will have to wait, then. Far be it from me to come between a woman and her principles. Tell me—what did you say to him? How did you deliver the great blow for your honour? And what was his response? I want every juicy morsel.'

Silvana rapidly recounted the whole episode. 'Aurelius Fortis stood there with a curl on his lips and a smug expression in his eyes, expecting me to grasp the proffered purse with both hands. I told him I wouldn't. Turned him down flat.'

'And you told him you wouldn't marry Eutychus.' There was a bleakness to her uncle's eyes as he gave the stack of tablets a wistful pat. 'Niece, you will never make a good twelve-lines player. You are far too honest.'

'What do you take me for? I am no novice to Baiae.' Silvana leant forward and looked her uncle directly in the eyes. 'I want to see the man suffer. I told him that I had every intention of marrying Eutychus. His offer made it obvious how much his family fear me. I told him I intend to squeeze every last *as* out of Eutychus before I go on to new pastures.'

Her uncle put his head in his hands. 'Silvana, what are you doing?'

'Administering a strong dose of medicine to Aurelius Fortis. The man needed a long-overdue lesson in humility. And I gave it to him.'

Uncle Aulus gave a low whistle. 'You are a brave woman, Silvana. Braver than you know. Aurelius Fortis used to have quite the reputation here in Baiae. Cool, calculating, taking tremendous risks, but possessed of the goddess Fortunata's favour in a way that one would swear he was her favourite son.'

'Then he is the worst type of hypocrite—seeking to deny his cousin activities that he enjoyed.' Fury bubbled up again in Silvana as she thought how pompous Fortis had sounded with his lip slightly curled and his eyebrow arched as he stood there, draped in his fine clothes.

'That is one way to look at it, to be sure.' Uncle Aulus made a temple with his fingertips. 'I have heard the injuries he suffered in the accident that killed his wife were horrific. A brush with death can change a man. Personally I suspect his old haunts reminded him too much of her, so he opted for the bigger stakes of Roman politics.'

'My way is the only way to look at it.' She refused to feel sympathy for Fortis. He had none for her. Silvana leant forward, clasping her hands together. 'He has had his lesson. Now I have no wish to have any more dealings with him. Do you understand me, Uncle?'

'He is a very rich man. Such men dislike taking no for an answer.'

'Uncle!'

Uncle Aulus held up his hands. 'All I am saying, Silvana is that I have rarely seen you react this strongly. I would not be surprised if he reappeared. Nor will I exclude him. People would talk. Besides, this is about more than you and Eutychus. It is about you and Aurelius Fortis.'

'I have no idea what you are talking about.'

Silvana drew her shawl about her shoulders and stood up as tall as she could.

Uncle Aulus waggled his eyebrows. 'And you call yourself a Baiae hostess. For shame.'

Everything was ready—her hair was elegantly pinned in the latest style with more tight curls and hairpins than a statue of Venus, her rose-pink gap-sleeved gown revealed enough to be enticing, and verged on the indecent. A cloud of scent surrounded her. She was the living perfect embodiment of the gossips' idea of a leading hostess of Baiae. Silvana tapped her fingers against the table. She could afford no mistakes. She had sent Lyde down to the quayside earlier and she had returned with the news that Fortis had not left as planned. The boat had slipped its moorings, but Fortis had been seen returning to his villa.

Silvana had little doubt that her uncle was right—Fortis would appear tonight. And she had the whole scenario worked out in her mind. How she'd ignore him, and show him that she had no intention of changing her behaviour.

'Silvana, Silvana!' Eutychus came up to her and grabbed her hands, spinning her around. 'Congratulate me.'

There was a different sort of air about Eutychus

this evening: a spring in his step, his dining tunic was tied much more loosely than before and he had taken to gesturing with his wrists. Silvana's hands went to her hair and tucked a hairpin in more securely. 'What should I congratulate you for?'

'I have broken with Mother. I have been telling you for months I would and I have done it.' He leant forward and the scent of sickly sweet wine wafted over her. 'I finally worked up the courage to tell her we are to be married. She started to have hysterics—crying and tearing at her clothes—but I would have none of it. I must have this woman, I said. Very fierce I was.'

Silvana stared at him in stunned disbelief. She should be rejoicing that Eutychus had publicly declared to his family his love for her, but a wave of depression washed over her. She thought she would have more time, time to torment Fortis, but in the end evade the direct marriage proposal. She had to do something, before her ruse was exposed. There had to be a way of avoiding a marriage that she knew would be a disaster.

'I have not said yes or no.' Silvana craned her neck, trying to look around his bulk. 'What does your cousin Fortis think of it?'

'He was there when it happened. Oh my goddess, my goddess, at last we can be together.' Eutychus caught her hand and held it to his heart.

'Where are you residing, Eutychus?' Silvana firmly removed his other hand from her waist.

'All suitable villas have been rented for the season. I couldn't stay just anywhere, so Fortis suggested I stay with him. He's redecorating his villa and needs my expert opinion. After the season is over, I am to return to Rome with him. Mother doesn't know about that, but when she does, there will be an explosion. Isn't that wonderful, Silvana?'

Silvana gave a weak nod. Eutychus appeared oblivious to Fortis's true intentions. He had allowed Eutychus to cut the *stola* straps, but remained in control of the situation, ready to curb any excesses. She had to applaud the subtlety of the man. But it also worried her. She tried craning her neck again. 'Where exactly is your cousin? Did he come with you tonight?'

'Fortis? I thought you would be pleased to see me.' A frown appeared between Eutychus's eyebrows.

'I am. I was wondering, that was all.' Silvana bit her lip.

What exactly was Fortis playing at?

She had expected a full-frontal assault against her. Or, at the very least, Fortis hovering about Eutychus's every move, playing the nursemaid. But despite staying in Baiae, he had declined to appear.

'Did you enjoy your walk with him this morning?' Eutychus asked with a slight petulant pout.

Silvana pressed her fingertips into her belt, seeking the familiar comfort of her Venus amulet. She should tell Eutychus about Fortis's offer. It was the perfect time, but the words stuck in her throat. Not now, when Fortis was behaving in a manner she approved of. Eutychus needed a steady male hand. She refused to destroy that relationship. And Fortis would have counted on her telling Eutychus. The corners of her mouth twitched. She would rise above this morning.

'You will have to ask him.'

'And he said to ask you.' Eutychus put a hand on her shoulder. 'Why are you being evasive? When we are married, you will have to behave differently—no more secrets. We must tell each other everything.'

'Should our marriage come to pass, we will discuss it then.' Silvana laughed, but the laughter died on her lips as she saw Cotta with a group of disreputable-looking men arriving and her uncle bustling up to speak to him. She removed Eutychus's hand as he glanced towards the new arrivals. 'Forgive me, Eutychus, there are other guests I must attend to.'

'I begin to understand, Silvana.' Eutychus reached out and gave her hand a squeeze. 'Truly I do. If there is ever anything I can do for you. I am your devoted slave.'

'Be a dear sweet boy, and get my chair, I think I shall be sitting at dinner, rather than reclining.'

Silvana watched Eutychus hurry off. With any luck, Fortis would decide that there was no point in seeking her out again. However, instead of cheering her, the thought vaguely unsettled her.

Fortis did not visit the next day or the day after but Eutychus appeared every night, full of his plans. It appeared Fortis had decided to play a waiting game, rather than risk a full-frontal assault in his attempt to separate her and Eutychus.

On the third evening Eutychus informed her Fortis and he were going to join a boar hunt the next morning and spent most of the evening going over the virtues of various hunting dogs with her uncle.

With a light heart the next day, Silvana went to the Baths of Mercury for a swim in the heated pool. Poppea, one of her main rivals, arrived soon after her and started regaling the entire hot room with her latest exploits and how she had legions of senators eating out of her hand, begging for the favour of her bed.

'I believe you are acquainted with my very latest conquests, Silvana.' Poppea touched her over-bright red hair. 'They are said to have been quite the admirers of yours.'

'Who have you ensnared this time?' Silvana asked, hoping Eutychus had not fallen into Poppea's claws. She did not relish having to rescue him, not with Fortis still in town.

'Drusus Cotta.' Poppea leant forward. 'And you know that lovely, lovely senator, Aurelius Fortis?'

'We are acquainted.' Silvana kept her face absolutely still.

'He was at my party yesterday.' Poppea smacked her bright red lips together. 'Quite the quiet one, him, but what a gorgeous set of shoulders. And legs that wouldn't quit. He will be good in bed, that one. You can tell from the size of his feet. Large feet, large—'

'You are more than welcome to them both, Poppea.' Silvana stood up and the bath attendant started to scrape her down. It would serve Fortis right if he became entangled with a grasping harpy like Poppea. She had already buried three husbands, decimated their fortunes and was on the lookout for the fourth.

'If you are sure…' Poppea touched Silvana's hand with a taloned finger. 'I would not want accusations of poaching on your hunting ground.'

'Neither man holds the slightest interest for me.'

'I shall hold you to that.' Poppea gave a husky

chuckle. 'I had my man of business make discreet enquiries and both of them can afford me. A woman has to think of her purse.'

Silvana felt her skin crawl. The best she could say about Poppea was that she was honest. Was this the sort of creature Fortis believed her to be?

'Did you know two merchants refused to give me credit for a length of purple silk that I had spotted?' Poppea gave a brittle laugh. 'Me? Can you believe it? Didn't they know I am guaranteed to find a new protector in a matter of days?'

'As you say, Poppea, I wish you good hunting.' Silvana tied her exercise robe securely under her breasts and left Poppea to gossip about the latest rumour about pirates and smuggling, a topic that produced much smacking of lips when she disclosed the city elders had sent a plea to Rome for help in catching them.

Silvana shut the door behind her with a satisfying bang. She then had a slight laugh about the idea of Poppea and Fortis. In many ways, any man she caught deserved the trouble she would bring.

Rounding the corner, she saw Fortis dressed in his exercise tunic. The tunic skimmed the mid-point of his thighs, revealing legs that were muscular and well shaped. Silvana tightened her lips. She admired his form as she might a beautiful statue or a picture.

It was his mind she objected to, and for her, a man's personality was as important as how he looked. But did his legs have to be such a dark shade of bronze and did the tunic have to show the muscles of his chest? Silvana realized with a start that she was staring. She turned her face resolutely away.

'Silvana Junia, what a delightful surprise.' A dimple showed in his cheek. His eyes looked her up and down. 'And looking in such splendid health. Tell me, are the gods treating you well?'

'Aurelius Fortis.' She gave a nod and prepared to pass on. 'I thought you had gone hunting…with Eutychus.'

'There was a slight change of plan. Eutychus has gone hunting instead with some friends of mine. My horse pulled up lame this morning.'

'And you decided to stay here. No doubt in pursuit of other quarry.'

'In a manner of speaking.' A shadow crossed his face. 'One could hardly call it hunting, but it does afford me a certain amount of satisfaction.'

'Ah well, one must takes one's pleasure while one can.' Silvana waved an airy hand. 'Live for the day. I always do.'

'Did you miss me?' His eye became deep dark pools of green. 'Eutychus said you were asking after me the other night.'

Silvana felt his charm lap at her will and refused to be drawn. She was physically attracted to this man, but it would pass. She simply wished her exercise robe went further down than her knees. She had to remember the other women like Poppea who were buzzing around him, hoping for a loosening of his purse. With him, the charm was probably effortless.

'Eutychus dined with us these past three nights. He informs my uncle and me of everything that happens in his life, including helping you choose the new frescoes for your dining room. You are tired of Bacchus and his nymphs, I believe.'

'Eutychus continues to sing your praises,' he said. The merriment had vanished from his eyes. Despite lounging against a wall, his body held the same watchful stillness that a wolf has before it starts to chase its prey. A pose to disconcert his opponent, making them behave in the manner of deer or rabbits. She had no intention of becoming a scared doe. Those days were long over. She had rubbed shoulders long enough with the harpies of Baiae. The question was how best to respond. She pursed her lips, and considered the possibilities. She had it.

'Did you doubt that he would? Eutychus is quite enamoured of me.' Silvana gave an exaggerated flutter of her lashes. 'And for my part, I continue to be very interested in the size of his purse. It really was kind of you to inform me of his devotion.'

'And yet I have not seen the formal betrothal offer. Eutychus must come to me first. I must have a hand in drawing it up. I positively insist as his guardian.'

Silvana put her foot down too quickly, stumbled. Her hand clutched at the frescoed wall, missed. Fortis's hand came and caught her elbow. The warmth from his fingers sent tingles up her arm. Every nerve ending in her body was aware of him. She moved and his fingers were gone as if they had never been there.

'We…we are waiting until he reaches his majority, then he will not have to ask his guardian for anything.' Silvana hated the feeble way it sounded.

'But he may still want my advice.' His lips were very close to hers. His warm breath ruffled her hair. What would his lips taste like? Honey? Her mouth ached with a dull sensation as the memory of the last time he stole a kiss threatened to overwhelm her.

'It is a risk I have to take,' she whispered back and tried to think of something other than the way his lips moved. She fought against the urge to explore them with her hand, with her lips.

'And do you like taking risks?'

'When the occasion demands.'

Fortis regarded the woman standing before him.

Her hair was caught back in a simple knot and her exercise tunic was moulded to the curves of her body. More fuel for the dreams that had haunted him these last few nights. Dreams of them swimming together, her body wet and slick against his. His hands entangled in her hair, pulling her face close to his. Dreams of primitive carnal desire that left his body aching and drenched in sweat when he woke.

He had stayed away from her, thinking it would pass, concentrating on the descriptions of sophistication Eutychus brought home every night, as well as revisiting old haunts from his youth, encountering the sort of harpies he knew Silvana must be. Then she appeared unexpectedly and she was the sea witch again, with her hair barely scraped from her shoulders and her face unadorned. He could feel the heat rising from her, calling to him. He wanted her, but on his terms, no other.

'Why didn't you tell Eutychus of my offer?' he asked in a husky voice that bore little resemblance to his own.

'Maybe I will…later. Maybe I am saving it for the appropriate time.' She fluttered her eyelashes, but her voice had dropped a note and her lips had become too red, too full. He wanted to draw her into one of the little private rooms that the Baths of

Mercury had for its clients who sought less public pleasures, and drink his fill.

'No, you lie.' Fortis forced himself to step back, breaking the spell that held him.

They stood a little apart, both gasping for air as if they had run a race around the exercise track.

'I have no idea what nonsense you are spouting.'

'If you were going to tell him,' Fortis continued relentlessly, pursuing his sudden insight, 'you'd have told him the first time you met with great crocodile tears and plenty of sighs.'

'Which is why you sent Eutychus to me.'

Fortis inclined his head. He had sought to separate the pair by getting to know Eutychus and showing him the other delights Baiae held, but Eutychus had resisted and Silvana had failed to behave how he had expected. The situation called for a different approach.

'Far be it from me to deprive you of such an opportunity,' he said.

'Crocodile tears are not my style.' Silvana snapped her fingers under his nose, anger surging through her. He had no right to affect her like this. 'I will tell him when the time is right, when it will do the maximum damage to you and your reputation.'

'I think not, Silvana Junia.' His eyes turned a deep sea-green, much the same colour as when she had first seen them. He ran a finger down the side of her cheek. 'Be careful of the games you play. You may not always win.'

'I am well aware that life is not a game of twelve lines.' She concentrated on smoothing the folds of her exercise tunic. 'Or maybe it was a thank you for the other night when you saw me home. It was something you didn't need to do.'

'That was and remains my pleasure. Rescuing sea witches is a speciality.'

Small tingles ran down Silvana's arms. She had to move, to get away or she was in danger of throwing herself at this man. Why him, when she had a dozen junior tribunes at her feet nightly, begging for her favours? No, she had to be attracted to the one man she despised and who despised her.

Why had Cupid decided to prick her with an arrow? She straightened her shoulders. Desire was one thing. Acting on it was another. She'd leave now while her dignity was intact.

'Ah, Silvana Junia, I was wondering when we might encounter each other.' Cotta's nasal tone boomed across the exercise yard. 'And you in deep conversation with a would-be protector. I had no idea you were such good friends. A word to the wise, my dear stepmother, his protection has often proved illusory.'

'Aurelius Fortis is Eutychus's cousin. You remember Eutychus.' Silvana refused to become angry. Anger would inflame the situation. She had to remain aloof.

'The young Eutychus—a simpering sort.' Cotta gave a short unpleasant laugh. 'I have no idea why you allow such young men to swarm around you, Silvana Junia. It is unseemly and causes talk.'

'Thankfully we are no longer related and you have no authority over who I see.'

'That could change.'

'Not if I have any say in the matter.'

Fortis allowed his gaze to flicker between Silvana and Cotta. Her back was now pressed against the wall and she looked ready to take flight. What exactly did Cotta want from Silvana? Could this be the explanation of why Silvana was reluctant to bid goodbye to Eutychus?

'Silvana, shall I escort you home?' he asked.

'My uncle's litter is waiting for me. If you will both forgive me…' She tucked a lock of hair behind her ear and walked away, head held high, the short skirt of her tunic swaying slightly.

'Quite the little tease, that one,' Cotta remarked. 'The stories I could tell you. All go in the dining room, no go in the bedroom is what they say. Why my late adopted father ever stayed married to her I don't know.'

'And yet it has not stopped you lusting after her.'

'I would hardly be a man if I didn't.' Cotta gave a distinct leer. 'Ah, but I forgot—wasn't your late wife a shining example of Baiae's womanhood?'

Fortis ground his teeth, but refused to give in to Cotta's deliberate provocation. An air of sleaze had hung around Cotta as a junior tribune. There had been unfounded rumours of other more valuable cargo being unloaded at the same time as Cotta's fortuitous discovery of the relatively minor smuggling. Rumours Cotta always vigorously denied. Fortis and others had never been able to conclusively prove the connection, but the suspicion lingered.

'That reminds me, Cotta, I am in need of some fish sauce, flower of the first harvest. A shipment of mine is several amphorae short.'

'And you would like to acquire them without paying tax? Is that it, Aurelius Fortis?' Cotta rubbed his hands together. 'I know how it is. It is at times like these men turn towards smugglers and pirates. It is why Rome will never get rid of them.'

'Rumour has it that you are the man to ask.' Fortis watched Cotta with hard eyes. After Merlus had returned in the early hours of this morning from a fruitless trip to Surrentum, he had narrowed the candidates down to three—Cotta, a senator from Pompeii and Junius Maius.

'Not me, Aurelius Fortis.' Cotta's smile became oilier. 'It would be Silvana's uncle you want to see. He is the man with contacts, the man who fixes things and has fingers in all the stews. You should remember me from our days in Bithynia, I have an intense dislike of pirates. Dirty filthy creatures. I simply understand why a man might be forced to use one.'

'You did always seem to have that uncanny knack of finding the hapless smuggler and claiming part of the recovered goods as a reward.' Fortis blew on his nails. 'I always wondered what else was getting through when we were busy with those small consignments.'

'The way you say it, Aurelius Fortis.' Cotta held up both his hands and widened his eyes, but the corners of his full lips turned down. 'Could I help it that Fortunata smiled on me and continues to smile? My business dealings have always stood in court.'

'A misunderstanding, then. I do beg your forgiveness, Drusus Cotta.'

Chapter Six

'What in the name of Jupiter Optimates do you think you are doing?' Fortis stared at Eutychus as he pranced around the atrium, stopping every few steps to swivel his hips and adopt an attitude.

'Practising my dance steps for tonight.' Eutychus raised his arm, and leant forward, with pursed lips. 'What does it look like?'

'A war elephant with a hangover.' Fortis laughed and shook his head. 'Here, let me show you what to do. You need to start out on your sword foot. It is all in the way you make the tunic sway.'

He rapidly executed a few dance steps and watched Eutychus's mouth drop open.

'Where did you learn that?'

'All my time has not been spent on the Senate floor, Eutychus.' Fortis gave a laugh. 'Now you try it. And when you twirl, keep your head upright. And remember your partner is not an inanimate object.'

'I think I have it.' Eutychus tried again and this time his movement showed much more polish and skill. 'Yes!'

'You did it, Eutychus.'

'I would have never done it without your help, Fortis.'

'Think nothing of it.' Fortis banished the thoughts about how Silvana would appear if she was clasped in Eutychus's arms like that, but the thoughts of how she would feel in his arms were harder to forget. 'I am sure Silvana will be proud of your skill when she dances with you tonight.'

'She won't be.' Eutychus missed a step. 'She never is.'

'What are you talking about?'

'I know what you and my mother think about Silvana.' Eutychus raised his hand, silencing Fortis. 'I overheard Mother detailing the whole thing to one of her friends with great relish yesterday when I was gathering the last of my things from her villa. Silvana's not like that, you know. They may tell tales about her, but Silvana is very aware of what is right and wrong. She never stays for the dancing. No, I lie. She danced one dance when I first arrived, with her uncle. Very prettily done, it was too.'

Fortis rubbed the back of his neck. How much did this young pup know? He thanked Minerva that he had decided not to tell Sempronia about his offer of gold to Silvana and her reaction. His aunt had never learnt when to keep her mouth closed. There was no telling what harm she could have done. 'You shouldn't listen at doors.'

'Old habits are hard to break. Besides, how else would I learn?' Eutychus gave an impudent grin. 'Mother thinks I wear a *bulla* and play at rolling nuts.'

'Other than not dancing, what virtues does your goddess possess?' Fortis said.

'She has a lovely singing voice, plays the lyre like a nymph and speaks Greek. Did you know she is very fond of geometry?' Eutychus fingered his goatee beard and practised another swivel of his hips. His interest in gossip appeared to be forgotten.

'What do you know about Silvana Junia and Cotta the Younger?'

'She doesn't like him,' Eutychus replied with a determined nod of his head as he attempted a tricky series of turns. 'She tolerates him for the sake of her uncle and her brother.'

'Has she told you that?'

'It is in her actions. I am sure she would have accepted my offer of marriage by now if it was not for her fear of upsetting her uncle. I watched her face go blank when Cotta came into the room the other night. I felt certain she was going to agree to my request, but then he showed up.'

'How does Cotta influence that?'

'He has some hold over them.' Eutychus again fingered his newly grown goatee beard. 'I heard Silvana and her uncle arguing the day before you arrived. He was insisting that Silvana go out on Cotta's yacht and Silvana said what a bloated war elephant Cotta was. It gave me quite a bit of hope. Cotta had been saying how Silvana would be in his power before the night was out.'

'And she wasn't.'

'No, and she assures me that she is giving my offer of marriage the attention it deserves.' He picked up a figurine of a sea nymph, balancing it on the palm of his hand. 'I am hoping she will give me her answer tonight. Marriages take a while to plan, after all.'

'I have changed my mind, Eutychus.' Fortis took the figurine from Eutychus and replaced the nymph on its shelf. 'I will come with you after all to the Junia compound.'

'Absolutely splendid. I am sure everyone will be delighted to see you. Aulus, Silvana's uncle, was asking after you last night. He wanted to know if there was any truth to the rumour that you were here about the missing shipments. Do you really think you can stop Draco this time?'

'What shipments would that be?' Fortis dusted a speck of lint from his dining clothes, feigning un-interest but every nerve was on edge. It was inter-esting that Silvana's uncle should have heard of his mission. Precisely where had he received the infor-mation from?

'The ones that Draco keeps taking. The amount he charges for safe passage is astronomical. I know a nest of pirates was cleared out earlier this year, but there are rumours that someone very high up in Baiae was up to his neck in it. A senator even.'

'Aulus Junius Maius would be well advised to keep quiet on the subject. I am here on holiday like many other senators.'

Eutychus's face fell. 'I thought you had come to see me.'

'That as well.' Fortis rubbed his hands together. Silvana had been left on her own long enough. Now was the time to ratchet up the pressure and ensure Eutychus was free from her coils. 'We don't want to keep your goddess waiting.'

Silvana sat on the stone bench in the atrium, ab-sentmindedly stroking Bestus and trying to forget her current obsession with Fortis's shoulders. Her earlier words to Poppea were a lie. She knew that. She had to trust Fortis was not one to be impressed by a slender ankle and timely dropped shawl. The black-and-white greyhound had laid its head on her knee and was looking up at her with big sorrowful eyes. 'You won't get any more honey cakes from me, Bestus. They're all gone.'

The dog gave a huge heartfelt sigh and settled at her feet. The late afternoon sun warmed her face and the sound of honeybees on the thyme filled her ears. She read the tablet Crispus had sent for the fifth time. Jupiter and Mercury willing, he should be back in Baiae within three days and he hoped she'd remembered her promise about no more scandals because he had a possible hint of a junior tribune's position, but he would tell her all about it when he arrived as he was her devoted younger brother.

Once Crispus arrived, she was certain her attraction to Fortis would vanish. She'd be too busy making sure Crispus had all the correct doors opened to him, and that he did not make a fool of himself with some of the women.

'Silvana,' her uncle called.

'I was about to put Bestus away before the guests start to arrive.' Silvana rose and brushed the crumbs from her skirt. 'And if you are wondering about the musicians, they are already here. If you listen, you can hear the lyre being tuned.'

'All that will have to wait. I have to go out.' Her uncle appeared wrapped in his darkest travelling cloak. 'One of my shipments has appeared on the horizon.'

'And you have to go now? But the guests are arriving.'

'And you are here to greet them. I won't be long, I promise, and what could go wrong? Dida used to be a gladiator. He can handle anyone who has imbibed a bit too much of Bacchus's favourite libation.' Uncle Aulus ran his hand through his thinning hair. 'You mustn't look at me like that, Silvana dear, it isn't what you think.'

'How would you know what I think?' Silvana looked hard at her uncle. It was unusual for him to miss the start of a party, particularly one just as the full season came into swing. 'Poppea was crowing about her conquests in the Baths of Mercury today, in particular Aurelius Fortis and how her entertainments are rapidly becoming the must-attend parties because of it.'

'Last time I looked, my dear niece, Aurelius Fortis had fine eyesight. And here I was thinking you wanted nothing more to do with him.' Uncle Aulus laid a hand on Silvana's shoulder. 'She would find it hard to enslave him. Poppea is all mouth and talon.'

'I am not worried about such things.' Silvana shrugged off his hand. 'I only hope he does. It would serve him right—accusing me and then becoming involved with one of the biggest harpies of all time. Now, will you please tell me why the great mystery of where you are going?'

'A shipment of spice from Parthia has arrived, and I want to get my agreed share. Last time they were three measures short, but Cotta has vouched for their honesty. Now all of our troubles will be sorted out.'

'That is what you always say, Uncle.'

'This time they will be. Trust me on this. If anyone asks where I am, say that I have had to go to Surrentum unexpectedly.'

'Surrentum?' Silvana asked, tilting her head to one side. 'That will take several days. Are we not better off cancelling the dinner party? Without you to host it, there is little point in holding it.'

Uncle Aulus sighed. 'I am not actually going. It is simply a ruse to keep those in ignorance away. Cotta has a great fondness for code names.'

'I had wondered…it seems Surrentum comes up a lot in conversation lately.'

'Do you know of anyone else who has gone there recently?'

'Fortis was going to go, but changed his mind and stayed in Baiae instead.'

'Though he certainly has not graced our table the last few nights, despite the invitation I sent.' Uncle Aulus tapped his teeth. 'Stronger measures may be called for.'

'Uncle! How could you after what passed between us?'

'How could I not? He needs the opportunity to see the error in his thinking. And exactly what did pass between you?' Uncle Aulus's eyes grew grave. 'What are you fighting against?'

'Nothing,' Silvana said, quickly, much too quickly.

'After his wife's death Fortis swore never to spend any time in Baiae unless he positively had to, or so the bathhouse gossips say. But then what do they know?'

'You were misinformed. He decided to stay.'

'Why do you think he did that?'

'I have no idea.' Silvana ignored Uncle Aulus's smug expression. 'We met briefly at the Baths of Mercury this morning. I encountered Cotta as well. Hostility exists between the two men.'

'And did you discuss Eutychus?' Uncle Aulus caught her hand. 'You can tell me every little detail and I won't tell a shade.'

'Uncle, your mouth runs as freely as the Tiber runs through Rome.'

'You wound me, niece,' Uncle Aulus said, clutching at his chest in a very theatrical way. 'As if I would ever interfere with your affairs.'

'I am not interested in Aurelius Fortis. Nor is he interested in me.'

'You do an awful lot of protesting over nothing.'

'Allow me to handle this in my own way.'

'Very well. I was simply asking.' Uncle Aulus wore a smug expression on his face. 'Indulge me if I happen to believe there is another reason for Aurelius Fortis staying. And for believing he will turn up to my dinner party in time. I plan to ask him to let me in on some of his money-making ventures. I am willing to bet all of his shipments come in on time.'

'How soon should I expect you back?'

'Before the evening is out, I will return...triumphant.' Uncle Aulus hurried off, calling for his manservant as he left.

'Are you ready, Eutychus?' Fortis stood dressed in his dining clothes. 'I thought to stop at your mother's on the way.'

'Do we have to?'

'She is your mother, Eutychus, and will remain your mother no matter what happens with Silvana.'

'Maybe I don't see it that way.'

'You should go to Rome and see what the city life is like on your own. There is a job for you in the grain distribution. A rather easy one—not much work, lots of wining and dining of senators. You'd enjoy it, Eutychus, you truly would.'

Eutychus wrinkled his nose and changed the subject towards horses and the prospects of finding a good team, one which could make Cumae and back without having to change at the Sibyl's cave. Fortis put his fingers together. It was too slow. Eutychus's birthday was approaching. He had to separate Silvana and Eutychus before then. Seduction was a possibility, but he had to consider the hurt and betrayal Eutychus would surely feel.

'Aurelius Fortis, I beg your pardon.' The new porter tugged at his tunic. 'There is a man to see you. He says it is urgent.'

Fortis saw Pio standing there, twisting his cap. His tunic bore distinct signs of having been worn for several days, if not since last Nones. The new porter pursed his lips.

'I know the man. You are to admit him whenever he requests it.' Fortis signalled to the fisherman, who hurried past the porter. The porter put his head in his hands and shook his head. Fortis gave a signal and Merlus quietly joined them, gliding up with scarcely a sound.

'My information was correct. They are attempting to unload the goods—spices as well as Egyptian silver. And Draco himself will be there to oversee the unloading.' Pio lowered his voice. 'Surrentum is a little inlet on the north side of the peninsula. I have sent word to the Prefect as we agreed.'

'This is far too easy, Pio. It is almost as if he wants to get caught.' Fortis toyed with his cloak. Pio was honest, he was sure of that. They had experienced enough together in Bithynia, but it did not mean that he had overheard correctly. He had to be sure. If he was to call out the army, he wanted them to discover something of substance, not simply a pair of illicit lovers on the sands. 'If you will remember the last time, your information cost Merlus a long fruitless voyage.'

'And he was seasick. Very vocal about that as well.' Pio gave a hearty laugh as Merlus called out a few choice insults. 'Tell me, why do you put up with his insolence? If he were mine, I would sell him immediately.'

'He is a good manservant.' Fortis dusted a speck of lint from his cloak. 'Now tell me your theory.'

'They say he is getting bolder and bolder.' Pio leant forward. 'It is supposed to be a large haul. He needs the money. You have managed to close down most of the other ports.'

'Perhaps, and perhaps not.' Fortis tapped his finger against his mouth. 'In any case, I want all the men detained. The Prefect is to release no one unless he has direct orders from me. Let's see who he catches this time.'

Pio took the signet ring Fortis dropped in his hand. 'You can count on me, Aurelius Fortis.'

Silvana glanced at the water-clock. She had expected her uncle back over an hour ago. The dinner guests had been well behaved, but now the after-dinner guests were arriving and a few had obviously stopped at a wine bar or three before deciding to come here. One grappled with Dida the porter, protesting how sober he was. Several others egged him on, shouting out bets as to who would win the contest

'Is there a problem, Dida?' Silvana glided over, wishing she possessed her uncle's jovial bonhomie that seemed to settle such disputes in a drip of the water-clock.

'This gentleman and his companions demand entrance, but I think they are better off suited in one of the brothels down by the docks.' Dida indicated an overweight pimply youth who was wearing a laurel wreath tilted over one ear and whose light purple dining clothes showed several wine stains.

'I want to give her a kiss. I want to kiss Silvana Junia,' the man slurred drunkenly and laid his heavy hand on Silvana's shoulders, trapping her before she could twist away. 'She kisses all the boys. They said so at the baths.'

'Then she can kiss me as well,' his companion slurred. 'We can make a threesome.'

Out of nowhere, a fist connected with her assailant's jaw and sent him reeling. His companion was sent flying after him.

'I trust no one else wants to make a slur on our hostess's reputation?' Fortis's quiet voice filled the deathly silent entrance way. The waiting men shook their heads while the other two got up and fled, the soles of their sandals making flapping sounds as they scurried down the street. 'Good, perhaps we can continue this evening in the manner befitting Romans, rather than barbarians.'

'I'm not—' Silvana's quip about not being in danger faded as she saw his muscular shoulders and trim figure. This time he wore dining clothes of the purest green silk. They moved and flowed with each step he took, accentuating the breadth of his shoulders. Silvana's breath caught in her throat before she remembered she was indifferent to this man. She swallowed hard and extended her hand. 'Aurelius Fortis, how kind you are to grace this party.'

'Eutychus and I would have been here earlier, but we were unavoidably detained. I trust our host will forgive us.'

'Your timing was perfect.' Silvana gazed after the two men. 'Dida's reputation is such that normally we are free from this type of disturbance, but obviously with so many new arrivals in town, a few think they can take liberties.'

'For that I am grateful.' He brought her hand to his lips for a heartbeat, before releasing it.

'Forgive me for being late, Silvana. My mother insisted we break bread with her.' Eutychus came forward. 'And do you know what just nearly happened—two men nearly knocked me down in their haste. They looked as if Hades himself was after them.'

'A minor disagreement over the correct way to greet Silvana Junia,' Fortis replied.

'Oh, good thing you have Dida, Silvana,' Eutychus said, 'or who knows what could have happened.'

'Yes, it was good that I have my protectors,' Silvana murmured, looking Fortis straight in the eye.

'I have my uses.'

He gave a slight nod, and Silvana found it impossible to think of anything but the strength in his shoulders. He cleared his throat. She remembered her duties, and the fact that she was supposed to be supremely attracted to Eutychus. She turned towards Eutychus and batted her eyelashes.

'Will you escort me to the dining room,

Eutychus?' she purred. 'Now that the disturbance has ended.'

'Tell me there will be dancing tonight?' Eutychus tucked her hand in his arm as they strolled towards the dining room.

'There is always dancing.' Silvana removed her hand as unobtrusively as she could. She had no wish to give Eutychus ideas. 'The servants are clearing the tables and couches back to the side of the room as we speak.'

'Splendid, splendid.' Eutychus rubbed his hands together. 'Now you can show me exactly how you dance, Fortis. You must see how he dances, Silvana. I thought my cousin all full of the Senate's business, but he assures me they dance in Rome as well as in Baiae.'

'Is there no limit to your talents?'

'What I do, I endeavour to do well.' Fortis's lips curved upwards. 'Even dancing.'

'Such a paragon of virtue.'

'Is your uncle here?' Fortis asked, scanning the crowd. 'I particularly wanted to pay my respects to him.'

Silvana's fingers curled around her gold necklace, seeking comfort from the amulet. Exactly why did Fortis crave a word with her uncle? 'My uncle had to go out unexpectedly. He was supposed to be back before now. It was why I was attempting to deal with the disturbance at the door.'

'Do you normally have to contend with drunken louts such as that?'

'My uncle received a laurel wreath for wrestling at the Olympic games in his youth. He can handle most of the junior tribunes.'

'But he wasn't here.'

'He expected to be back.' Silvana wiped her hands on her skirt. 'He could return any time.'

'Is there anything we can do?' Fortis asked, his eyes becoming grave.

'Nothing,' Silvana said around the sudden hard lump in her throat.

'This is dreadful!' Eutychus's face fell. 'Who will lead the first dance? Junius Maius always leads the first dance.'

Silvana looked around the rapidly growing throng of people. They were here in part for the dancing. To cancel that would be a sign something was wrong, and it might take months before her uncle's reputation recovered. But who could take the honour? As hostess, in theory she could, but she dreaded to think of the scandal, and given the timing of Crispus's return, he would be engulfed in it. 'I haven't given it much thought. Do you have any suggestions, Eutychus?'

She took care to bat her eyelashes at Eutychus, and make sure her tone was honey sweet. Colour rose in his face, turning him quite pink. 'I could.' Eutychus gulped. 'I really could. Tell me I can, Silvana. You won't regret it—'

'No!' Fortis broke in. 'Besides your dancing, it is your status. You would be placing Eutychus before a number of senators and he is no relation to your family as betrothal terms are not yet agreed.'

Silvana winced. In ways she wished she had never started this war with Fortis. Were the betrothal terms the reason he had reappeared? He said it so casually. Had he now decided to agree to Eutychus's request, and, if so, where did that leave her? She had no intention of marrying Eutychus, but what if her uncle insisted? Silvana smoothed her gown. It was a bluff. Had to be.

'Do you have an alternative suggestion, Aurelius Fortis? Are you volunteering for the position?'

'He should do it. No one would comment.' Eutychus clapped his hands together like an overly excited schoolboy.

'If you desire it.' Fortis stroked his chin. His eyes sparked with a sudden green flame. 'As a solution, it does have a sort of naïve charm to it. I have the status, and it is the sort of thing Junius Maius would approve of. Eutychus as my cousin shall be the next in the line.'

'Thank you.' Silvana inclined her head and looked away from his eyes. There was something about them, something that made her feel vaguely nervous and unsettled, reminding her of the game of twelve lines they had played. She thought she could contain him then, and had lost badly.

'I have no wish for Eutychus to make a fool of himself.'

'It is the result I am interested in, not the reason.' She met his gaze and noticed he had impossibly long lashes for a man. She signalled to a servant for her uncle's wreath. 'If you are going to lead the dance, you had best pay homage to Bacchus. It would never do for the leader of the dance to appear without a laurel wreath.'

'I have no wish to offend.' He bent his head and she placed the dark green laurel wreaths onto his black curls. 'Tell me, Eutychus, what do you think of your cousin now?'

'Absolutely splendid.' Eutychus's bottom lip trembled. 'But why do you never crown me with laurels, Silvana?'

'No doubt when you lead the dance, you will wear the laurel, Eutychus,' Fortis said before Silvana could say anything.

The first notes of the lyre and cornu sounded and Eutychus dragged Fortis on the floor. Silvana watched in amusement that rapidly faded to grudging admiration as Fortis flawlessly executed the complicated footsteps and manoeuvres required for the dance. He had no hesitation about leading the chain of men first this way and then that way. His dark green tunic swayed and swirled revealing the outlines of his muscular thighs. The laurel wreath that always looked so ridiculous on her rotund uncle suited Fortis and his dark looks. She saw several women look admiringly at him and the way his body moved as one with the beat of the music.

Silvana's mouth grew dry as a warmth starting glowing deep within her. It was the way he danced, his hips swivelling in rhythm to the music, a wild pulsating beat that grew faster each time the line of men circled the dance floor, their feet stamping in perfect time. Their tunics swirled, revealing slightly more of their legs than strictly necessary. A faint glow shone on their faces. Fortis's eyes held an emerald gleam as if he lived for the music and the music lived for him. Silvana found it impossible to tear her eyes away from his body as he led the ever-growing group of men around the dance floor.

The direction of the dance changed. Fortis came towards her, his eyes caught and held her. His laurel wreath had slipped to a rakish angle. He made a half-gesture towards her in time to the music.

An invitation?

She shook her head, but he repeated the gesture, this time with a wide smile and a slight jerk of his head.

She took a step forwards, her body swaying in time to the music. He was close, so close. Only two more steps. A clang jarred across her nerves. Her slipper had hit a goblet, sending it rolling out on to the floor. Silvana stopped, confused. How could she dream of doing such a thing? The scandal it would cause, if she gave into her desires and started dancing with an unmarried man in public, would reach Rome and beyond.

She raised her cup of wine to her lips and drained it, seeking the solace of the sweetened liquid. It was madness of the blood brought on by over-anxiety about her uncle. In another heartbeat, she would have gone out there to join him. With a trembling hand she set the cup down and escaped into the coolness of the garden.

The night air brushed her cheeks, taking away the heat, giving welcome relief. She gulped mouthfuls of air and her breathing became steadier. The slight damp soaked through her slippers but she refused to care. The pulsating beat was a distant noise. Her hand grasped the trunk of the olive tree, drawing strength from it.

'Here. You look pale.' Warm fingers pushed a

cup into her hands. 'Drink this. It will make you feel better.'

'I already had a cup of wine, Fortis,' she said.

'Drink it.' His tone allowed for no refusal. 'It will put the roses back in your cheeks.'

She raised the cup to her lips and the honey-sweetened wine filled her mouth before tracing a fiery path down her throat. She lowered the cup and handed it back to Fortis. This time their fingertips briefly touched, sending a pulsating warmth through her. He did not move away, but stood close enough to touch, if she dared reach out a hand.

'I thought you would be dancing.'

'The junior tribunes have thrown off their mantels, one has divested himself of his tunic and is in his loin cloth. The dance appears to have inspired them.' Fortis gave a soft laugh and moved a step closer. She could see the small beads of sweat gleaming in the lamp light.

'But not you?'

'One dance with them was enough to remind me of my misspent youth. Let Eutychus and the others enjoy themselves. Soon enough they will have to grow up.'

'Do you miss it?'

He shook his head. 'No, by the time I left Baiae, I had attended too many parties, seen too many drunken fights. I was glad of the rest.'

'There is gaiety in music.'

'I prefer the sort that comes from within, and is not contained in an amphora of wine.'

Silvana stared at him, aware the sounds of the lyre had faded, and all that was left was the lonely plaintive wail of the cornu. The dance was over. She was safe.

'Thank you for saving the party. I am in your debt.'

'Then I have a boon to ask of you.' His voice flowed over her.

'What do you want?'

'Dance with me.' His hand caught her fingers, held them still in his firm grasp. 'The musicians are playing another tune. Listen.'

Silvana tilted her head to one side. This time the music was slower, sweeter, with a dreamy, almost lyrical, beat. Her body swayed slightly. Fortis clasped her hand and started to lead her towards the open doors.

'Out there in that crowd?' She started to pull away, but his grip tightened, holding her, preventing her from leaving. 'You must be mad! I am trying to avoid scandal, not cause it.'

He shook his head. 'Out here in the garden then, just us two. You want to dance. I know you do.'

Silvana struggled to take a breath. Her body swayed to the rhythm of the lyre. The music entered her body, pulsing through it. She wanted to do this with every fibre of her being.

'Are you a coward? Are you going to refuse me this one little request?' he asked, and held out his other hand.

Chapter Seven

Mutely, Silvana took his outstretched hand, linking her fingers with his, warm, soft, yielding to the pressure. Her hair had escaped and now curled invitingly at her temples as her eyes sparkled with hidden lights, beckoning him forward. As the lyre started its tune, desire rose within him, intensifying. He longed to dip his head and taste her lips, but he had to go slowly, to ease her along.

He forced his feet to move, beginning the grape-vine. Silvana hesitated, halting, threatening to pull away as a crease appeared between her perfectly plucked brows. She mistimed a step and stumbled.

'Follow my lead, Silvana.' He gave her hand a squeeze. 'I won't let you fall.'

She gave a barely perceptible nod and moved out into the silver moonlit garden.

'I am ready.'

He raised their joined hands to shoulder height and started to move, his feet doing the intricate steps in time to the music.

Silvana followed along, head held high. Slowly at first, as if the steps were half-remembered, and then, as she grew in confidence, her feet began to move faster and faster.

Fortis manoeuvred her around an old olive tree, causing her to spin around, her skirt lifting and flowing over her shapely ankles. A soft laugh of pure happiness escaped her lips. She stumbled slightly and Fortis brought his other hand up to her waist, steadying her. All movement stopped. The music became a distant melody.

Silvana heard the pounding of her heart in her ears. She was powerless to do anything but stare up at him and the shadowy planes of his face. Then she dropped her gaze, rearranged her shawl more tightly about her shoulders. 'I am a bit rusty at this, I am afraid.'

'You did want to dance.' His voice was silk over her arms. Seductive, smooth, making her remember the touch of his lips.

'As a girl, I loved to dance, but my late husband forbade it. I was to be a beautiful statue, above all such things,' Silvana said, ducking her head to avoid his penetrating gaze. She only had to lift her mouth a little and she'd touch his lips. 'When I was widowed, I was determined to do all the things he had forbidden.'

'Including dancing.'

'Uncle Aulus felt a woman dancing would make his parties seem too much like a brothel, but I was determined.' Silvana found she could smile at the memory now, but at the time, she had felt like her world was falling apart.

'And who won?'

'Uncle Aulus and I compromised, once a year is enough as we don't want to give his parties the wrong tone. Slightly risqué, not all-out debauchery.'

'Dancing…'

Her eye shone with hidden mischief and she put a finger to her lips to silence him. 'Dancing is seldom accomplished standing still in the shade of an olive tree. Even a novice like me knows that.'

'No, but…' His lips were closer. He raised her chin. His green eyes loomed large and she could see the faint stubble of his beard. Would it be soft or bristly? Did she dare? A trembling like the breeze rustling through the olive leaves filled her. Her body started to arch towards him.

A sudden loud twang from the lyre resounded, discordant, sharp, changing the tempo. She jumped away, her back hitting the bark of the olive tree.

'We are supposed to be dancing, shall we?' she said, trying to ignore the racing of her heart.

Without waiting for an answer, she forced her feet to move, feeling the cool gravel underneath her sandals. Quick firm steps back out into the moonlight. Out here, she would not be tempted.

'And how many men have you danced with in the moonlight?' he asked as they made a second circuit of the garden.

Silvana pretended to ponder the question.

'I could tease and say thousands, but I believe you are the first.'

'And do you plan to make a habit of it?'

Their footsteps slowed imperceptibly until they were standing, swaying gently. A white statue of Venus gleamed silver in the moonlight. The lyres sounded softly in the distance. The scent of jasmine rose and mingled with a scent Fortis knew he would for ever associate with Silvana. She raised her brown eyes to his. Her lips were full, and begged to be kissed. He needed to kiss her.

'I should go back.' Her hand threatened to slip from his. She would go and vanish like the night. She turned, took a step away from him.

'Stay.'

She halted. Her gown slipped slightly off her shoulder but she did not bother straightening it. Her red lips parted as if she wanted to say something. Fortis cupped the back of her head, drew her unresisting body towards him. 'Please stay.'

He brought his mouth down on hers and felt it tremble. Slowly he nuzzled her lips, a gentle kiss.

She sighed against his mouth and her hands came up to his shoulders. Her mouth parted slightly, and he tasted the soft sweetness that had teased his sleep-filled brain since that morning he had found her, dripping with seawater, on the harbour wall. The warm honey taste.

Her hands reached up and encircled his neck. Fortis increased the pressure and her mouth opened further and he was able to drink his fill. Her head tilted back, exposing the slender column of her throat. His lips traced a line down to the hollow where her heart sounded. He rested his head there, listening, allowing her scent to envelop him.

'There are blossoms in your hair making you look like you were taking part in the rituals of Flora and those ended a month ago.' Soft laughter echoed in her voice as her hands plucked at his curls. 'I hate to think what Eutychus and the rest will say you've been up to.'

'I don't care,' he growled, pressing his lips against the spot where he could hear her heart racing. 'They will be too busy dancing to notice I am here with you.'

'We should go back.' Her hands continued to brush the blossoms away.

'We should do nothing of the sort.' He cupped her face with his hands and smiled down at her. She didn't move, but stood there waiting.

One by one, he plucked the hair pins from her head, and allowed them to fall to the ground, until her honey-gold hair was a curtain around her shoulders. His fingers combed her hair, bringing it to his mouth. 'Your hair is like gold and scented with roses.'

'Fortis.' Her whisper was no more than a breath.

His lips claimed hers again. This time there was no need to rain soft kisses, her mouth opened and their tongues touched. There was a certain innocence to the way she kissed that surprised Fortis. He would have thought a woman of her notoriety would be an expert in the art of kissing. Then he brought his arms around her hard, seeking to blot out all memory of other men. Her body responded by arching. The tight buds of her nipples brushed his chest through the thin cloth that separated them.

She gave a soft moan in her throat and her tongue entered his mouth, imitating his. He cupped her buttocks and pulled her tighter against him, heard the gasp in her throat as she felt his need pressing into her. She wriggled against him. Her hands entangled themselves in his hair and pulled his face closer. Her tongue traced the outline of his mouth.

His body hardened to an aching, throbbing need, urgent, insistent, unwilling to be ignored. He wanted to lift her skirts and press himself into her body. He wanted to have her, hear her moan in her throat when she reached the point of no return. The thought made him ache harder. His breathing echoed hers, short, sharp, and he felt his body begin to lurch towards that point where he would lose control, something he had not done since he had been an *adulescens,* younger than Eutychus.

All this from a kiss.

He forced his body to retreat, tore his mouth away, drew a shuddering breath. Lifting her chin, he stared into her deep eyes, seeking confirmation that she had felt something as well and she wanted him in the same way. Her fingers stroked his cheekbone with a faint fluttering touch, hesitant, but then firm, cupping the back of his neck, pulling him towards her. His control slipped. With a growl deep in his throat, he reclaimed her lips.

'Fortis, where have you disappeared to?' Eutychus's voice floated towards them. 'At least six tribunes want to learn your dance steps. I have promised them that you will show them, as you showed me earlier.'

Fortis swung around, his hand instinctively hiding Silvana's face against his chest. He laid a finger against her lips. If she kept silent, there was a possibility they could keep their encounter hidden. A quick glance down showed how thoroughly he had kissed her. Her hair hung in waves about her shoulders, and her mouth was full and red. His body wanted her as he had wanted no other woman. He wanted her in a hundred, no, a thousand different ways, and somewhere where he could pursue his desire without fear of interruption.

'We'll talk later, Eutychus.'

'Who are you with? You are not the type to commune with the gods.'

Fortis cursed. He had not meant for this to happen. Not now. Not like this, but he had to accept what the Fates had given him. He gave Silvana's shoulder a squeeze and hoped she'd understand. She gave a slight nod. He stepped out of the shadows and faced his cousin. 'What are you doing out here?'

'Looking for you.' Eutychus had a triumphant gleam on his face, proud and alert. There was a crowd of young tribunes around Eutychus. Most were drunk. A few swayed. 'I told my friends you would teach them the dance, the turn.'

'Some other time. It takes more concentration than this lot possesses. The musicians are about to strike up another dance.' Fortis gave a nod towards the yellow pool of light in the doorway. Behind him, in the shadows, there was a distinct crack of a twig.

'Somebody else is there,' one of the crowd called out.

'Come, come, whoever you are.'

'Can you dance as well?'

Fortis crossed his arms, blocked the way.

'Back to the party, Eutychus. Take your friends with you. There is nothing for you out here.'

Eutychus opened his mouth as if to protest. He attempted to peer around Fortis as the moon came out from behind a cloud, briefly illuminating the garden. His eyes widened, and Fortis saw a flash of hurt as Eutychus hurriedly stepped back and away from the shaded laurels.

'I understand,' he said in a high tight voice, not unlike the one he had used when he confronted his mother. 'I need to go.'

Fortis wanted to do many things, most of all to have the ability to turn time back. He had wanted to end Eutychus's devotion to Silvana, but not like this, not in this manner. His insides twisted.

'This is not the time or the place for dance lessons,' he said quietly.

'Back to the house, boys. I think the porter will open an amphora of wine if we ask pleasantly.'

Eutychus gestured with his arm and the crowd started to disperse.

Fortis let out a breath. There was a slim chance nobody had noticed who was standing in the shadows. Eutychus's hand caught Fortis's wrist. His eyes were anguished, but his face had a hardness that had not been there before.

'Hurt her, and I will cut your heart out, cousin.'

Fortis gave a barely perceptible nod and watched his cousin walk back towards the light. He fancied Eutychus's step was a little more firm, a bit more determined.

'Would you mind telling me what you were doing there?' Silvana's hands were busy straightening her hair.

'I didn't think you or I needed another scandal.' He paused. 'There will be no scandal. I can guarantee you that.'

'For once, I agree with you. The last thing I need is another scandal.' Silvana dropped to the gravel and started searching with her hands. 'I appear to have lost a hair pin.'

'I prefer you with your hair down.'

'I can't go back in there with my hair about my shoulders as if…I and you…' She glanced up from the ground and her voice faded away.

Fortis pulled her up and placed a finger over her

lips. 'No one is asking you to go back in there. I would consider it very unwise.'

'Unwise in what manner?'

'I will send everyone home. You can have retired with a headache, worried about your uncle. No one will question it.'

Silvana hesitated. Fortis gave her a little push towards the outside stairs.

'Go now before your guests take it into their heads to start swimming in the fountain.'

She started towards the outside stairs. Her footsteps were quick and her gown swirled about her legs in the moonlight.

'I don't make a habit of kissing men amongst the laurels,' she said over her shoulder.

'I could tell.' He resisted the urge to recapture her and carry her to her room.

'As long as you know.'

'And, Silvana, my opinion has not changed—you would be bored within ten days if you married Eutychus.' He paused. 'However, if you ever decide you wish to become my mistress, the position is open.'

The dining room and *tablinum* still bore signs of last night's party. The bits of debris and scattering of spills did not worry Silvana. They would be clean and sparkling for tonight. But the atmosphere was all wrong, a strange and collective stillness hung over the villa, almost as if the house was holding its breath. Uncle Aulus had failed to return home or send word, despite his promise.

Last night after the guests departed, she had laid awake, waiting for the creak of the door and boom of his voice as he called for a servant to help with his sandals, but nothing, not even a whisper. This morning, she had sent both Dida and Lyde out to see if they could glean any gossip. Both had returned with nothing to report.

Silvana leant down and replaced a cushion on a couch, so it hid part of a stain. The party had been a bit wilder than when her uncle was present. She hated to think what might have happened if the guests had not left when they did.

Fortis had been as good as his word. All the guests had departed before she had time to straighten her hair and gown, and repair the damage the kiss had caused. She wanted to regret the kiss, but her body refused to let her. She shuddered at what he must think of her. Properly brought-up Roman matrons, even widows, did not kiss like that in the shaded nooks. All she had done was confirm his belief that she was a loose woman, a woman unfit for his family. No doubt he believed all the wild tales about her had to be true. Hadn't she confirmed it with one passionate kiss?

She had to be grateful that he had stepped between her and Eutychus, shielded her. He could have so easily turned her towards the crowd, shown Eutychus what she was. She despised herself, but she knew if she had another chance, she'd taste those lips again, melt in his arms.

Later, after her uncle returned home safe, she'd go to Eutychus and explain to him as gently as possible that there was no hope for something between them. She loved him like a sister, not as he deserved to be loved. He needed to find someone else. Out there, a woman who needed him waited to be discovered.

She made a face. Surely Cupid, that mischievous god of lust, had been working overtime when he pricked her with his arrow.

'Silvana Junia, the aide to the Prefect requests an interview,' Dida the porter said, breaking into her reverie. 'It is official business. He refuses to wait.'

Silvana smoothed the folds in her deep pink gown as a sudden stab of fear ran through. Uncle Aulus? Or worse, her brother Crispus? Had some tragedy befallen him on the Appian Way? 'Did you inform him of my uncle's absence?'

'It is about your uncle that he has come.'

Silvana nodded, and tried to ignore the sudden clenching of her stomach. Silently, as she waited, she offered up a prayer to Minerva and Juno that her uncle might yet come home safely. She started to pace the room and then realised that would betray too much. She had to stand and wait impassively, not allow her imagination to run wild. It could all be a mistake.

The aide strode into the dining room, his metalled sandals striking the mosaic tiles with a ringing sound and his deep red cloak flowing behind him. Silvana relaxed slightly as she recognised him from several of her uncle's parties. He had a fine voice and she had once accompanied him on the lyre, but his name escaped her.

'It is good of you to see me at such short notice, Silvana Junia.' The aide raised her hand to his lips. 'You are truly radiant this morning.'

'You told the porter you had news of my uncle.' Silvana withdrew her hand as gently as she could, and wiped it against her gown.

The tall soldier shifted in his sandals. He took off his helmet and held it awkwardly at his side. A crease appeared between his eyebrows. 'I come as a friend, as someone who has enjoyed your hospitality many times.'

'Where is my uncle? Is he alive?' Silvana's hand clenched at her side. Whatever happened, she would not scream. She would remain upright.

The soldier's face cleared. 'Yes, ma'am, he is alive, but—'

'But what? Where is he?'

'He is at the garrison.'

Silvana's legs suddenly refused to hold her and she sank down on the couch. Her mind kept repeating—he's alive. Nothing else mattered, except her uncle was alive. A new fear clawed at her belly.

'How badly is he injured? I must know.' She laid a hand on the soldier's forearm. 'As a friend, and you are a friend, you must tell me.'

The soldier's eye became fixed on a point above her head. 'He is in protective custody. He was found, with a number of others, consorting with a pirate.'

Silvana stifled a gasp. She could easily imagine what protective custody was and how her uncle would be treated, despite his status.

'There has to be a mistake. My uncle would never do such a thing.'

'He was captured in the act of receiving spices from a known pirate and associate of Draco. The pirate is ready to testify that your uncle is Draco's main Roman contact.'

'But that is wrong.' Silvana clasped her hands together. 'It is wrong. My uncle would never do anything like that.'

The soldier withdrew a scrap of papyrus from his

belt. 'He managed to write a few lines. Things he would like you to send back with me.'

Silvana reached out and with numb fingers took the scribbled note. Her uncle listed a number of items, and ended by saying sorry. She stared at the words until they started to swim. 'This is a ghastly mistake.'

'I live and pray that it is, Silvana Junia.' The soldier looked straight ahead. 'All the times I and my brother officers have enjoyed his hospitality, never dreaming he would betray Rome in such a manner.'

'Can I go to him?'

'That will not be possible. The Prefect is very proud of his catch. He only arrived in Baiae last Ides and already he has done more than most.' The soldier stood to attention. 'He is a stickler for discipline and for following the rules.'

'How many people know?'

'Not many. Your uncle and the others were surprised in the early hours.' The soldier gave a small shrug. 'But you know how small Baiae is. The story will be in the public houses before the general bathing time, I would guess.'

'I will send the things he requires.' Silvana drew a deep breath. Her mind raced. Everything she and her uncle had worked for was in ruins. She clearly remembered what happened two years previously when a senator had been caught aiding and abetting pirates. All his property was confiscated. His wife and children had to go into exile in Spain. The scandal would ruin any chance Crispus had. She knew her uncle was innocent. The problem was how to get the Prefect to listen to her. 'And tell my uncle I will do all I can.'

'I will tell him. He said that you were a good woman, the sort of woman Rome could be proud of.'

Silvana stared at the plain stone wall of the garrison's gatehouse. Nothing was coming in or going out. No carts, or even men. The whole fort wore a hushed air. Beyond the gatehouse she could see the Via Princeps that led to the headquarters and to where the Prefect must surely be.

After the soldier left she had not waited, but had called for Lyde and they had hurried to the fort, but little good had come of it. None of her entreaties to the guards had worked. The Prefect had stubbornly refused to see her. Otherwise occupied, was what the guard had said.

There had to be a way. If only she could see the Prefect, she could explain that a terrible mistake had been made.

'Silvana Junia, it is unusual to find you here.' Cotta's nasal intonations grated across her already stretched nerves. 'Is something the matter?'

Silvana placed a hand to her head, willed herself to be calm and turned to face her stepson. It was worse than she had feared. On his arm hung Poppea Cornelia, wearing the expression of a sleek well-fed temple cat as well as a new purple-and-gold gap-sleeved gown and matching *stola*.

'Yes, do tell us, Silvana. I cannot remember the last time I saw you in such an unbecoming hairstyle or without a *stola*,' Poppea said.

Cotta whispered something in her ear and Poppea dissolved into a series of gasping twitters as she clutched his arm.

'I had no idea you two were such friends,' Silvana said.

'It is a recent friendship, stepmother. I do hope you approve.'

'I should think you two were very well suited to each other.'

'I'd like to think we are.' Poppea drew a finger down Cotta's arm. 'You should see the new bracelet he gave me.'

Poppea displayed a gaudy silver bracelet bedecked with Egyptian hieroglyphs.

'It is quite unusual.' Silvana opted for a diplomatic answer. 'Foreign.'

'She begged me for it.'

'And you do so like it when I beg.' Poppea gave a simpering smile and a wink. 'I do it very well.'

'And I would agree with that.' Cotta preened his heavily embroidered toga.

Silvana turned her head. She hated to see the depths to which Poppea had sunk. Poppea would not see it that way. She saw it as a business deal, a using of her assets to allow her to live in the manner she wanted to.

'There has been a great deal of activity at the Aurelius compound this morning.' Poppea batted her eyelashes, but her tone held a certain malicious delight.

'Why should that be of any interest to me?' Silvana refused to show any emotion, but her mind raced. What was Fortis up to?

'A little bird told me that your young swain was seen taking a horse very rapidly in the direction of Rome.' Poppea gave a cat-like smile. 'I do wonder what it is about.'

'I assure you, I have no idea.' Silvana gave a shrug of her shoulder, but she hated the idea that somehow she had inadvertently hurt Eutychus. She had not intended the kiss happening and wished she had had the opportunity to say so.

'There appears to be very few people entering the fort this morning. None of the usual carts and people on foot,' Cotta said. 'Do you have any idea why, Silvana?'

'One hears rumours.' Silvana made a little fluttering motion with her hands. If she admitted the truth Cotta would foreclose on the loan. Undoubtedly, the interest rate would have increased and the value of their property decreased. Somehow she needed to convince the Prefect that he had made a mistake.

'I heard a rumour that Aurelius Fortis was on good terms with the Prefect,' Poppea said. 'Maybe he can discover if it is true that they have actually captured pirates.'

'Aurelius Fortis is on good terms with a good too many people,' Cotta harrumphed. 'If you had known him back in Bithynia when we were tribunes, you would never have considered him destined for any greatness. The only thing he lived for then was horses and the gaming tables.'

'They say he changed after his wife's death.' Poppea gave another one of her twittering laughs. 'Of course, Murcia and I were friends—not great friends, but friends. She was a sly one, that one, wrapped him around her little finger. Such a dreadful accident and a waste of vibrant life. Did you know she was planning to leave him? She had confided in me that she had found a better-placed senator.'

'You are a veritable fount of information, Poppea.'

Cotta toyed with a strap on Poppea's *stola* as she fluttered her lashes demurely. 'Perhaps you would like to come on my yacht.'

'I do wish you better luck, Cotta. Maybe this time your dinner companion can't swim,' Silvana said as the pair sauntered off, happily exchanging gossip.

She regarded the forbidding gatehouse once more. Too much activity. Within a few hours, the whole town would know of her uncle's crime and then the requests for money would start and then there would be the offers, offers that would have nothing to do with marriage and everything to do with a protector. Pain throbbed at her temple. She had to do something while she was able to make a choice. She drew in a breath. There was one avenue she hadn't tried.

Chapter Eight

'And to what do I owe this visit, Silvana? And so early in the morning?' Fortis rose from behind his scroll-strewn desk. There was a small ink blot on his right hand and a red mark on his cheek as if he had rested his face against his hand as he wrote. Approachable, not forbidding. The knots in Silvana's stomach relaxed. She could make this request and save her uncle from scandal.

'I need your help,' Silvana blurted out, not waiting for the pleasantries. 'You must help me, Aurelius Fortis. You must.'

'Take a deep breath. What is so dreadful that you have come to visit with your hair escaping from its netting and without your *stola?* Have you come alone?' Fortis's eyebrows drew together in a frown.

'My maid is waiting with the porter. It appears they are third cousins on Lyde's father's side.'

Fortis came towards her and ushered her on to a couch covered in cushions and blankets. His simple white tunic made his skin even more golden than usual. His warm fingers lingered on her shoulder for an instant longer than propriety demanded.

'I am certain you did not come to discuss your maid's ancestry with me, as fascinating as it may be.'

'Last night soldiers came upon my uncle and arrested him for consorting with pirates.' Silvana gave a great hiccup. Her hands twisted the end of her belt. All the pretty speeches she had devised on the way to Fortis's vanished as if they had never been. Sitting here in this study with Fortis's deep gaze on her made it all to real. This was not a Fury-induced dream or even a play, this was real and if she was not very careful she would never see her uncle again.

"I had heard rumours that the pirates intended to land Egyptian silver and spices." His eyes were hard and unyielding.

'My uncle has been accused of receiving spices. No one has mentioned silver—Egyptian or other-wise." She covered her face with her hands, willing her body to stop shaking. She could do this. Make the request. Offer the bargain. He had to agree.

Within an instant Fortis had placed his arms about her and she rested her head against the crisp linen of his tunic, listening to the quiet steady rhythm of his heart. Several hot tears slipped from the corners of her eyes.

'I am sure it is not as bad you think,' he said after her sobs had subsided. 'Your uncle is a patrician and very well connected. There is little the Prefect can do, even if it is proven that your uncle has conspired with pirates.'

'The new Prefect is determined to make an example of him,' Silvana said into his chest. 'It is very hard for a man to appeal to Rome if he has been crucified.'

'You are allowing your imagination to run away with you.'

'Crucifixion is one of the penalties for pirates. When Julius Caesar strung up the pirates, did anyone complain? And rather than being punished for acting outside the law, Julius Caesar has gone from strength to strength. They say he is going to become an *aedile* next—after that, who knows?'

'This is an entirely different matter.' His hand stroked her hair. 'Now look at me. Your uncle is a Roman citizen, an equestrian and a patrician. No Prefect will risk his career by quickly punishing him, and particularly not one as ambitious as this one.'

Silvana raised her head and looked at the growing blotch on his tunic. She wanted to trust his soothing words.

'I am making a mess of your tunic. I am afraid my make-up is running everywhere.' She took a handkerchief from her belt and dabbed ineffectually at the spot where her head had lain. The spot only grew bigger. Silvana felt the hot prick of tears again. Even something as simple as cleaning a spot she made a mess of.

'Leave it.'

Silvana's hand froze in mid-air. 'I was attempting to help.'

'I have other tunics. The fuller can easily whiten this one.' Fortis's hand closed on hers and he gently returned it to her lap. His arm came around her and held her body against his. 'Tell me why you have come. I doubt it was to spill paint and powder over my tunic. How do you wish me to help? What do you need me to do?'

Silvana drew a deep breath and gripped her thighs with her hands, her nails digging into the flesh through the thin linen of her gown. She had to make her request properly, make sure he understood what she was offering.

'I need you to go and see the Prefect and explain. I have already tried, but he is refusing to see me.'

'Explain what?' Fortis tilted his head to one side, assessing her.

'Explain that my uncle is innocent.' Silvana's hand

twisted some of the material of her gown into a tight ball. He had to help her. He was her last hope.

Fortis's eyes narrowed. 'How do you know he is innocent?'

'The aide who came to see me said that Uncle Aulus was arrested for trafficking with pirates. Uncle Aulus is accused of being the main go-between in the area for the pirates. He would never do such a thing. He couldn't—not after what happened to him.'

'What happened?' Fortis leant forward. His hand gripped Silvana's. There was an edge to his voice. 'You can tell me. Why would your uncle never traffic with pirates? Plenty of men do.'

'Several years ago, just before my father married me to Cotta, Uncle Aulus, his wife and young son were captured by pirates off the coast of Sicily. My uncle survived the ordeal, but his wife and son died. Since that day he has never had anything to do with such creatures. Vultures, he calls them and wonders when the Senate will take concrete action, instead of spouting mere words.'

'But your uncle is renowned as a dealer of cargo, a man with a finger in all the stews and intrigues.' Fortis tilted his head to one side. Was this another of Silvana's games? Her uncle was in trouble, he did not doubt that part of the story, but how deeply was he involved?

'He only invests in legitimate businesses.' Silvana sat bolt upright, her eyes flashing. 'He likes to know what is going on, but he won't invest if he thinks pirates are involved. Can you imagine what it was like for him to watch his wife die?'

Fortis closed his eyes. His lips became a thin white line. 'I don't need imagination.'

Silvana bit her lip and forced her hands to stay still. 'Then you will understand why my uncle behaves in the way he does. He follows the teaching of Epicurus—living for the day. But whatever the temptation, he refuses to have anything to do with pirates. It would dishonour the shade of my aunt.'

'And why have you come to tell me this?'

'Because you have status. The Prefect will listen to you. You are an ex-queastor of Rome. Status impresses him.'

'Your belief in my abilities is touching.'

'Even if you cannot free him, then I am sure you can arrange to see him, and get his wounds seen to.'

'He is wounded?'

'Roman soldiers are not noted for their gentleness with pirates or their supporters.' Silvana regarded the charcoal brazier across the room. Her mind kept conjuring up images of Uncle Aulus beaten and in pain.

'If your uncle is innocent, set up as you claim, who is the culprit?'

'Drusus Cotta the Younger,' Silvana said without hesitation. 'I would stake my life on it.'

'Your life is too precious to waste.' Fortis made a note on a tablet. 'Do you have any concrete proof? Proof I can offer a court? A hidden hoard of Egyptian silver?'

Silvana shook her head slowly. 'No proof...only a feeling. You must help me.'

'And what will you give me if I do this for you?'

He had asked the fatal question. Silvana's palms and mouth were dry. It was time. She had to make her offer and wait. Hopefully she had not misread the situation.

'I knew you'd expect payment, so I have come to offer you a deal.' Her voice sounded high and strained to her ears.

'What sort of deal?' Fortis reached out and traced his finger along her jaw. 'I should warn you that Eutychus left this morning for Rome. He suddenly discovered that my offer of a job in the Senate was a great deal more appealing than staying here after what he saw last night out in the garden.'

Silvana jerked her head away and stood up. Fury coursed through her veins. How dare he! The anger grew as a suspicion took hold. She had naïvely danced her way into his plans. Such a fool.

'Last night was planned?'

'Last night was a pleasant interlude.' Fortis came to stand behind her. He did not touch her, but the warmth of his body was just behind her, flooding her senses, causing her anger to be replaced by something equally as elemental—desire. Silvana knew all she had to do was to lean back the smallest portion and she'd encounter the rock-solid muscles of his chest. She forced her body to stay still. 'Unexpected and all the more enticing for it.'

'You knew what was going to happen when you kissed me.'

Savage hands turned her around. His green eyes blazed a fire. 'I kissed you because I wanted to, not because I thought Eutychus would find us. I did everything in my power to protect the boy. I did not want him to become disillusioned in that way, in the way I knew he eventually would.'

'And now that he has…'

'I won't deny my pleasure in being right. You were not made for him.' He gave a crooked smile. His hand touched her shoulder, pulling her shawl up. 'I did warn you of the danger of trusting in a young man's affection without the betrothal papers being signed.'

'You presume much!' Silvana spun away from him, retreated to the other side of the room. She should never have come here. She had trusted him, believed that they had reached some sort of under-standing last night, a friendship of sorts. But every-thing was a sham. He had coldly kissed her to prove a point and she had melted in his arms.

'But you are highly attracted to me.' He followed her, his eyes softening slightly as his fingertips brushed her shoulders, sending tremors along her arms.

She hurriedly wrapped them about her waist. 'I have no idea what you are talking about,' she lied.

'I would like to see you deny that you did not find my kiss infinitely more enjoyable than any Eutychus might have bestowed on you. Shall I have to demonstrate again?'

In another heartbeat she'd be begging for the touch of his lips again. She turned her head and concentrated on the frescoes, willed her heart to stop racing. She refused to think about the deep dark warmth of his kisses, until everything was settled between them, until he had agreed to arrange for her uncle's release. She had to remember why she was here and what she wanted to achieve.

She forced her lungs to fill with air, achieved a measure of calm. Turned back to him, poised with a smile on her lips. 'If you were convinced that your methods would work, then why did you offer me money to drop Eutychus?'

His arms fell to his side. The soft beguiling look vanished to be replaced with a much harder, more mocking expression.

'You were right about one thing, Silvana, that day on the quayside. I wanted to take the easy way. I have spent the last few years using my money to solve problems, running away from life.'

'And now?' she whispered, afraid of what he might say, afraid of what he might not say.

'I am not sure what I want.' He ran his hand through his hair. 'If you are not here to see Eutychus or for the money, what are you here for? What sort of help do you want? There are matters that require my attention.'

Silvana ran her tongue over her lips. Did she dare reveal her true reason? She had to concentrate on the man who held her in his arms last night, the man who had ravaged her mouth, not the austere senator who stood before her with his arms crossed.

She had made her decisions standing before the fort. Any man she went to was bound to ask for payment and she had only one thing left to bargain with. She wiped her hands against her gown, smoothing the folds. Cotta had made that clear on the boat that night. She had to choose. To save her uncle she had to sacrifice herself.

Silvana squared her shoulders and stared directly

at Fortis. She refused to falter. Her uncle's life depended on it. 'The Prefect will see you. He will have to listen to a former queastor. If you are able to free my uncle, I will become your mistress.'

Fortis stared in disbelief at Silvana. Her hands were pressed together and her chin upright, proud. Her rose-pink gown bore creases and tear splotches. Gone was the perfect hostess from last night and in her place stood the woman he had rescued from the sea. Vulnerable, yet defiant and determined. A sudden overpowering desire to protect her swept over him.

He knew the situation. Pio had reported back on the arrests—Junius Maius and a few of the more feckless fish fanciers of Baiae along with three hapless seamen, and not a single one of them a head of a pirate clan or even a captain. Sacrifices to appease Rome. He knew how he was supposed to act, but he intended on playing the game his way, rather than by his unknown opponent's rules. The only thing the opponent had done was to show him Junius Maius's innocence. That and to have Silvana appear like a ripe plum, willing to trade her body for her uncle.

'Why?' he asked between gritted teeth as he fought to hang on to his self control. 'Why are you offering me this?'

She stood proud. Her chin lifted, but she allowed

her shawl to drop and Fortis was afforded a view of her creamy neck and the start of where her breasts swelled.

'My body is the only thing I have to bargain with. If my uncle is convicted, we will lose everything. I want this solved before my brother arrives in Baiae. I want no stain on him or his prospects.'

'Why not bargain with the Prefect?' Fortis forced the words from his lips. He had to know to be sure. The stakes in this game were very high, but he intended to force them higher. 'Or do you think he might not like your body?'

Silvana blanched and then her face contorted with fury. 'You were the one who asked me last night. Then I had no reason to take you up on your offer. I am not a courtesan who is willing to sell her body to the highest bidder. I came to you because of what we shared last night. You told me I had only to say the word and you would take me for your mistress.'

Then she waited, every nerve straining to hear his response. He had to do this. The silence grew deafening.

'You want to save your uncle.' The words were said slowly, but she could not read his expressionless face.

'Is it wrong to want to save my uncle? You offered me money in an attempt to save your cousin.'

Fortis winced at the memory. He also knew he

wanted this woman in his bed, and his body didn't care very much how he got her there. He had experienced some of Silvana's potential for passion last evening and he wanted to make sure it was not extinguished.

'Are you willing to become my mistress if I go and see the Prefect? It seems a large price to pay for such a small thing. If you asked when you were making a mess of my tunic, who knows what I would have done for a woman in distress.'

Her lips curved upwards. 'Crocodile tears are not in my repertoire. I normally never cry.'

'Then I am to feel honoured at the stain on my tunic.'

'If you manage to get my uncle released without a stain on his character, it will save both my uncle and my brother.' She lifted her chin and stared him directly in his eyes. She stretched out her hands. 'You are my last hope, Aurelius Fortis. I can no longer think of my own honour. I must consider the honour of my uncle and my brother.'

Fortis was tempted to ask Silvana what her brother or uncle had done for her, but no doubt she would have a ready answer. If she wanted to sacrifice herself for them, who was he to stop her? And if he refused her, there was always the possibility she would find someone else.

A stab of jealousy shot through him. He did not want to think about Silvana being with anyone else.

Cotta's words from the baths whispered in his mind—she was all go in the dining room, but no go in the bedroom. Did Silvana seek to cheat him? If so, she would find him a more difficult proposition than the junior tribunes she entertained at her uncle's house.

'And you will openly be my mistress, even though it may cause a scandal?'

Her tongue moistened her lips. She hesitated, her eyes going towards the door. Then she straightened her back and her direct gaze met his. 'Yes. It might harm Crispus a bit, but not as much as if my uncle was crucified. A minor scandal to prevent a major disaster.'

She moved to him and put her hands on his chest. Her oval face was upturned and her lips were like ripe cherries ready for the plucking, tempting. An invitation, one his body wanted to accept, but Fortis could not rid himself of the feeling that she was merely upping the stakes in the game. Flirtation and titillation were second nature to her. Nightly she indulged in the game of making men's heartbeats pound, so that they would return again and again to her uncle's parties.

Taking her to bed would end the hold she had over him. Once he had experienced her charms, she would no longer exert a hold over him. It was the best thing he could do. 'Yes can mean many things. Say it, Silvana.'

'Yes, I will openly be your mistress, once I know my uncle is safe.'

'And should I trust you?'

He reached out and brushed her cheek, saw the shiver run through her and her pupils dilate slightly. She wanted him as well. He could taste it in the air. She stepped back and allowed her shawl to drop to the floor with a silken sigh.

'I swear on my father's and mother's shades. You do this for me, have my uncle released without a stain, and I will be your mistress. Once my uncle is home, I will come to you. You simply have to name the time.'

'I have another plan.'

Fortis rested his chin on the tips of his fingers. It was time to up the stakes once more. He reached over, grabbed a scroll and scribbled a few words on it. He rang for Merlus and gave him instructions to take the missive to the Prefect.

Merlus raised an eyebrow, but said nothing, for once, merely bowing as he closed the door with a click.

Fortis rested against the desk, his foot swinging in the air while Silvana stared at him, head tilted to one side.

'When the Prefect gets my note, he will release

your uncle. It was under my orders that he decided to start targeting those who traffic with pirates. I have fulfilled my side of the bargain.'

Silvana's eyes grew wide. 'Can I trust you?'

'You could play *micatio* in the dark with me.' Fortis used the Roman phrase for indicating that he was an honest man, one who would not cheat and call out the wrong number of fingers in the gambling game. Fortis put his hands behind his head. How far exactly was Silvana prepared to go? He would find out and then send her home with an admonition not to play such games in the future. A quick sharp lesson.

'You decided to take up my offer and become my mistress. Very well, I accept your terms. Seduce me.'

Silvana stared at Fortis where he lounged with his hands behind his head, a self-satisfied expression on his face. His tunic stretched slightly across the broad expanse of his chest. Her body all too clearly remembered what it felt like to have his mouth on hers. A warm glow filled the centre of her. Yes, she wanted this man, but she had no idea how to go about the finer details of seduction. She had not thought beyond getting him to agree to have her uncle released. She had assumed he would take the initiative.

'Seduce you?' she asked and was horrified to hear her voice squeak.

'As you are auditioning for this role, I would expect my mistress to be more than capable of seduction.'

Silvana swallowed hard. It all became blindingly obvious—he expected her to fail and back down. But then where would it leave her—in his debt and vulnerable. It was quite possible he intended to demand something else when she failed. She had to do it. She had to do it for Uncle Aulus. A little voice in the back of her head called her a liar. She wanted to experience what it felt like to be joined intimately with him, with this man in front of her, whose kisses banished all other thoughts from her mind. She rubbed her temples. She had to concentrate.

'The setting is not what I had anticipated.' She gave a light laugh and allowed her hand to trail along the side of the couch. 'A bit stark and austere.'

'And you were expecting my bedroom?' A slow smile spread across his face. 'Or the bath?'

'It would have made things easier. Somewhere more conducive and comfortable.' Silvana's mind raced. It was as good an explanation for her lack of finesse as she could grasp. 'Somewhere we won't be disturbed.'

'We won't be disturbed in here, I guarantee it.' His voice dropped to a husky whisper. 'And the couch you are busy fondling has other uses.'

Silvana jumped away from the couch as if it had

bitten her. Her mind filled with images of entangled limbs. This should not matter. She knew dozens of women who conducted discreet affairs. She had been accused of it enough times. But the fact remained she had never done it. Somehow she had managed to avoid the traps. Now she had managed to get herself in the one situation she had sworn she would never be in.

What exactly did he expect her to do? Her fingers felt numb and uncooperative. And he was looking at her with a raised eyebrow. She had to do something.

Her hands went to her head and pulled the few remaining pins out of her hair, allowing it to tumble down to her shoulders and waited. No movement from Fortis. He lounged on the desk, waiting.

Exactly what did he expect from her? Silvana hesitated. She could leave now, but she had given her word. She had agreed, and she could hardly confess that she had not the least idea about how to seduce anyone.

Silvana's fingers fumbled on the knot in her belt. It refused to budge. She swore softly under her breath and tried again, turning her back on Fortis, her fingers working feverishly. It gave way and fell to the ground.

She managed to get two of the fastenings undone, then the third stuck, refusing to budge.

Her fingers pulled hard. A loud tearing echoed in the room as the fastening bounced to the floor and rolled under the couch. Silvana stared at it in dismay. She could hardly go scrambling around looking for a lost fastening. She was supposed to be in the midst of seducing this man and nothing was going right.

'I can't do this.' Her hand plucked at the hole in her gown. 'It is all going wrong.'

Warm fingers wrapped around hers and held her hand still, captive. She lifted her arm and he released her, trailing his hand along her shoulder.

'I find the best place to start with seduction is by asking the other person what he wants.'

His voice tickled her ear, doing strange things to her insides. Melting her fears and doubts. Making her body become the white-hot flame of hope.

Silvana turned. There was a gentle expression in his eyes where she had expected mockery. He made no attempt to take her in his arms. Her body quivered.

'What do you want?' she whispered.

'I want you in my arms on that couch, our limbs entwined.' His hand smoothed the locks of hair from her face, a gentle movement, but one that created a small fire deep within her. Silvana wanted to reach up and feel his stubble against the pads of her fingers but she forced her hands to remain at her sides.

'Are you going to seduce me?' Her voice sounded thick and strained to her ears.

'If I must…' He dropped a kiss on her nose. 'Let me show you how I propose to go about it, then you will know the next time. You should be a properly trained mistress.'

A properly trained mistress. Silvana knew she should make a light-hearted sophisticated remark, but none would come. He expected her to be experienced. She was tempted to confess, but her confession would ruin everything. She had given her word. She had to trust Venus everything would work out, that her instinct and wit would guide her. That somehow she would emerge triumphant at the end.

'As you have a definite idea, perhaps you should show me.' She twisted an arm around his neck, smiled her most seductive smile up into his face and saw an immediate glowing response from his eyes. She could do this. She had given her word. 'I am always willing to learn…new tricks. It could be enjoyable for the both of us.'

'It could indeed.'

His hands deftly undid the remainder of the fastenings and her gown slithered slowly over her curves to the ground, and became a pool of rose-pink. She stood before him, wondering, not daring to move a muscle.

Would he like what he saw? Her under-things were practical—a breast band and a sleeveless tunic, hardly the items men's fantasies were made of.

He placed a butterfly-light kiss on her lips, one that teasingly promised something more. He cupped her face in his hands and held her, his face but a breath away, teasing her, tormenting her. Her hand tightened around his neck, pulling him downwards, seeking that caress again. Briefly, too briefly, his lips lit upon hers, but then moved about her face, nuzzling and caressing her cheekbones, her nose and eyelashes. Unhurriedly exploring, sending little pulses of warmth throughout her body. She tightened her hold and recaptured him.

This time, his mouth opened for a long slow kiss, one that made the little pulse of warmth grow into a raging fire. Silvana heard a slight moan and knew it was hers, felt him stiffen and begin to draw away.

All the warnings her mother had given her flashed through her brain. She had been too forward. A man did not want a forward woman. She pulled her mouth from his. Her hands dropped to her sides.

'I didn't mean…' she began when he looked at her with questions in his eyes. 'A Roman woman should be…'

His hands reached out, pulled her close, making

her body arch against his so that she could feel the ridge of his arousal pressing into her.

'The most important rule I have,' he said against her neck, 'is that you experience as much pleasure as I do.'

'But—'

'Silvana, I know the nonsense that is drummed into the heads of Roman women.' He put his finger under her chin and lifted it so she could see into the depths of his green eyes. 'How they are not considered proper if they move a muscle in bed or enjoy themselves, but consider you are no longer proper. You have agreed to be my mistress, and I want you to experience pleasure.'

His hands smoothed down her back, stroking her. She turned her face into his neck as warm waves crashed over her. He was thinking about her and not just himself.

'Kiss me, Silvana, the way I know you want to.'

She leant forward, gently as he had done and then more firmly, tracing her tongue around the outline of his mouth. His lips parted, drew her tongue into the warm interior, capturing it, holding it there while heat exploded inside her.

When he lifted his head and released her, her lips ached with a delicious warmth. He rubbed the back of his knuckles over them and the heat intensified, filling her, driving her onwards.

She drew a shaky breath and started to recapture his mouth. He shook his head, demanded she stay still. His lips nibbled a trail down her neck and stopped at the base of her throat. Slowly, tantalisingly, he brought his hands up to cup her breasts.

His thumbnail drew little circles on her breast with ruthless precision, teasing the nipple to a hardened point. She gasped as a tingling sensation coursed through her, intoxicating her as if she'd drunk an amphora of the finest Falerian wine.

'Do you like that?'

She nodded, helpless as her breasts grew large and full, straining against the breast band that held them. With each breath she took, the band grew tighter, more confining. Her hand pulled impatiently at the cloth, but his fingers captured hers. He eased the tunic from her shoulders and down her curves, until she stood wrapped only in the linen band.

His fingers pushed at the material until the tip of her dusky pink nipple peeked out. He bent his head and closed his mouth around the nipple, sending spasms through her. Her hands gripped his forearms as her knees gave way and her body became molten. He eased her down onto the silk cover of the couch and back amongst the heavily embroidered silk cushions. Their softness enveloped her, held her cocooned.

'Your turn.' Her voice was a husky whisper.

'If you wish.'

He slowly raised his tunic, inch by inch exposing the hard muscles of his body. His chest was golden smooth and dusted with black hair, contrasting with the whiteness of his loincloth. With a deft hand, he undid the fastening, and the cloth dropped.

She stifled a gasp at the size and thickness of him. The enormity of what she was about to do washed over her. Would he be gentle? Considerate? The time for explanation had passed. She had to hope it would not be as bad as her mother had predicted when she sacrificed her three remaining dolls to Venus, her final act of childhood before she married. She had to do something, say something, but the words refused to leave her throat.

She reached out and traced the jagged scar that ran down his right side.

'A souvenir from the Appian Way.' The corners of his lips turned up and he settled himself next to her, his bare leg running down the length of her thigh. 'If you take a corner quickly with spooked horses, your chariot will overturn. Trust me on this.'

'It looks painful.' She concentrated on the scar, and tried to ignore the sensations that were building inside her.

'It was. It is why I always take care and double-check my reins.' He put a finger under her chin. 'Does it repulse you?'

Mutely she shook her head and put out her hand to feel the warm flesh.

His hands slid down her body, exploring her curves, grazing her nipples, travelling ever lower until they hovered above the apex of her thighs. She felt his fingers become entangled in her triangle of curls and gave a sharp gasp as liquid fire spread through her. Her hands tugged at his shoulders.

He put a finger on her lips. 'Remember— pleasure. Give into the feeling. You see what touching you there does to me.'

She glanced down and saw his shaft had thickened further. Her mouth became dry. She wanted to say, to explain about the past, but the words wouldn't come. If she told him the truth, he might stop and her body craved his. She wanted him.

'You will let me touch you there.'

She nodded, unable to speak.

His fingers skimmed her curls. Her hips lifted slightly, seeking his touch. He slipped his finger inside her folds and a broad smile crossed his face. Delicately he drew apart her thighs, revealing her hot moist inner core.

'You are very tight,' he whispered in her ear. 'Relax, my sea nymph. Relax. Relax here.'

His fingers stroked her with long strokes until they found her pulsating nub, circled around, then started their journey again. A slow figure of eight. Gently but firmly his hand worked until she was racked with waves of intoxicating pleasure. Her body surged upwards, as her body demanded release. Her hands grabbed his shoulders as her head thrashed about on the silken cushions. Then a sweet languor filled her and she looked into his deep green eyes, eyes dilated with passion.

'Do you want more?'

'I…I would like…'

He raised himself up on his elbows and gave a very masculine smile. 'See if you like this better.'

His mouth made a warm wet trail down her belly to where his finger played. His tongue flicked out, touched her innermost spot, circled round and suckled. The world became engulfed in spasms.

Silvana heard a cry and knew it was from her own throat and all the while his tongue played in her soft warm folds. When she thought she could bear no more, he slowly came up her body and then guided her hand to his shaft.

'Touch me. See how you make me feel, Silvana.'

Hard iron beneath a coat of silk. She gave him a stroke and saw his eyes dilate. Then she became bolder, her hand closing around him, holding him, feeling him come alive. She started to move her hand back and forth. A low moan issued from his throat. She stopped, withdrew her hand, hesitating.

'I need you. Now.'

Without waiting for her response, his knees pushed apart her thighs and he entered her. Hard. Fast.

A searing pain that seemed to go on for ever rushed through her. Silvana winced, wanting to pull away, tried to, but Fortis had driven himself into her and continued to drive himself further in. Where there had been pleasure and warmth, there was only a deep burning ache. She gave a muffled cry as her hands beat against him.

Fortis stopped, surprised. He cupped Silvana's face with his hands. 'Silvana,' he breathed. 'I would have been gentler, if I had known.'

Shuddering overtook him and he lay still, impaled in her. His body collapsed against hers, heavy, weighing her down, pinning her to the couch.

Why had she thought this was a good idea?

She shut her eyes tightly as the misery washed over her.

Chapter Nine

Fortis eased his body out of Silvana's. The enormity of what he had done hit him. He should have known the instant he slipped his finger inside her. She had been too tight, too narrow for it to have been only fear. He had concentrated instead on her sleek wetness, her little cries of pleasure instead of the obvious truth.

Silvana Junia was anything but a fallen woman, one who took her pleasures lightly. She was a virgin.

Once he had encountered her maidenhead, it had been too late. His body had raged out of control, driven him onwards. Her shoulders bore bright red stripes where his hands had gripped her. Fading, but visible.

What had he done? Taken her with less finesse than a callow untried youth. She should have been opened slowly to pleasure, and instead he had slaked his lust.

He reached over and covered himself with his

tunic. Then he pulled the covers up to her chin, hiding her magnificent body and all the while her brown eyes regarded him with an accusing stare.

'When were you going to tell me?' he asked quietly.

'Tell you what?'

'You were a virgin. You have never experienced full sexual intercourse.' Fortis forced the words from his mouth.

She flinched, her mouth twisting, but she said nothing.

'You should have told me before,' he said, touching her hand where it gripped the coverlet. 'I deserved to know.'

'Would you have believed me if I had?' Her toneless voice filled the room as she pulled away from him. 'Tell me honestly, what difference would it have made?'

Fortis considered the question. He wanted to draw her close and tell her that he would have believed her, but that would be a lie. He would have thought she was playing games again, that somehow she was attempting to trick or cheat her way out of their agreement. That it was another raising of the stakes in the very high-risk game they were playing. And he would not have believed that she had been married for three years, and yet had remained untouched until he took her.

Impossible, but true.

No wonder she looked at him through bruised eyes and with a wary mouth. A wave of remorse swept over him.

'No,' he said, regarding the fresco of ships behind her. 'I am not sure I understand even now, but I cannot deny the evidence of my own eyes, of my body.'

She sat up, wrapped her arms about her knees and her dark golden hair fell like a curtain between them.

'My late husband was a very proud man but very elderly. His days of playing in Cupid's groves were long past, but he had no desire for anyone to know, least of all the man who would be his heir.'

'Is that why he married you?'

'I know what was said about me.' She held up a hand, stopping him. 'Some of the gossip was true. My parents were in debt and they sold me. I was bought as he might purchase a beautiful statue—to be admired, to be petted and trained in the art of being a hostess. He wanted to possess me. I was his oh-so-charming companion. He encouraged me to flirt, and to be pursued. The fact that men begged for my favours fed his ego.'

'Were you happy?'

'I was fed, and well clothed. I found a talent for amusing conversation.' She gave a delicate shrug of her shoulder. 'My parents were pleased. They had married their daughter to a Senator. All their money troubles had ended. Their status had risen.'

He touched her shoulder and this time she did not shy away. A small victory.

'How long did this continue?'

'Three years. I lasted longer than his previous wife, but there was starting to be talk. His eye had fallen on another young woman, and there can be no doubt I would have been passed like a present to one of his more favoured clients. But he, like my parents the year before, fell ill and died.' She raised her head. 'I cried at the funeral.'

'But all the rumours, all the affairs.' Fortis ran a hand through his hair, making it stand on end. 'You are the notorious Silvana Junia.'

'I was married. My husband knew I was a virgin. He warned me when we made our pact—he'd disown any child I had. I would have been ruined and my family along with me.'

'And you accepted that?'

She gave a bittersweet smile. 'I had very few choices until after Cotta the Elder died. There was my younger brother to consider. There was always the possibility that Cotta might choose to adopt him rather than the man he formally adopted on his deathbed.'

'And then what happened?'

'Luckily, Uncle Aulus returned and became my

guardian rather than Cotta the Younger. We were able to reach an agreement—I became his hostess and he would allow me to choose my husband when I was ready and not before.' Her hand flipped her hair back. 'Or at least that was what was supposed to happen until two months ago.'

'Are you still intent on marrying Eutychus?' Fortis tried to ignore the stab of jealousy that shot through him.

'I would hardly be in your bed if I were.'

Fortis regarded Silvana. Her dark blonde hair flowed over the couch. She rested her determined chin on her hand. He had been so wrong about her. He had believed all the stories, rather than the evidence of his own eyes. He should have trusted his own instinct. Unfortunately, he, and only he, had made her into the only thing she wasn't. He had made her into a courtesan. Once it became common knowledge, she would have lost all chance of respectability.

His insides twisted. Apollo help him, his body wanted her again. Once was not nearly enough. It would never be enough. He had to do something, before he gave in. 'Tell me, was everything abhorrent to you?'

She tilted her head to one side. A myriad of emotions crossed her face. Fortis's fingers itched to draw her into his embrace, but if he did he would make love to her, and just now she would be too sore to enjoy it properly. He could not risk losing control again. Had he ruined her?

'No, not everything. Just the end.'

'It only hurts once.' He padded over to a jug of mint tea and poured some on a cloth. Then held it out to her. 'Here, clean yourself. You will feel better for it.'

Silvana bit her lip. Her story repulsed Fortis. She should have never given into her impulse. Her passionate response had driven him away just as her mother had warned.

'I ought to go,' she whispered, ignoring the cloth he offered her. Misery welled up inside her. 'My uncle will worry if I am not there when he gets back.'

'Hush.' Fortis put a finger to her lips, but she turned her face. 'Things are not as bad as you fear.'

'What do you mean?' Silvana hugged her arms tighter about her waist. All she knew was that she had a terrible ache in her middle and a feeling that she had made the biggest mistake of her life. Why had she ever thought this was a good idea? And what was worse, she knew if Fortis kissed her, she would be in his arms again, demanding a repeat performance.

'No one knows you are here except your maid. She can remain ignorant as well.' Fortis held out the cloth again. 'Use the cloth and clean yourself off.'

She glanced down and saw the flecks of blood on her thighs. A small cry escaped her lips. 'Lyde wouldn't talk. She has never said anything.'

'You are supposed to be an experienced woman of the world. How long has your maid been with you?'

'A year or two.'

'She would find such a thing too unusual to keep quiet. It would come out by accident.' He reached out and touched her shoulder, a gentle touch. 'You cannot afford to take the chance. You don't want Cotta the Younger claiming that you have no right to whatever you inherited from your late husband.'

Silvana gave a slight nod. She had not considered it from that angle. Her hands closed around the wet cloth, the coolness seeping into her fingers.

'If I have to wash you, Silvana, we will end up entangled again on that couch.'

'And that would be so bad?'

'Yes.' He rubbed the back of his neck. 'I am trying to do the correct thing.'

Silvana cleansed her thighs with fierce movements. The area between her thighs was sore and her body ached as she drew her gown about her. She didn't bother looking for the lost fastening. Her shawl would hide the damage until she returned to the villa. This whole adventure had been a mistake, yet, Venus help her, she wanted to feel his arms about her and his lips against her hair. She wanted to feel like something more than a body he had used, but he stood there, eyes averted, dressed in his unbelted tunic, the spot where she had laid her head earlier clearly visible, a reminder of how she had found comfort in his arms.

'I need to go. My uncle will be wondering where I am.'

He gave a nod and she knew if she had the least bit of encouragement she'd rest her head against his chest again. He did nothing, but continued to stare at her with an unfathomable expression.

'Should there be a child…' he said as she put her hand on the door.

'You needn't worry,' she replied with more confidence than she felt. 'I am a widow of Baiae. We know all the remedies.'

Her throat closed around the words and she knew them for a lie. If a child did come as a result of this morning, she would welcome it. She longed to hold a child of her own in her arms. Of all the whispers about her, the cruellest ones had been that she was barren, unable to give her husband a child.

'I should have guessed.'

'I believe our agreement is at an end.'

'Silvana.' His voice sounded strained. He stood there with his head bowed. If he had given her one sign, she would have run into his arms, but he didn't. He stood there, unmoving. 'I wish this morning had been different.'

'It wasn't your fault, but mine.'

Silvana left the room before she threw herself at him when he so clearly didn't want her. He wanted someone different, someone who was all the things she pretended to be.

Voices. Male voices. Silvana paused at the door of the *tablinum,* listening. In the few hours since she had returned from Fortis's she had changed, reapplied her make-up, had Lyde try a new hairstyle and regained her composure, but she had not been able to have a private interview with her uncle, as he had departed for his afternoon at the Baths of Mercury.

One voice was clearly her uncle's—but the other?

Silvana's heart stopped. She shook her head to clear it. After the way he couldn't wait to push her from his house, it would not be Fortis's voice, but the low-timbred voice sent tingles along her spine.

She was hearing things now!

She would deal with Fortis when they next met. He had probably already departed for Rome, back to his well-ordered life, leaving the tawdriness of Baiae behind.

Whoever it was, she would handle this evening with

grace and aplomb. She was an accomplished hostess with the latest witticism ready to drop from her lips.

She pushed open the door and stepped into the olive-oil-lit room.

'Uncle—'

The two occupants turned around. Silvana's stomach dropped. Against all reason, her instinct was correct. Fortis was here, dressed in his dark green dining clothes, conversing with her uncle as if it were the most natural thing in the world.

'Silvana, we have been discussing you.' Fortis brought her hand to his lips. She resisted the temptation to snatch it away as even the gentlest of touches sent pulses racing through her body. 'I was saying how well you coped with the party last night. Things nearly got badly out of hand.'

'Silvana is an accomplished hostess.' Uncle Aulus glowed with pride. 'Truly an asset to this house or indeed any house. The times I have thought—where would this house be if not for Silvana's social skills? She is the sort of woman who would bring favour to any household.'

Exactly what had her uncle and Fortis been discussing?

Her uncle sounded in full matchmaking mode. Silvana moved away from Fortis and tried to regain control of her mind. She had to draw on her years of training. No man had ever affected her like this before. She deliberately turned away from Fortis and faced her uncle.

'I had thought you would have been here when I returned, Uncle,' she said, going over to the shrine and righting one of the silver statues of Mercury, a little act, but one that gave her a chance to regain her composure.

'You know I made a vow after I was ransomed never to miss the fourth day before the Ides bathing session at the Baths of Mercury, Silvana.' Her uncle made an expansive gesture with his apricot handkerchief. 'Apollo and the rest of the pantheon of gods willing, I have yet to do so. One has to maintain one's standards or we shall have the barbarians at the gates of Rome in no time. Don't you agree?'

'Without standards, one surrenders to the barbarian hordes,' Fortis said with maddening complacency. 'I can understand your uncle's desire to appear there. Many had questions about his adventures. Rumours were flying around the bathhouses.'

'Wicked baseless rumours, which I did my best to dispel.' Uncle Aulus leant forward. 'Did you know that Cotta was putting it about that I had been the main go-between for Draco and his band of pirates. Me? A lifelong upholder of Roman virtue, I ask you.'

'Your uncle is very passionate about such things.'

'As I have said many times, Uncle Aulus is no friend to the pirates.' Silvana inclined her head.

Fortis looked away from her gaze first and Silvana felt she had won a victory of sorts.

'I discovered Fortis there quite without a dinner invitation.' Uncle Aulus beamed as if he had brought Silvana a present. 'I refused to take no for an answer.'

Silvana smoothed her skirt and did not meet Fortis's eye. Surely he could have found a reasonable excuse. This dinner would be torture for both of them. He had shown that he had no desire for her after their encounter, and she…she certainly had no desire for him.

'I fear our dinner will be simple tonight. I have cancelled any plans for tonight's entertainment.' Silvana glared at her uncle, who glanced up to the ceiling and circled his thumbs around each other.

'I can eat without music, Silvana. It has been known to happen before.' Uncle Aulus made a little mocking bow. 'The things I do for my niece and nephew. Now, if you will entertain our guest, I will go and see what is keeping the wine. I promise you, Fortis, once tasted, this vintage is not soon forgotten.'

'In the circumstances, it is probably best.' Fortis inclined his head, but made no other attempt to move towards her. She watched his long fingers, and tried to banish the memory of them stroking her. She had to concentrate on the future, not the misbegotten past. 'Your uncle already explained that you are waiting for your brother to arrive when I accepted his invitation.'

What else had her uncle explained? He had the air of mischievous Cupid about him as he positively skipped out of the room, calling for Dida and the key to the cellar.

'Why did he invite you?'

'He heard about my leading the dance and Eutychus's hurried departure. The news is apparently common currency in the bathhouses. Speculation runs riot, from Eutychus and me fighting a duel, to you offering your body in exchange for gold. To refuse such a sincere request would have invoked comment,' Fortis said in an undertone as the servants bustled in, carrying ewers full of perfumed water, closely followed by another two couples—elderly friends of her uncle. 'No other reason, I swear it.'

Silvana gave a nod. 'He is attempting to play Cupid. If it was not so laughable, I would cry. Will it be you or me I wonder, who informs him that such a match has no possibility of ever happening?'

'If that is your opinion, I must share it,' came the cryptic reply. Fortis started to speak to the two other men, acquaintances from the Senate.

Silvana automatically greeted the new arrivals, but her mind was racing ahead. Her uncle appeared intent on matchmaking and was unlikely to listen to reason. The last thing she wanted to do was to confess the true state of affairs between Fortis and her.

Uncle Aulus was easygoing in many things, but before they had begun this enterprise, he had made her promise that she would not have affairs, that the gossip would have no foundation. Now, in order to save him, she had broken her promise. And while what Fortis and she had shared this morning could not be called an affair, it did have the power to undermine everything.

'You look shocked, Silvana,' her uncle said, sidling up to her. 'What have I done to disturb you this time? We are about to go into dinner and I have yet to see a pretty smile on your face.'

'I would have thought you would be more discreet. You nearly lost everything and here you have invited people as if nothing happened.'

'What would you have me do? Hide my head in shame?' Her uncle shook his head. 'I did nothing that most men in Baiae have not done. My only regret is that they were pirates rather than actual traders. To think the Prefect actually thought I would do such a thing. However, he is young and inexperienced. He knows now. So many people came to my aid.'

'Exactly how many people did you contact, Uncle?'

Her uncle rocked back and forth, started counting on his fingers and then gave a helpless smile. 'Some things are best left unsaid, niece. I have spent long enough in Baiae to know where a few bodies are buried and to have helped bury a few more. My true friends remember that. I regret you were worried. It worked out in the end.'

'The guard at the garrison would not even let me see the Prefect.'

'You are a woman, dear. I told you to stay at home. Everything was under control and so it proved. You should trust your uncle.' Her uncle tossed his apricot mantle back from his shoulders. 'Now, about you and Fortis—you will recline next to him. Your colouring complements each other. Such a good-looking pair.'

'I am pleased you are back home—safe and well.' Silvana reached over and gave her uncle a kiss on the cheek. 'But your blatant attempts at matchmaking are doomed to failure, Uncle.'

'Aurelius Fortis is unattached and has a fortune, Niece.' A crease appeared between her uncle's eyebrows. 'He appears far from indifferent to you. Why should I not attempt to engineer a match?'

'You are mistaken. He is not interested in marriage…or me,' she added quietly.

'Silvana, you can be selectively blind.'

'Men such as he do not take women like me for their wives. They marry women for their connections. We have no connection that Aurelius Fortis could want.'

Uncle Aulus was silent, pulling his upper lip over his teeth and pursing his lips. He started to say something, then stopped. He placed a hand on Silvana's bare arm. 'You will have to marry some time, Silvana Junia. I won't live for ever and you don't want to become like Poppea—staring into the mirror, for ever wondering if this will be the day that the wrinkles show. When life throws you a ring, catch it and hold on to it with all your might.'

'You are a romantic.' Silvana gave a small shake of her head. There would be no moving her uncle, but he was destined for disappointment. There would be no happy ending for her and Fortis. 'Aunt Anna spoilt you for anyone else.'

Her uncle gave a wry smile before turning his piercing gaze on her. 'Why, Silvana? Can you give me one good reason why I should not attempt to make a match between you and Fortis? He is wealthy, good looking and desires you.'

The reasons why not crowded in her brain. It would be far too easy to blurt out what had happened this morning, but she had no idea what her uncle's reaction would be. How would he feel to find out that she had indeed played the courtesan, had in truth become more like Poppea than he could imagine in order to get him released from custody? She pressed her lips together, holding back the words.

'We don't suit,' she said at last, choosing the mildest excuse she could think of. 'He is far too manipulative for my liking.'

'And you are not?' her uncle murmured, beckoning Fortis with a wave of his hand. 'See, he comes to speak with you. Be charming, Silvana.'

Silvana pretended she had not heard the last remark. She stepped backwards and collided with Fortis. Her entire body radiated warmth. Silvana clamped her lips together. All the cleansing and scraping she had done, certain she would be unaffected the next time she encountered Fortis. But the merest hint of a touch and her body was aflame, remembering the passion they had shared.

'You are unhappy about me dining here,' he said without preamble.

'You overheard my conversation with my uncle.'

'I saw your face.' Fortis touched her elbow. 'Believe me—I will not say a word about what passed between us this morning.'

'Then why are you here?'

'What better way to show your uncle has been cleared of all involvement with pirates than for me to dine at his house?'

'But my uncle asked you here.'

'I went searching for your uncle. His habits were easy to discover. And he was very willing to oblige. There was a small risk, but I felt the probability of the outcome worth it.'

'Your logic is flawless.'

'It is what makes me such a formidable opponent.' A faint smile touched the corners of his lips. 'When I play, I play to win.'

'Shall we progress into the dining room? I believe my uncle has begun the procession.'

By the time the dessert of figs, dates and cheese arrived, Fortis's nerves were stretched to breaking point. His fingers itched to find another excuse to brush against her shoulder. When he managed to extract the dinner invitation from Junius Maius, he failed to consider that Silvana might actually be put as close to him as she was. He wanted to prove that he did have control over his body, but with each breath she took, he could feel his control slipping a little more.

'Shall we take a turn around the garden, Silvana?' he asked.

Her fingers closed around a date as a faint rose appeared in her cheeks. 'The garden?'

'Your uncle assures me there is a very fine olive tree and the crickets have begun to sing.'

'Dinner has finished.' Silvana nodded to where the servants were unobtrusively clearing the table and refilling the cups with wine. 'I thought perhaps to recite a bit of poetry or perhaps play the lyre as the evening's entertainment.'

Junius Maius waved a lazy hand. 'Go with him, Silvana. Show him the garden. I can live without the Greek poets for a few days longer.'

'Your uncle shows no objection.'

'But I do.' Silvana rose and kept her skirts carefully away from him. 'I know what happened in the garden last evening.'

'And you are afraid it might happen again?' Fortis tucked her arm in his. 'On my honour, I will do nothing you do not wish to do.'

Her cheeks became a delicate rose pink. A small thrill ran through Fortis. She was not indifferent to him. He would have her again. And this time, it would be done carefully and slowly until she dissolved with pleasure. He intended on laying siege to her until she gave in.

'I will go because my uncle wishes it, and to explain my reasons why not would involve too much.'

Silvana stormed through the doors and into the garden. Fortis followed at a more leisurely pace. He stopped to pick up her discarded shawl. When he reached her, he dropped it on her shoulders and felt her body tremble underneath his fingers. Relief swept over him at this confirmation of her feelings for him. He could win, if he tried.

'There was no need to do that.' She rearranged the folds of the shawl to cover her shoulders more securely.

'I wanted to. You should not risk a chill.'

'In Baiae? In May?' She shook her head.

'One can't be too careful.' He smiled down at her. Her mouth look enticing, enchanting. 'I am sorry there is no music tonight.'

'Dancing is not something I do often.' She turned her back on him and plucked a white rose. Her fingers crushed the petals, releasing the fragrance. 'White roses are for secrets, you know.'

'I know.'

'I thought we had agreed I was no longer your mistress.'

'If you were my mistress, I would expect you to dine with me...alone.' His hand covered hers, captured the petals, held them before allowing them to drift silently to the ground. 'Your uncle at the baths asked me if my intentions were honourable.'

'He had no way of knowing. I saw no one when I returned. Lyde knows nothing. I told no one.' Her eyes searched his face. 'Tell me he knows nothing of what passed between us.'

'Someone besides Eutychus saw our kiss in the garden.'

Her face cleared and she snapped her fingers under his nose. 'A kiss means nothing. My uncle knows that. Men have stolen kisses before.'

'Nevertheless, I told him my intentions were honourable. I have no reason to ruin your reputation.'

'Slightly late for that.' Her mouth twisted and he felt his heart contract.

'It was a mistake, one that I would rectify if I could.' His fingers tightened around hers. 'I had no wish to hurt you Silvana.'

'You have realised that you are not all powerful.'

'Tell me the harm in admitting to being human.' He placed his hands on her shoulders. 'I made a mistake, Silvana, but I shall never regret taking you into my bed.'

Silvana's mouth opened. Fortis started to draw her unresisting body towards him. There was only one way of ending this senseless argument between them. His mouth ached to feel her lips under his, to taste the sweet cleanness of her.

Chapter Ten

A warm curl of desire snaked through Silvana. Her body started to arch towards Fortis as she lifted her mouth. His lips were inches away, silhouetted in the moonlight. A sudden clattering of hooves against the cobble stones and shouts from the porter and other servants filled her ears. Silvana took a stumbling step backwards. She clutched her shawl and rearranged it more tightly over her shoulders.

What had she been about to do? Give her lips to him? After the humiliation of this morning? He had made it very clear what he thought of her.

He stood there with his arms outstretched, ready to gather her in, tempting her. She gave her head a slight shake and he allowed his hands to fall to his sides as his face became a bland mask.

She had no idea what sort of game he was playing now. And it was a game, she was certain. He had not liked the fact she had left. It had nothing to do with her personally. She was a challenge who had to be conquered. Then he would leave. It could be the only explanation for why he was here now.

'Silvana—'

Silvana held up her hand, silencing him. She loathed that her body ached to surrender to him again. So soon after the ache of this morning! She wanted to feel his mouth against hers and experience that first deep shuddering release. Now that she was no longer a virgin, the pain should be gone.

Where had her will power gone? Her sense of propriety?

She needed to regain control of the situation and her body. She forced a light laugh from her lips, the perfect hostess once again. 'See the servants hurrying about—someone has arrived.'

A tall bareheaded figure dressed in a travelling cloak appeared in the doorway and her heart leapt. Even though she had not seen him for over a year, there could be no mistaking her brother. She started to run, but Crispus met her halfway, catching her in his arms and spinning her around.

'Look at you. How big you have grown!' she exclaimed. 'My little brother has grown to honourable manhood. Crispus, you don't know how I've longed for the day.'

A faint frown appeared in her brother's eyes as he looked her up and down. 'You are the same. I can hardly see you through the paint and elaborate hair-style you insist on wearing these days.'

Silvana pressed her lips together. She had hoped her brother had changed, but he seemed intent on following those who believed in old-fashioned Roman virtues. Virtues? Prison sentences more like it—men could do as they wished without censure and women were to be seen and not heard. She gave a polite smile and a shrug. 'Why would I change? Baiae suits me.'

'You must be Silvana's brother.' Fortis advanced towards them. 'You both have the same smile. I'm Lucius Aurelius Fortis.'

Crispus's eyes widened as Fortis clasped his forearm in the customary greeting. 'The queastor? I have heard of you. Your name is often bracketed with Cicero's and Cato's as an honourable man. Such a pleasure to meet you.'

'Nonsense. You are relieved that you don't have to scold your sister for the company she keeps.' The words were lightly said, but Silvana could see the hardness in Fortis's eyes.

Crispus's cheeks flushed and he dropped his gaze. 'One hears things. My sister's doings are widely reported. The whole school spoke of them. How she entertains men with her conversation and dancing.'

'You should never believe everything you hear. You will have to endure much worse if you want to go into the Senate. It is a snake pit—full of comment and innuendo. See how Julius Caesar behaves. He ignores the comments about his private life.' Fortis laid a hand on Crispus's shoulder. 'Trust your sister to do what is right.'

Silvana looked away as her throat closed around a hard lump. Fortis had championed her and he had judged her harshly before. What had made him change? Or was it simply guilt speaking because he had discovered the truth in such a dramatic fashion? He certainly had not believed in her virtue when he offered her money to dump Eutychus. It did not matter. He had defended her, and defended her to her brother, who ought to know better than to believe such stories in the first place. She longed to ask Fortis for his reasons, but now was definitely not the time or place.

'What do you intend to do with yourself now that you have returned home?' Silvana linked her arm with Crispus's. 'Have you given much thought of how you are going to obtain a junior tribune's post? Which important men you want to meet? Most will appear at Uncle Aulus's over the coming months.'

'I intend to race horses.' Crispus pulled away from her and stood belligerently with his fists on his hips. 'And win.'

Silvana blinked and shook her head. Her brother had always been concerned about becoming a junior tribune. It was why she sought to avoid scandal and cultivated those men that might be useful to him. Now he was going to throw it all away on horse racing.

'Surely, Crispus, there are other ways your time could be better employed. What about giving orations in the marketplace? Your skill might be noticed and you could catch the eye of a lawyer.' She glanced at Fortis for support.

'Racing does not seem to be a sober pastime,' Fortis commented, 'for someone determined to avoid scandal. You would be better off doing as your sister suggests.'

'What does she know about anything? It is her fault that I am in this mess.'

'Crispus, what are you talking about?'

'It is the only way I have to quickly renew the family's fortune. Drusus Cotta contacted me at school and informed me of my uncle's profligacy.' Crispus pointed with his finger. 'I am under no illusion about the state of my finances and I have some small skill with horses. There are often informal chariot races in and around Baiae, or so a schoolfriend informs me. It is a respectable pastime, a time-honoured tradition. I won six races at school. Best in my year.'

'Chariot racing in Baiae is not for the faint-hearted,' Fortis said quietly. 'It is very different from schoolboys racing improvised chariots around a small circus. Some of these men could be professional if they were not patricians.'

'And you would know something about it.' There was an arrogant tilt to Crispus's chin.

'More than you would ever guess.' Fortis laid a hand on Crispus's shoulder. 'A bit of friendly advice—don't go seeking races until you have the measure of the participants.'

'Do my ears deceive me or has my darling nephew returned to the family fold?' Uncle Aulus hurried in and clasped Crispus to his chest, calling for another amphora of wine to be opened. 'If I had known you were arriving, Crispus, I would have had the musicians play a composition of welcome. Alas, your sister only allows me to hire them, rather than own them.'

'In some things, it would appear my sister shows good sense. I wish she did in all things.' Crispus gave a little clap. 'Come, Uncle, see what I have brought you from Rome.'

He began to supervise the unloading of his trunks, ordering Dida and the other servants about in a loud tone.

'He doesn't mean to be proud,' Silvana remarked at Fortis's questioning look. 'He is young and my father's debts were more than we originally thought. I fear the school he attends has made him a bit severe.'

'You indulge him.'

'He is my only brother and young. He will learn. And he does have a fair amount of common sense.' She tucked a tendril behind her ear. 'I wonder what is behind this sudden passion for horse racing. He has never shown much interest before. I don't believe Cotta means him to profit.'

'In that I agree with you.'

Silvana noticed the atrium had fallen silent again. Fortis was standing near enough to touch. There were many things she wanted to say, but she had no idea where to begin. All she seemed capable of doing was staring at him.

'Silvana! Where are you?' Crispus's voice floated on the evening's breeze.

'I should return to the dining room. My brother…' Silvana put her hand to her throat.

'Enjoy your brother's company.' Fortis touched a finger to her lips. 'We will speak later.'

When Silvana rose the next morning, she discovered Crispus in the *tablinum*. He gave a quick smile and put down the pan pipes that he had been blowing. His fair hair curled slightly at his temples, giving him the look of a young cupid.

'This is how I remember my sister,' he said going to her with his hands outstretched. 'How I like to see her. Plain and unadorned. You have no need for paints and pots of wine dregs. Yesterday it looked like you were wearing a theatre mask.'

'Crispus, it is good you've come home, but please understand, I am happy here. I choose what I wear and how I paint my face.'

'Silvana, it has been hard for me. All the stories I hear. The whole of Rome gossips about you. You are more notorious than Clodia Mettalia and her sisters.'

'When have there not been stories?' Silvana crossed her arms. 'If you want to blame someone, blame our late parents. They were the ones who sold me to Drusus Cotta the Elder. They and you benefited from the work my late husband sent our father's way.'

Crispus flushed. 'You were not nearly so scandalous then.'

'Yes, I was,' Silvana answered quietly. 'You were protected from it. The harpies picked over everything I did and the latest gowns I wore. It was a regular sport with them. You are five years younger than I am. You can remember if you try.'

Crispus wrinkled his brow and gave a helpless shrug. Silvana pinched the bridge of her nose. She had been longing to see him and now she wanted him to leave.

'The gossip does pain me, and, Silvana, it is affecting my chances to obtain a respectable post as a junior tribune.' He grasped her hands and held them to his heart. 'And I do worry about you. It cannot be good for you.'

Silvana withdrew her hands. 'Did your worries about me start when Cotta the Younger contacted you? You made little mention about your fears when you were last home. Suddenly all your letters are about when will I settle down and stop behaving improperly and the first thing you say to me is that I am wearing too much make-up.'

'Maybe it is because I am older, but I will say that Cotta did first mention it to me and then I went to hear Cato speak on the necessity of keeping to the old values. Many of my friends agree with him.'

'And will theses old values and new friends get you the post you desire? There will be more senators and people with influence here in Baiae than anywhere else this summer. There always is. Trust Uncle Aulus to find you one.'

'Uncle Aulus has lost his touch, or so Cotta informed me. Do you know how much he owes? The best people are no longer offering him contracts, and good rates for shipping.'

'Where are Cotta's old values when he cavorts

with Poppea?' She hit her fist against her palm. 'The hypocrisy of it all.'

'Cato has already refused to look at my application because of Uncle Aulus and you. That is what Cotta told me.'

'I am your sister, your flesh and blood, the one who used to come in and comfort you when the Furies attacked your dreams and Jupiter rode his chariot across the sky. Remember?'

Crispus made no reply but began to talk very rapidly about his plans for the summer and his passion for horse racing. Silvana sighed and allowed the conversation to turn. It worried her that her only brother was easily led. She had seen too many young men ruined on the shoals of Baiae. And what sort of game was Cotta playing? His sole interest was increasing his immense fortune. She did not want her own experience to cloud Crispus's chance of finding a position, but her instinct was that her erstwhile stepson was up to no good.

'Has your brother discovered any chariots to race?'

Silvana turned from her perusal of silks in the market place to find Fortis standing quietly at her side. His white toga with large purple border contrasted with his golden tan. The memory of how his skin felt against her fingers flooded through her. Ruthlessly she tried to suppress the feeling. It had been more than ten days since he had left her uncle's dinner party and she had not had word from him. She had convinced herself that her attraction to him had died, and had instead concentrated on regaining the routine of her life. However, all she had to do was hear his voice and the tingles started on her arm again. There was a difference between being attracted to someone and doing something about it.

Her hand trembling slightly, she replaced the length of blue silk shot with gold thread back on the market stall. She would show him that he no longer affected her. Their intimate association was over.

'My brother is rediscovering Baiae much as you have been. The town has many delights to tempt the newcomer.' She winced. The words sounded jealous and they certainly revealed far more than she intended. She signalled to Lyde that they should leave.

'I have had to be away, discovering the delights of warehouses in Pompeii, Cumae and Puteoli.' Fortis named two of the ports around the Bay of Naples. His eyes crinkled. 'It is pleasant to know my presence was missed.'

'I never said that.' Silvana ducked her head.

The merchant intervened, going on about the rarity of the cloth and how lovely she'd look in it, particularly lovely for the man standing next to her. She made a show of declining the cloth, but could not help giving a last lingering touch to the smooth cloth, allowing it to slide through her fingers.

'Allow me to buy that for you.' Without waiting for an answer, Fortis directed the market-stall owner to send the entire length over to the Junius compound.

'That is too much,' Silvana protested

'Are you going to deny you want it? The colour will go well with your hair.'

'That is not the point.' Silvana tapped a finger against the stall. She found it impossible to deny that she coveted the silk. She had gone to the stall several times over the last few days simply to gaze at the material, but with the current state of their finances she could not afford it. She had to worry about finding the money for Crispus's junior tribuneship before she even thought about replacing any of her gowns. Thus far, none of Uncle Aulus's leads had come through. There was always a good reason why they could not oblige. Silvana wondered if somehow, her uncle's precarious financial position was known.

'Wearing a gown because it enhances your beauty is the best reason I can think of for buying a length of cloth.'

'I refuse to accept a gift like from you, from any

man. The news will be buzzing from bath house to bath house before vespers are sounded.'

'And that is a problem?'

'Crispus would like me to become less scandalous. I have been trying hard.' It was an excuse and she knew from the look on his face that he knew it as well. She could hardly explain that to accept a gift like from him would be to declare she was his mistress.

'Do you always do as your brother asks?'

'He and my uncle are the only kin I have. Once my uncle crosses the River Styx, it is quite likely my brother will become my guardian. It means that I need to take his wishes into account.'

Fortis nodded. He leant across to the market owner, changed the order and rearranged for the cloth to be delivered to his villa. 'You may pick it up later.'

His eyes offered a promise of pleasure. Silvana swallowed hard as her body remembered the last time she had gone to Fortis's villa. She raised a trembling hand and tucked her shawl more firmly into place.

'I have no intention of ever going to your villa again.'

Fortis lifted an eyebrow as he trailed a hand along her arm, creating little fires of warmth. 'You know, I do love challenges. What will bring you back to my villa, I wonder?'

Silvana ran her tongue over her lips. She had to take control of the situation and turn it into a light-hearted flirtation. The only trouble was that her body desired the seduction.

'I thought we had agreed our brief association was over.' Silvana turned and resolutely started back towards the compound. What had been between them was over. She was not going to make a fool of herself a second time.

His long legs easily matched her shorter strides and he appeared not to notice her determined snub.

'Isn't it funny how two people can experience the same thing and remember it in such different ways?'

'Are you saying that you have a different memory of what passed between us?' Silvana stopped dead in the middle of the street. She and Fortis were finished. He had ended the association. 'Our bargain has been completed.'

He made a wry face. 'Sometimes, it would appear I say a great deal too many things. You are right. I agreed that you fulfilled your side of the bargain.'

'I am glad we both share the same memory then.' Her breath had become rapid and shallow. She could hear her heart beginning to pound in her ears. Surely Fortis would not have noticed the change. She needed to sweep on before she started to beg.

His fingers gripped her elbow, propelled her along

to a quiet shadowed portico of an anonymous temple. He turned her towards him.

'This is what I remember.'

His lips swooped down and took the breath from her mouth before she had time to think. Hard, insistent. Silvana fought against the power of the kiss and the feelings that were building in her. As if he could sense her inner turmoil, the kiss changed and became beguiling, teasing, tempting a response. Her body arched forward of its own volition. Her limbs threatened to give way and she clung to his shoulders, her breasts brushing his chest.

'What were we arguing about?' Fortis asked, lifting his head, and his deep green eyes crinkled at the corners. 'Remind me.'

'I did not start the argument.' She paused to catch her breath and then continued in a calmer tone. 'I was simply examining some cloth. There is no harm in examining cloth.'

'You will look lovely in the cloth almost as lovely as you do without any adornment on your body.'

Silvana made an irritated noise as a quick flash of pleasure coursed through her. She took a step backwards and her back touched the cool pillar. 'You can keep the cloth. I stand on my own two feet. I have no intention of returning to a living statue again.'

'And two of the prettiest feet I have ever seen.'

Fortis's hands reached for her again. Her mouth tingled. Her nipples contracted to hardened points and she felt her body arching towards him once again, welcoming his touch.

'Madam, where are you?' Lyde called. 'Your brother is coming. There is a large group of men with him.'

Silvana withdrew further into the shadows. To be caught in a shadowed portico in the embrace of a man—the scandal would be repeated with lip smacking delight from now until September. It would ruin any chance of a relationship she had with Crispus, and they were starting to get along in the way they had done before she had married Cotta the Elder and he had still worn his *bulla* about his neck. She sneaked a peek at Fortis, who looked entirely unrepentant.

As the group drew closer, Silvana realised the noise she had taken for high spirits was actually far more quarrelsome. Crispus appeared to be arguing with some man about Silvana and her virtue.

Silvana started forward, ready to defend her honour.

Fortis's fingers curled around her arm, keeping her within the shadows. He shook his head.

'That is me they are discussing, and he is my brother. There has to be something I can do.'

'Stay here. You will cause your brother more embarrassment if you reveal yourself.' He moved his body so it was between Silvana and the group, shading her from view. 'Let the young cub win his sword.'

'But he is unfamiliar with the ways of Baiae.'

'He'll learn. He has to, unless you want him to be tied to your skirts in the same fashion Eutychus was tied to his mother's.'

Silvana looked up and saw the deep green of his eyes, and the protest died on her lips. Fortis was correct. She could do little to help Crispus and her presence would probably cause a greater scandal.

The noise grew louder and she hid her face in Fortis's toga, felt his strong arms come around her and hold her, his heart thudding in her ear, nearly drowning out the sounds of a scuffle.

Fortis's fingers lifted her chin. A smile crossed his features. 'Everything is fine. They have passed by.'

'What happened?' Silvana peered round him into the empty street. 'Is my brother all right?'

'One blow to his opponent, that is all. The conversation has now turned towards the merits of gladiators. If you had stepped out, the conversation would have returned to gossip about you. Your brother can hold his own.' His eyes became serious. 'Silvana, Merlus is shadowing him and has been for the last ten days.'

'But why?' Silvana breathed.

'When your brother arrived, he mentioned Drusus Cotta had been advising him to race chariots.'

'I don't see that that is any concern of yours.' She noticed his arms were still about her, holding her waist with a light touch, sending little ripples down her back. She stepped away and tried to regain control of her body. Why had Cupid's arrow pricked her so hard?

'I have seen Cotta play this little trick before, always to gain advantage over someone.' A muscle in his jaw twitched. 'He is up to something. He never does anything without a motive. What does he desire from your brother? What does your brother have?'

Icy cold washed over her. She knew the answer. Having failed to get what he wanted that night on the bay, Cotta had decided to strike at her in another way.

'It is not my brother. It is me, or rather my inheritance from his adopted father, in particular a property on the island of Capri.'

Silvana put her hand on the cool concrete column in the centre of the portico. The time for secrets had ended. She had to trust someone. Things were more than she could handle on her own. She had Crispus and his future to think about and Fortis appeared to care about what happened to her.

'It is why I was on his yacht that night. My uncle

was very foolish. He allowed himself to become in debt to Cotta. A trifling amount at first, but Cotta charged a huge rate of interest and then lent him money. It all started because a shipment of spices failed to arrive from Egypt. My uncle had invested in it on Cotta's advice.'

'The same shipment the Prefect caught your uncle with, the one supposedly from Draco the pirate?'

'Yes. My uncle thought it was lost. Once the word got out, Cotta threatened to call in the loan.'

'A loan your uncle can no longer repay,' Fortis stated.

'Once one of his other shipments comes in my uncle will be able to pay off Cotta, but it is May and the real shipping season has only just started.' Silvana tucked a strand of hair behind her ear. She had to make him understand.

'Then why did you have to go to Cotta?'

'Uncle Aulus knew Cotta had the power to make things difficult. He sent me to Cotta to plead his cause, but Cotta laughed. He was going to take me away, and marry me for the property on the island of Capri, once he knew I wouldn't give it up.'

'But why not sell it and be done with it? Cotta can be a powerful enemy.'

'I could never do that. It was where my late husband was born. He made me swear that I would keep it unless my very life was in danger. It is to be my decision and mine alone.' Silvana laced her hands together, and placed them under her chin. 'And I always keep my promises. Cotta the Elder was good to me after his fashion.'

'Has Cotta always been interested in the property?'

Silvana frowned, trying to remember. 'After my husband died and the Vestal Virgins released the will, Cotta the Younger contacted me with a less than generous offer. I refused to sell. I did not hear anything until February of this year—about the time Uncle Aulus unwisely gambled on a shipment of spices. Is it significant?'

'Little pieces of information form a complete mosaic. But it is intriguing.'

'Annoying is more like it. Sometimes, I wonder if Cotta deliberately targeted Uncle Aulus because of me, because he disliked being refused anything.' She gave a small shrug as his face did not change. What had she expected, for him to tell her fears were real? 'But mostly, I tend to think he is a scheming louse who would not hesitate to sell his grandmother.'

'If your brother arranges to race Cotta, get word to me.' Fortis adjusted his toga. His face seemed remote and austere. 'When you leave here, go home.'

'Where are you going?'

'I have to see a man about a boat. I can foresee a boat journey in the near future.'

'I had no idea you could see into the future.'

'Reading the signs is easy if you know where to look.' Fortis sobered. 'I like to be prepared. Remember about your brother. Contact me and I shall see what I can do.'

'It will never happen. Crispus is much more sensible than that. He is not easily manipulated.' Silvana said the words with more force than she intended.

'Who are you trying to convince—me or you? Never say never. Other men have been caught.'

'Kindly refrain from judging my brother as you would the others.' Silvana pressed her lips together. If she kept saying it enough times, maybe she'd believe it. She had to believe it. 'Crispus is different.'

'Be careful, Silvana.' Fortis laid a hand on her shoulder. 'Crispus is young and hot-tempered.'

'Leave my brother out of this!' Silvana cried. She stared at him with her hands on her hips. 'What do you want to do—say I told you so? It won't happen. Crispus is more intelligent than that. He has me to guide him. I am here for him. I don't leave such things to others.'

'I won't dignify that remark with a response. But ask yourself who you are angry with.'

Fortis turned and strode down the street. Silvana

watched him go and then put a hand to her head. She wanted to gather up her skirts and run after him to apologise, but he had already disappeared around a corner.

Chapter Eleven

'What in the name of Minerva are you attempting to do? Spin?' Crispus asked the next morning as Silvana's thread snapped for the third time and the spindle bounced across the floor.

Silvana hurried over to snatch it from Bestus's jaw before the greyhound decided it was a toy.

'We need blankets for the guest bedroom. I thought to do my part.'

'Spinning is not one of the things you are renowned for, Sister. And you look exhausted. What sort of Furies drove your dreams?'

'Witty conversation will not clothe servants.' Silvana piously bent her head and concentrated on re-attaching the wool to the spindle. She was not about to discuss her dreams of Fortis with anyone. Every time she had closed her eyes last night she had remembered the way his mouth felt over hers and her body had grown hot with anticipation until at last she had fallen into a dreamless sleep. She had thought spinning would be a simple enough task for a dream-addled brain, but the spindle seemed determined to prove her wrong. 'My skills are rusty, but my fingers will remember.'

'That won't be necessary. I can recall how much you loathed and detested spinning as a girl. You once tried to bribe me to spin a pile of wool for you.' Crispus grabbed both her hands. He smiled, that exceptionally beguiling smile he used to have when they were both little and he had stolen honey cakes from behind the cook's back. 'I have found a solution to our problems.'

'Let me guess.' Silvana tapped a finger against her lips. Crispus had such a smile on his face. It had to be something important. 'You have been given a junior tribune's post from…the senator who dined with Uncle Aulus, the one who asked you all those difficult questions about Bithynia.'

'Alas, no,' Crispus said, putting his hand to his brow in mock sorrow. 'But Uncle is working on it and he is very hopeful. No, this is even better.'

'Tell me, then. The excitement looks ready to bubble out of you.'

'Congratulate me, sister.' Crispus struck a pose much like the statue of Hercules in the temple on the waterfront. 'I am to race Cotta for Uncle's debts.'

'You are going to do what!' Silvana stood up. Fortis's warning thundered in her brain. She shook her head. She had to have heard wrong. Crispus was not that stupid. She had seen Cotta race several times when her husband was alive. He had a real talent, particularly for winning at the very end. There had been rumours of his cheating, but Cotta's connection with her husband had ensured the rumours vanished. 'Who put such a nonsensical idea in your head? Sometimes, Crispus, I swear you act more like you are eight than eighteen.'

'Nobody put the idea in my head. I thought of it myself. Last night when several of the lads and I were sharing a drink.'

Silvana released a breath. It might all be a scheme, something dreamt up between jugs of increasingly soured wine. She had heard similar boasts before many times at her uncle's parties. Then when Helios started to ride his chariot through the skies again, the words were forgotten in heavy snores and aching heads. Surely to Venus, Minerva and Juno, this had to be the case with Crispus.

'And just who were these lads? These drinking partners?' Silvana crossed her arms and tapped her foot.

'Friends. One or two from school and men I have met at Uncle's parties and others.' Crispus gave a wide smile. 'You'd like them, Silvana. They are a good bunch. Very supportive of the idea.'

'The ones who tried to beat you up yesterday? The one you felt necessary to knock down with a punch? And you complain about the company I keep!' Silvana attempted to keep her voice down to a mild screech.

'How do you know about that?' Crispus leant forward. 'Which little bird has been telling tales? It was nothing, I swear it.'

Silvana stopped. She had no wish to explain any more than strictly necessary to Crispus about her convoluted relationship with Fortis. 'You should know there are no secrets in Baiae. Your doings are regularly reported to me.'

'That doesn't matter.' Crispus made a sharp motion with his hands. 'Once I learned of Uncle's growing debts to Cotta there was only one thing I could do. I had to challenge. Our family honour must be restored.'

Ice gripped Silvana. What had her brother done? She shook her head. She must stop jumping to conclusions. He could be made to see reason. It would be like when he was a boy and he threatened to jump across the Tiber to prove he could fly. 'But this is all talk, Crispus. You haven't actually encountered Drusus Cotta, have you?'

'The boys and me, we ran him to earth at Poppea's

house.' Crispus's face glowed. 'You should see the furnishings! Gold and silver, with slaves spraying little bottles of perfume into the air.'

'I know what Poppea's house is like.' Silvana wrinkled her nose. 'What did Cotta say when you challenged him?'

'He was surprised. He tried to back down, refused to entertain the notion. Told me I should go home and play with my marbles. The other diners laughed at that. I hate being laughed at, Silvana.'

Silvana gave a slight nod. She only hoped for once Cotta was being kind. Surely even he could see how people would talk if he bested a youth. 'You left then, Crispus. Tell me you left.'

'Leave? I did no such thing! I am a Junius. I have my pride. I called him a coward and challenged him again.' Crispus stuck his thumbs in his belt. 'This time, his face turned purple and he accepted!'

'He accepted?' A numbness crept over her. She had hoped that this was some sort of bad dream, but she knew it wasn't.

'Of course he did. Everyone was telling him to.'

'How could you, Crispus?'

'You needn't fear, Silvana.' Crispus reached out and covered her hand with his, giving her an indulgent smile. 'All will be well. I am an excellent chariot driver. Everyone says so.'

Including Cotta? It was far too easy and smacked too much of Cotta's manipulation. The ostentatious refusal in front of witnesses, and then being reluctantly forced to accept the challenge. He did not have to do that. He could have had Crispus ejected with a wave of his bejewelled hand. No, Cotta accepted because Cotta wanted to. He was desperate to race Crispus. But why? It did not make any sense.

'And what happens if you lose? What are you going to give up?'

Crispus scuffed his sandal in the dirt. 'You would have to ask that.'

'It is because I want to know.' A sudden fear gripped Silvana. 'You haven't offered yourself as a member of his gladiatorial troupe?'

'Silvana! What a thing, of course not. I offered that estate I inherited from Father in the north of Italy.'

'Crispus! It is worth far more on the open market than the money Uncle Aulus owes. It is your main inheritance and has been in the family for generations.'

'Keep calm. I am not going to lose.' Crispus leant forward and Silvana could smell the faint aroma of sour wine. 'I had to have something to get him to rise to the bait. Cotta did not want to race me, but it was the only way I knew to get the money back. Everyone was goading me about it.'

Silvana put her head in her hands and tried to

control her temper. She wanted to beat her hands against his chest and tell him to listen to reason. She wanted to shake him until he saw sense, but he was too big. He was no longer smaller than her. She had to tread carefully. She took a deep breath and forced her shoulders to relax.

'Say you understand, Silvana.' Crispus gave a sheepish smile and held out both his hands. 'You know how these things happen. A man has to protect the honour of his family.'

'How could you do such a thing!' She slammed her fists together. 'I won't let you, Junius Crispus. You must stop this madness. You lose that race and you will have no land. You will cease to be an *equites*.'

'It was the only way. I have my pride as well. Besides, I am not going to lose. Cotta is not very good at racing. He injured his arm before the last Ides.'

'Here now, here now, what is all this noise? How is a body to sleep?' Uncle Aulus came in, tying his belt about his tunic. 'Why are you shouting, Silvana?'

'My sister has no understanding about what I have done.' Crispus crossed his arms and smiled smugly. 'I have saved the family honour.'

'You have done nothing of the sort!' Silvana wrapped her arms about her waist and started pacing the room.

'There is another way. Cotta indicated he would

take that piece of land you inherited from his adopted father. Its price is about the same as the debt, and nobody else would want it as it adjoins his land. But he needs to hear it from you. Apparently you insulted him the last time he asked.'

'I have already told Cotta. That piece of land was given to me in trust. It is a reminder of my former husband.'

'And I am your flesh and blood, Sister.'

'What has my nephew done?'

'I promised my estate in northern Italy to Cotta if I lose against him in a chariot race. But I have no intention of losing. Silvana is becoming hysterical over nothing.' Crispus gave his most winning smile. 'It was such a simple way of clearing your debts, Uncle, I wonder why you did not think of it before. Racing chariots is the easiest thing in the world.'

'You had no right to do such a thing!' Silvana cried again, and held out her hands to her uncle. Surely her uncle had to see sense. He knew the odds. He knew what happened to men who lost.

'I have every right! It is my property.' Crispus's bottom lip stuck out.

'You have not come of age. Uncle Aulus is your guardian.'

Uncle Aulus ran his hand through his hair. 'You

made this bet, Crispus? Without my knowledge or consent? Your sister is right. A bet made by an in-experienced youth does not have to stand. Cotta will understand. He is a reasonable man. You may apolo-gise, if you like.'

'I did it for you, Uncle. I had no wish to see you suffer the indignities of having to hold these dinner parties any more, waiting for scraps of information to fall your way, for men to gamble too much and to dance. I can't apologise and ever hold my head up again. Surely you must see that.'

'You show great courage, Crispus.'

'And you did say that I could take charge of my inheritance.' Crispus snapped his fingers. 'Silvana, he did agree—three nights ago.'

Silvana closed her eyes, but all Uncle Aulus did was to give a weary sigh.

'Uncle, since when did you give Crispus the power to negotiate such things? He is under age. He has no business wagering his inheritance.'

Her uncle shrugged and looked away. 'I may have said something when I had too much to drink. Forgive me, Silvana, I thought he only wanted to make sure that his inheritance was safe. It was only a scroll of intent.'

'A scroll of intent?' Silvana went to her uncle and shook him. 'Tell me what you did.'

Crispus caught her arms, and held her back. She freed herself from him.

'Cotta told me it would be a good idea. He wouldn't even entertain the idea unless I had Uncle's consent. It was best to keep everything legal. And then it was my idea to have the bet written down as well. I had no wish for him to cheat. Here, read it for yourself.'

Silvana rapidly read the bet. It was a binding wager between Cotta and Crispus. If either chariot should fail to race, the other would win through default. The winning driver would get her uncle's debts, but if Crispus's chariot lost, he would give up all claim to the estate in northern Italy.

'Crispus, you should not have done this.' Silvana sank to the couch and pressed her palm into her forehead as a pounding pain crashed over her.

'I am not going to lose, Silvana. You are getting upset over nothing.' Crispus gave an indulgent smile and a perfunctory pat on the shoulder. 'By tomorrow evening, all this worry and hysterics will have been for nothing. And Uncle will have his loan forgiven.'

Silvana paced the small chamber in the Baths of Mercury. The smiling nymphs on the frescoed walls appeared to mock her. Unable to bear the tension, she had left Crispus and Uncle Aulus to their self-congratulatory smugness and had sent a tablet to Fortis, asking him to meet her here before the seventh hour.

She had waited beyond the seventh hour. Several couples, looking for a place to be alone, had peeked in, but she had refused to move despite the pointed stares and eventually they had departed, tittering and cooing together.

Now she wondered if Fortis would even show up. Perhaps it was better this way. She was used to having to fend for herself. She drew a steadying breath. She'd leave now, before she did something foolish, like begging him to find a way to stop the race.

'You sent a very mysterious tablet.' Fortis entered the room, his bulk making the room seem small. He wore a simple tunic, but the material was much finer than normal working men's tunics, moulding to his body and hinting at the hard muscles underneath. All too clearly. 'Requesting a meeting at a place known for its discreetness.'

'If you are here to make jokes and snide remarks, you can leave.' Silvana turned towards the frescos. She had been sorely tempted to throw herself into his arms and all he could was make jokes.

'Silvana, tell me what is wrong. Why the mystery?'

Silvana pressed her palms together. She thought the Baths of Mercury was the best place—private, yet not private. Nothing would happen here. She held her head high, refusing to flinch, despite his stare. 'I wanted to apologise.'

'Have you done something that offended me?' Fortis crossed his arms and leant against the door-frame. 'Pray enlighten me.'

Why was he making things difficult?

'When we last met, you made certain observations about Crispus. Things I utterly rejected. But you were right about my brother. He is very naïve.' She halted the torrent of words and regained control of her voice. She would be calm and dignified. 'He has allowed himself to be caught in Cotta's coils in record time. He challenged Cotta to a race.'

She bowed her head and waited for the mocking superior words. Instantly, Fortis was at her side. He put his arm about her and she relaxed into his warmth before straightening and walking over to the nymph fresco. More than ever the nymph's smile seemed over-bright and false, as if she too was under considerable pressure to appear happy and blithe, without a care in the world when, in fact, her world was collapsing around her.

'I take no pleasure in being correct, Silvana.'

A wave of guilt passed over Silvana. She had been so sure that he would take the opportunity to loudly proclaim his righteousness. Her finger traced the line of the nymph's robes. It would be easier if he had been sardonic. It would have given her something else to fight against, instead of her all-consuming desire to collapse into his arms, feel his mouth against hers.

'Is there anything I can do?' He was close behind her. His breath caressed her neck, beckoning her. 'Why did you ask me here, Silvana? Why did you feel the need to apologise in person? Here in this place known for its trysting lovers?'

'If I had remembered that little fact, I would not have invited you here.'

'And here I had hopes you wanted to renew our relationship in the most open of all possible ways.' There was a distinct mocking gleam in his eyes. Against whom, Silvana couldn't tell.

'You were the one who ended it,' she stated bluntly, refusing to allow her cheeks to grow hot under his gaze.

'I believe we agreed to different memories.'

The words were on the tip of her tongue, dismissing him. When she had first sent the tablet, she had thought she would ask him to help her, to find a way to stop Crispus, but, after she had arrived, she realised to do that would be to surrender. She had nothing left to bargain with. She moved away from him, away from his body, and then turned to face him. Her hands gripped the amulet of Venus that hung from her belt. She drew a deep calming breath. She'd start again. This time, she'd explain properly.

'I wanted to explain in person and to apologise for doubting your words.' Silvana held out her hands, palm upwards. 'That is all. It would appear you know my brother better than I do. To be caught so soon. My words were in haste and error.'

'What has Cotta done to your brother?'

Silvana wrapped her arms about her waist. It had seemed easy before. A few words, that was all she would have to say. He'd mutter some sardonic remark and then they would part on better terms than they had previously. It frightened her how much she wanted to confide in him. But she had to tell someone. Briefly she explained what her brother had done, and what the stakes were.

Throughout the recital, Fortis's face did not change, but his body became more guarded. He tapped his finger against the wall. 'Cotta will set out to win at any cost. Is there something you want me to do?'

Hold me.

She forced her shoulders to be straighter and concentrated on the nymph fresco. 'There is nothing you can do. I have already made my mind up. I know what Cotta wants. When my brother loses, I will make him an offer.'

'What makes you think he will take it?' His eyes became hard green stones and his lip curled slightly as his gaze raked up and down her slim form. 'I understand he already has a mistress.'

Silvana clenched her hand, ready to strike him. How dare he misinterpret her words! She had wanted to see him, to talk through her plan and all he could do was make cutting remarks. 'I will offer him the property on Capri that he desires. As you say, he has a mistress, and an expensive one at that.'

Fortis flinched as the words cut into him. He should not have taunted her, but the thought that she would willingly give her body to another man, that he had somehow started her down a road where she abandoned all the standards she had held, inflamed his temper.

'Why did you summon me here, Silvana?'

'Because…because I wanted to have someone I could talk it over with…someone whose counsel I trusted. Obviously I made a mistake.'

She prepared to sweep from the room. Fortis knew if he let her go, he'd lose her for ever.

'What do you want me to do, Silvana? Challenge Cotta?'

'I am not sure.' Silvana started to pace the room, agitated.

Fortis reached out, gathered her hands in his and

held them to his chest. 'Whatever you want me to do, you only have to ask.'

She shook her head slightly and gently withdrew her fingers. 'It was a mistake even to contact you. I must stand on my own feet.'

Fortis regarded Silvana. She was standing there, proud yet vulnerable, refusing to see her own weakness.

Fortis could all too clearly see what was happening. When Crispus lost, and Fortis knew he would, Silvana would give up the property that she had promised her former husband to only sell if her life depended on it. She would also give up her pride. He knew what it had cost her to come to him that day when her uncle had been imprisoned in the garrison, and how he had treated her.

He wanted to draw her into his arms and whisper that everything would be fine, but that would be a lie. There was only one way that he could guarantee he had a say in the outcome. 'When are they racing?'

'Tomorrow at the fifth hour. The race is along the road to Cumae. When they reach the Sibyl's cave, they are to head back to Baiae. The person to return first to the Forum wins.'

'I will lend him my horses for the change at Cumae as he has only one set of horses and your uncle's are not very good.' Fortis placed his hands on his thighs and stood up. A plan was beginning to formulate in his head. There was an outside chance Crispus could be made to see reason, but he first had to win his trust. However, he had no desire to give Silvana any false hope, give her any reason to refuse him. More than anything he wanted to take her in his arms and kiss away the fear, but that would complicate matters. He needed to build her trust. 'The greys have the stamina and speed. It will help even up the race.'

'Your horses? But you don't race.'

'I don't race now. Seven years ago, I raced many times to Cumae and won.' Fortis stared at the frescoes. He could remember Murcia loving this room, and her excited squeals that one of the nymphs looked like her. He could also remember her cries of pain as the chariot tumbled over, a reckless race, a reckless wager and an untimely end. After that, he vowed not to race, but to use his energies for good. 'My judgment on horse flesh has not diminished.'

'Crispus assures me that his pair are swift. Some of the swiftest seen in Baiae for a decade. Why will he need to change?'

'They are swift, but they don't have the stamina for the race. Merlus told me about them last night.' Fortis ran his hand through his hair. He had to convince her that he meant to help, if only she would allow him to. 'Crispus has won a few small races with them. Enough to give him confidence, I suppose, but nothing against real opposition or over any great distance. It has made him over-confident. He needs another pair of horses for the return journey.'

'Are you sure about that?'

'Cotta will change horses. Everyone who races to Cumae does,' Fortis said with an arched eyebrow. She had lived in Baiae for how long? Surely she was not that ignorant of the finer details.

'I wouldn't know.' Silvana gave a small shrug. 'I don't race. I dislike the speed of chariots.'

'One scandalous thing you have failed to do.'

'Did your wife race?' Silvana asked. Her direct gaze seemed to pierce into his soul. 'It is how she died, isn't it?'

'Murcia challenged me. Our chariots collided on the bad bend just outside Baiae. She was attempting to pass. She was thrown and her neck broke instantly. She did not suffer.'

'It wasn't your fault.' She touched his shoulder. He closed his fingers over hers and gave them a brief squeeze. 'Accidents happen all the time.'

Fortis stood up and brushed a piece of lint from his tunic. He would swear Silvana was a witch. He had not talked about Murcia in seven years, and he had no intention of beginning now. He refused to dishonour her memory. What was in the past should stay there.

'Perhaps you are right, but Crispus will still need a fresh pair of horses. Where will he get them from if not from me?'

Silvana's dark blonde hair had sprung free from its confines and little ringlets encircled her face. She rubbed the back of her neck. 'Crispus is determined to do this his way. His horses will have to be enough. They are very swift.'

'Crispus will be the first to reach the Sibyl's cave, but he won't be the first to return to Baiae—not without a change of horses.'

'You are willing to do this?' Silvana said, standing. She tucked one of the loose curls behind her ear. She seemed irresolute. 'I will tell him. Maybe he will listen to me.'

'It will be done, Silvana. He can speak to my trainer. It will give him the best opportunity.' He held out his arms, willing her to walk into them. To trust him to take care of her and see her through this.

Her tongue traced the outline of her mouth. She took a half-step, and then deliberately she turned her head and spoke to the fresco. 'Yes, I can see that. It makes sense. I still don't see why you are willing to do this for him.'

Not for him. For you. Because of what I did.

'I heard from Eutychus last evening.' Fortis regarded the crown of her head. 'He sent a tablet. He asked to be remembered to you. He is settling well. Rome is hot, but there is enough going on. He has shaved off his goatee beard.'

'He did look ridiculous with it.' Silvana's infectious laugh rang out. She paused. When she had come into this room she had thought never to laugh again, but there was something about sharing her worries with Fortis. He made her feel as if her worst fears were not going to come to pass. Her eyes searched his face. 'You are doing this for Eutychus, aren't you? He told you to look after me. I should have seen this before.'

His lips parted as if he was about to say something and then he firmly closed them. He reached out and touched her hand, a butterfly touch. 'The horses will give Crispus a chance, Silvana.'

'I was right to trust you.' She bowed her head and concentrated on the end of her belt. 'I am very used to being alone.'

'You are not alone now.'

His words flowed over her like soothing balm, warming her. She wanted to believe them, but she was frightened. What would happen if she trusted him? Would he go away and leave her? One more disappointment.

'I will be when you depart, when you return to Rome.'

Fortis shook his head and let the remark pass. This was not the time to explain what he intended. He had to be patient. He wanted Silvana to come with him, because she wanted him, not out of gratitude for what he had done. 'If Crispus loses, do you want me there when you confront Cotta? In case he decides to cause trouble.'

She hesitated and then a slow smile spread, lighting her face with an inner radiance. 'Yes…yes, I would like that very much.'

'I will be there.'

He walked away from the room and towards his demons and the ghosts of his past. For too long he had avoided them, taking comfort in his work in the Senate. Now he had to confront them and win. He had to for Silvana's sake. He had to give her a future.

Chapter Twelve

'Can you tell me again what you intend to do, master?' Merlus said as Fortis strode towards the stables the next afternoon. 'You are being very mysterious.'

The fierce afternoon sun beat down on the cobblestones, and the heat rose, curling around Fortis's ankle-strap sandals. It was a day for sitting in the baths and relaxing, not for going out and trying to prevent chariot races.

'First you lend your horses to a jumped up youth who can barely wipe his own backside,' Merlus continued, not waiting for Fortis's reply, 'and then you demand to meet the man before the race.'

'I want to make sure he will not saw at the blacks' mouths. If he applies too much pressure, they may overturn the chariot. Particularly as he comes out of Cumae and encounters the uneven paving.'

Merlus nodded, but his expression showed that he didn't believe a word. He opened his mouth to say something more, but shut it as Crispus emerged from the stable. Fortis glanced over at the boy. Gone was the arrogant youth who had berated his sister for daring to cause a scandal that first evening. Instead he stood, leaning against the stable wall, shoulders slumped and toe drawing a slow line in the dirt.

At Fortis's shout of greeting, he glanced up and half-raised an arm. He wiped his hands on his tunic and started across the dusty stable yard towards them, carrying his helmet in one hand.

'He looks worse than a tiro about to meet his first opponent in the ring,' Merlus said in a low voice.

'What are you talking about, Merlus?'

'I have seen that expression many a time before. Tiros in particular, but one or two gladiators as well, come to think of it.'

'What are you talking about, Merlus?' Fortis repeated.

'It is like they know what the Fates have in store for them and just give up, like. All the fight goes out of them. It's them eyes that gives it away. Always my trainer says look at the eyes, you can tell within a heartbeat who is going to win the bout and who ain't. And this here race ain't going to be won by someone like him.'

Fortis shook his head at the doom-filled predictions spilling forth from Merlus. 'That will be enough, Merlus. Crispus approaches.'

Merlus lapsed into a gloomy silence.

The youth came closer, staggering slightly. Dark pink wine spots stained his tunic and Crispus's face was a sickly shade of green. He stumbled over a stone, frowned and then came forward with great care and precision.

Fortis tapped his fingers together, revising his earlier prediction. Even with the horses, it would be doubtful if Crispus made the first checkpoint, let alone the Sibyl's cave. To keep a chariot upright took every ounce of concentration and sometimes, even then, it turned over.

'Crispus, are you ready to race? The starting horn will be blown in less than an hour.'

Crispus swayed, sought to balance himself and nearly tumbled. Merlus rushed forward, but Fortis shook his head and the manservant stopped. Eventually Crispus appeared to master the art of walking and strode the final steps to Fortis, clasping his forearm in greeting.

'Cotta will rue the day.'

He raised his fist in the air and then crumpled to his knees and was sick. Fortis allowed him to lie there for a little while, but when he showed no inclination to move, he picked him up by the tunic and set him on his feet.

'You know why you are racing?'

'Don't matter now.' Crispus wiped a hand across his mouth. 'Sil…Silvana will make good the money. I heard her say so. She looks after me. My sister does. Always has done. Not going to fail anyway. Prove to everyone the Junius family is capable of great things.'

'But it doesn't matter if you do lose, does it? It is not you who is going to suffer.'

'What do you know about it?'

Fortis's mouth twisted. He should leave this youth to learn the consequences of his actions, but it would only propel Silvana further down a road she had not wanted to set out on. Crispus had no real stake in the outcome of the race. It would be his sister who would suffer because she would misguidedly try to protect her brother. What Crispus needed was not protection, but a cold hard dose of reality.

'You are in no fit state to be in charge of horses,' he said calmly, looking Crispus directly in the eye.

'Says who?' Crispus came up and prodded Fortis in the chest. 'I can drive the horses blindfolded.'

Fortis picked the finger off his chest as if he were picking a piece of lint off his toga.

'It is not very clever poking me in the chest, but as you are young, I will let it pass.'

'You and who else?' Crispus put his hands on his hips as his bottom lip stuck out. 'You are here to laugh at me.'

He looked Crispus over from the curls on his head to his scuffed sandals. The stench of sour wine hung about his person and the stains on his tunic were more numerous than Fortis had first thought. What Silvana had done to deserve a wastrel like this for a brother, he had no idea. She should allow him to lose his estate. It would be the making of him, force him to do something for another human being, rather than have everything given to him on a plate. But Silvana would destroy her future to protect him. Fortis held out his hands. 'I am here to help, Junius Crispus.'

'Who sent you? My sister?' A crafty gleam appeared in Crispus's eyes. 'She always wants to take over anything I do. That's why you sent the horses, isn't it? If you had asked me, I would have told you Castor and Pollux can last the full race. I told Uncle Aulus, but he wouldn't listen.'

'He shows some signs of sense.'

'What did you say?' Crispus poked him again in the chest. 'I didn't hear you.'

This time, Fortis reacted, grabbed Crispus by the tunic. It was only the thought of how Silvana would react if her brother was torn limb from limb that held Fortis's temper in check. He let Crispus go and the youth fell to the ground, wiping tears of self-pity from his eyes.

'You don't want to race, do you?' Fortis said between gritted teeth. 'It is why you are trying to pick a fight with me.'

'I have no idea what you are talking about.' Crispus hiccupped twice. 'I take exception to your attitude.'

'You listen to me.' Fortis rested his fists on his hips. 'You will go to Cotta and back down. You and I will offer him a deal for your uncle's debts—a schedule to repay them from the funds for your northern Italian estate. It will all be done quietly.' Fortis started towards the part of the stables where Cotta's horses were held. 'There may be time to solve this problem sensibly. You may not have to lose your estate.'

'No.' Crispus stamped his foot. 'I want to race. I will race. You can't stop me. It is my life that is at stake. Not yours!'

Fortis halted, maintaining control of his temper by the thinnest of margins. The muscle in his jaw jumped. In the background, he could hear Merlus's low whistle and shout, 'Take it from an old hand, lad, when the master's eyes are like green glass, you run for cover.'

'You fail to understand. You have no choice, Junius Crispus.'

'It's my race, I tell you. Mine and I am going to win. You can't stop me!' Crispus swung a wild punch that glanced off Fortis's shoulder and then started flailing madly with his fists, tears streaming down his eyes. 'I have to win. You don't understand. I gave my word.'

He aimed a kick, connecting with Fortis's shin.

'That was not a good idea, mate,' Merlus called. 'I think you had better apologise.'

'Why? I have nothing to apologise for. He started it. Coming here, ordering me around.'

'You are right,' Fortis replied, regarding the youth. 'I can forgive one punch, but not two.'

Fortis's fist connected with Crispus's jaw. Crispus gave a low moan, crumpled to the ground and then lay still. Fortis regarded the prone body.

'What are we going to do now, master?' Merlus came to stand beside him. He poked Crispus's body with his sandaled foot. 'Have you killed him?'

'He lives. I doubt Silvana would forgive me if I had accidentally killed her brother. She does seem to have an inexplicable attachment to the wine-soaked creature. But I fear Cotta will declare the race forfeit if Crispus does not show.'

'You should have thought of that before you struck him.' Merlus rolled his eyes and knelt down beside Crispus, starting to fan him. 'Up you go, Sunshine. Next time, think before you use your fists.'

'No, keep him with you.'

Merlus allowed the body to drop to the ground with a thump.

'Keep him with me? Out here? Have the Furies touched you?'

'You can do it. Better yet, put him in Castor's stall and keep him there. Sit on him. When his sister appears, you can give her custody if she wants it.' Fortis bent down and picked up Crispus's discarded helmet. He gave a salute to the body. 'I promise you, Junius Crispus, I will do everything in my power to see that the race is won and your family's honour is restored.'

'Wait, wait.' Merlus pulled at his hair with his hands. 'Where are you going?'

'Somebody has to race.'

'But why? Is it because you suspect Cotta is in league with the pirates? You have actively avoided racing before now. Always, always, you say no.'

A pair of large brown eyes appeared before Fortis. He refused to explain it to Merlus. Let him think what he wanted to. It made life easier. He had Silvana's honour to think of. Silvana's future was far more important to him than any phantom from the past.

'I have my reasons, Merlus.'

For a race that had only been agreed the day before, word had spread remarkably quickly.

Crowds lined both sides of the road to Cumae and stretched as far the eye could see. Everyone from Poppea, in her new gold-shot-purple silk gown to Fortis's aunt, Sempronia, appeared to be here, ready to comment on the biggest race so far this season.

Everyone, that was, except Fortis.

She had scanned the crowd, and nowhere had she seen the familiar broad shouldered figure. A lump of disappointment rose in her throat. She had not realised how much she had counted on seeing him until he was somewhere else.

She should have known better than to ever depend on anyone. Silvana pinched the bridge of her nose. She would get through this afternoon and then she would do what the Fates decreed.

'Have you seen Crispus at the stables, Uncle?' Silvana asked, elbowing two young men out of the way to stand by him.

Her uncle did not meet her eye, preferring instead to make a show of straightening his toga. Silvana repeated her question, this time tugging at his toga and forcing him to look her directly in his eye. Beads of perspiration broke out on Uncle Aulus's forehead and he wiped it repeatedly with a handkerchief.

'I have seen Crispus, yes,' he admitted at last. 'Earlier.'

'There is a problem.'

'Not a problem, exactly, more of a condition.'

Silvana swallowed hard, her mouth tasting bitter. She had not dared see Crispus, afraid her nerves would unduly influence him. She had lain awake most of the night, imagining what it would be like when he lost, what she'd have to say when she confronted Cotta. Surely, her late husband would understand that she could not allow her brother to ruin his life.

'Uncle Aulus, I have a right to know. He is my baby brother. What in the name of Apollo has happened to Crispus?' She paused as a chill ran down her back. 'He can still race, can't he?'

'Dida found an empty amphora of wine in Crispus's room this morning. Not a good vintage, you understand, but one which you open late in the evening. The sort that gives a nasty head if taken undiluted.'

'Are you saying Crispus is drunk?' The enormity of the situation began to sink in on Silvana. If Crispus was drunk, he might not even make the first bend in the road. Not only would he lose, but he would become the laughing stock of Baiae. It would become a tale to be repeated over the dinner tables with great relish, the sort of tale that would cling to his toga for years to come. 'How could you let him get drunk? You gave him the amphora. Don't bother to deny it, Uncle.'

Uncle Aulus hung his head.

'It appeared to be a good idea at the time. Something to steady his nerves. The boy was shaking like a leaf last night. He knows what he has done, Silvana, but there is no stopping him, even if I wanted to. He signed that scroll and had it witnessed. He needed something to calm his nerves.'

Silvana crossed her arms. 'But why, Uncle? You know as well as I do alcohol gives only false courage.'

'He wants to prove himself, Silvana—to show the world that he can amount to something, but then the reality hit. Be patient.'

Uncle Aulus put a hand on her shoulder, but she shrugged it off.

'It's not him I am angry with. A whole amphora, Uncle?'

'I never ever thought he would drink the whole thing—merely a glass or two and straight to sleep. That's what I told him.'

'He won't prove himself like this. He will create a massive scandal. Everything he worked for gone on the strength of a few glasses of sour wine.'

'I gave him something to sober him up, but it appeared to turn him a bit green. He should be fine come race time.' Uncle Aulus wiped his forehead with his handkerchief. 'That is if he doesn't find another amphora.'

'Uncle.' Silvana gave an exasperated shudder as

her uncle shrugged and then began to answer a senator's question on the betting, assuring him that he had heard Cotta would fall at the last turn.

Silvana tapped her sandal, but her uncle studiously ignored her. She frowned, trying to decide what her next course of action should be. Her uncle was no help and, despite his promise, Fortis had not bothered to show up. She had not realised how much she was counting on seeing his face until he wasn't there. She would have to depend on herself as she had always done. She started to edge her way out of the crowd. A pink parasol briefly blocked her way. Silvana retraced her steps and started to sidle out the other way.

'Where are you going, Silvana?' Uncle Aulus's fingers caught her sleeve. 'The race is about to start. See, the cornu players are getting in position. I will say that Cotta does know how to put on a good spectacle.'

'To see Crispus. If he is in no fit state, then someone else will have to drive the chariot. I refuse to give into Cotta that easily.'

'And that someone would be?' Uncle Aulus ran his hand through his thinning hair. 'I would do it, Silvana. Truly, I would. I want Crispus to win that wager. The young fool should never have made it. But my knees have never been the same since the pirates freed me and, well…wouldn't Cotta declare the race over, if he does not race Crispus. Think about that, Silvana.'

Silvana shifted uneasily. From what Fortis had said at the Baths of Mercury, she knew Cotta intended to win—by fair means or foul. He had picked his target well. 'Cotta does not mind who he races as long as he wins. I read the scroll, the same as you. The words only say a race on this date. It does not say the drivers' names. Uncle, we have to do something.'

'They are bringing our chariot out now.'

Uncle Aulus pointed to the starting area where the grooms were leading the familiar silver and blue painted chariot out. Crispus's horses pawed the ground and tossed their heads. The man holding the reins stood straight and sure, proud.

'All your fears were for nothing. Those horses look to be real goers. See, Crispus is even wearing my lucky helmet.'

Silvana stared at the tall man who was in Crispus's chariot. Despite his helmet being jammed on, his shoulders were broader, and the way he held his body more commanding.

Fortis.

Every sinew in her body told her so. It had to be. He turned his head and their eyes met, held. He gave a slight nod and a touch to his helmet before the stamping of hooves drew his attention back to Crispus's pair.

Silvana clapped her hand to her mouth, glanced again at Uncle Aulus, who was urging Crispus forward, shouting advice on how to handle the notorious bends at the start of the race, and seemingly oblivious to the change in drivers.

Was she the only one to recognise him? Silvana laid a hand on Uncle's Aulus's arm. 'Uncle Aulus, it is not Crispus.'

A blare of trumpets drowned out Silvana's words and Uncle Aulus went on shouting encouragement.

Cotta appeared, dressed in purple robes with a crown of laurels on his head. He waved grandly to the crowd and threw a handful of coins. The young children scrambled forward to pick up silver and copper coins.

'Look at that, will you! Who does he think he is? The jumped-up son of an *aedile*. Where does he think he is? The Circus Maximus in Rome? I can remember when he was desperately trying for any junior post.' Uncle Aulus harrumphed. 'Cotta is a bloody arrogant fool. The sooner Crispus shows him his mettle the better.'

'Uncle Aulus, the driver is not Crispus.' Silvana forced the words from her throat.

'Have you had a touch of the sun, Silvana? Don't you think I know my own nephew? Go to it, Crispus!'

When Cotta saw the man in the other chariot his wave faltered slightly. He leant over and barked a few words. The other driver seemed not in the least perturbed as he pointed to the finish line and shrugged.

Cotta jammed his helmet on, and imperiously gave a signal that both chariots were ready.

Both chariots started to edge forward, held back by the combined efforts of trainers and grooms. The crowd hushed as the *aedile* gave the details of the race. Silvana offered one last prayer up to Mercury.

The starter held his white handkerchief aloft. The crowd held its breath as the horses pawed the ground. Silvana watched the handkerchief, fluttering in the light breeze.

Why didn't he let it go?

Just when she thought she could bear it no longer, the handkerchief drifted gently down.

A loud blast from the cornu rent the air and the horses surged forward, breaking free of their trainers as the roar of the crowd became deafening.

'They're off!' Uncle Aulus shouted, grabbing Silvana's arm. 'By Mercury, what a start! The race is on!'

Chapter Thirteen

Fortis's arm muscles bulged as he pulled back hard on the reins, trying to steady the black horses. The noise from the crowd and the sudden blast of the horns had sent them into a frenzy, leaping forward, hooves pawing the ground. The chariot lifted off the ground and crashed back to earth with a disconcerting thump. Fortis swayed back and forth, struggling to keep his balance as his body first hit one side of the chariot and then the other.

'Steady, boys,' he called out softly. 'We will soon be through this crowd.'

Neither horse gave any indication they had heard but continued to run as if a horde of demons were chasing them, living up to their reputation as some of the swiftest horses in Baiae. Swift but without discipline, and definitely lacking in stamina. Crispus had bought a disaster waiting to happen. He should have left Crispus to his well-deserved fate, but the consequences for Silvana were too great.

A wall surrounding a villa loomed in front of him. Fortis forced his body to the left. The black horses turned at the last instant, and the wheels of the chariot scraped the stone.

The chariot tilted first one way and then the next. He could feel the chariot begin to slip to the right, one wheel tipping. He leant all his weight to the left, heard the thud as the chariot righted itself and then the steady movement as the wheels began to turn smoothly and the road opened in front of him.

'Easy now.'

He had opted to have the reins wrapped around his body as professional charioteers did. This meant he could cut them with a knife and jump to safety if the chariot started to run completely out of control. At the moment they were stretched tight from his body to the bit, alive with the pull of the horses.

He looked ahead and saw Cotta had taken an early lead. Fortis smiled grimly, concentrating on the road. It would be dangerous to try to pass here. There was a spot halfway to Cumae where the road suddenly opened up and he could pass. Now he merely had to pace his horses, keep Cotta within his sights, and wait for the over-confidence to appear.

* * *

Silvana watched Fortis's horses bolt as the race started, unlike Cotta's smooth start. Had Cotta known?

With an inexperienced chariot driver, the chariot would have overturned. She dreaded to think what would have happened if Crispus had been holding the reins. But Fortis turned the horses away from the crowd. Then, in a blink of an eye, the chariots disappeared in a cloud of dust, impossible to tell who was in the lead.

'It will be several hours before they return,' Uncle Aulus said, rubbing his hands. 'Crispus was a bit reckless with his team. They appeared to be wildly out of control.'

'That was not Crispus.' Silvana wrapped her arms about her waist.

'What do you mean? Of course it was Crispus. Are you sure you have not had a touch of the sun? I know my own nephew.'

'It was Aurelius Fortis.'

Silvana passed a hand over her eyes as a pounding attacked her head. When she had gone to Fortis she had not expected him to drive the chariot. She could never envision a situation where Crispus would give way. His pride in his own abilities was too great. Something had to have happened to Crispus.

'Now, are you coming to the stables with me to find

out what happened to my brother or are you going to stand there with your mouth open catching flies?'

Uncle Aulus stood with his hands on his hips, surveying the road. 'But Aurelius Fortis never races. He gave up racing when his wife died.'

'He is racing now.'

'That is very interesting news indeed.' Uncle Aulus rubbed his hands together. 'Where can I go to put a small wager? I had the pleasure of seeing Aurelius race many years ago.'

Silvana closed her eyes and willed her temper not to explode. Uncle Aulus appeared to be oblivious to what was actually happening—talking about wagering small amounts of money when Fortis held their entire future in his hands. 'Uncle Aulus, isn't there enough riding on this race?'

'True, but the omens have improved.' He leant forward as a broad smile crossed his face. 'I would go so far as to say that the omens are excellent for you receiving an offer.'

'You are spouting myths and legends again. Next you will be telling me you saw a dryad in the woods.' Silvana fastened her shawl more securely about her shoulders. Fortis had no wish to marry her. Marriage was out of the question.

'You have no real appreciation of the subtler things in life, Silvana.' Uncle Aulus trotted along beside her as she walked rapidly towards the stables, ignoring the stares from curious onlookers.

'I am going to find Crispus, and maybe, just maybe, I can salvage something from this mess.'

'But mark my words, Niece—Fortis has made a fairly public declaration about his intentions towards you.'

Silvana tried to ignore the war elephants that had suddenly taken hold in her stomach. Was guilt the only reason Fortis was racing? If he won, he would gain control of her uncle's debts, and could dictate terms. And if he lost… Silvana did not want to think about him losing, but in many ways it might be the best solution. She could pay off the debt to Cotta and not be beholden to Fortis. Silvana pressed her fingers to the bridge of her nose. Except she did not want him to lose. She wanted him to win.

She looked where people now sauntered across the roadway, chatting and laughing, but a few heartbeats before, Fortis had fought to keep Crispus's unpredictable team under control.

But, more importantly, she wanted him to survive!

When Fortis rounded the last bend before the open countryside, Cotta was slightly ahead of him. The gold detail on his chariot gleamed in the sunshine, the rumble of a second pair of chariot wheels against the stone pavement resounded in Fortis's ears.

He bided his time, holding the horses back as the narrow road snaked through the various outlying villas. The roadside was marked with indentations from scores of previous crashes. Even today, several forlorn chariot wheels lay half-submerged in a ditch.

The road opened up, straight and smooth. Fortis flicked the reins, urged the blacks forward. The horses responded instantly, adding an extra burst of speed. He pulled level with Cotta, who gave him a furious look.

'Thought you'd have it your own way? That was quite a neat trick you pulled at the start. You knew these horses were skittish around the sound of trumpets, didn't you? It was why Crispus could afford them.'

'Believe me, the witch isn't worth it.' Cotta laid his whip into his horses. Flecks of white foam spilled from the horses' mouths as they attempted to sprint forward.

Fortis gave a merest flick to his reins, and his horses surged forward with effortless ease. He drew level with Cotta again. A sudden sting lashed at his shoulder. Fortis forced his body not to react, not to move to the side and spin the chariot out of control. 'That was a mistake, Drusus Cotta. You have made it personal.'

'Nobody takes what is mine.'

'Why do you have such a grudge against Junius Crispus? Or is it his sister you are interested in?'

'You are sure of yourself.' Cotta gave him a furious glance. 'You wouldn't listen. Same as my father. No one humiliates me. She refused me.'

'We shall see.' Fortis gave a low whistle. Castor and Pollux passed Cotta with ease.

Cotta let out a frustrated yell.

The road narrowed and Fortis concentrated on negotiating a bend, rather than looking back and savouring his triumph. The race had a long way to run.

'Crispus? Where are you, Crispus?' Silvana picked her way through the silent stable yard. No sound.

Silvana wrinkled her nose and stepped around a pile of horse manure. Where was Crispus? She needed to find him before the race ended. She had to find out exactly what had happened. But no one appeared to be here. They were all at the finish line, putting bets on the racers.

She was about to leave when she heard a series of loud snores. She quickened her footsteps and went into a stall. Her eyes widened.

'Get off him, you brute.' She tugged at the large man sitting on the prone figure of her brother. The man had his feet outstretched and hands behind his head, seemingly content to watch the world pass by while her brother was held prisoner. 'What do you think you are doing?'

'Obeying orders.' The man scratched his head. 'Watching the world go by.'

'Get off my brother this instant.'

'If you insist…but my master is not going like this.'

'I do very much insist.' Silvana tapped her foot as she remembered where she had seen him before. Fortis's servant.

The man slowly rose and dusted himself off, his gladiatorial tattoo clearly visible on his forearm. Crispus gave a low moan and then an even louder snore.

'He's hurt! What have you done to him, you…you *infamia!*'

'I reckon it is more the drink than the punch that is causing this,' the man remarked in a helpful tone. 'My master packs a good punch, but he shouldn't be laid out for this long. 'Tis more likely to be the wine he consumed.'

'Aurelius Fortis punched him? Why? What reason could he have had to attack my brother?' Silvana took a step backwards. The pain in her head increased.

'Could be because he was attacked or could be because he objected to his tone. Me personally, I like to think he did that young lad a favour. He was scared, see, and he was going to lose the race. Understandable in the circumstances. Even forgivable.'

Silvana knelt down in the straw and dust and shook Crispus's shoulder. Immediately the stench of sour wine assaulted her nose. Crispus gave another great snore, but did not bother opening his eyes, waving with his hand and mumbling about breakfast. All sympathy for him vanished. 'He's drunk.'

'Like I said, it was more the wine than the punch. If you want to lay people out, ensure they will not rise, you have to make the back of the head hit the ground with a good thump.'

'Spare me the details.' Silvana held up her hand. 'Get me a bucket of water.'

The man returned with a bucket of water. Silvana grabbed it and threw it over Crispus.

'What did you have to do that for?' Crispus cried, spluttering as he sat up.

'I hope you are ashamed of yourself. Drinking before a race! You were in no fit state to be in charge of horses.'

'Does your voice have to be that loud?' Crispus looked up at her, water dripping off his nose. 'My head feels like Vulcan has been pounding it with his hammer and tongs.'

'Good.' A small sense of satisfaction coursed through Silvana. Crispus deserved to suffer for the trouble he had caused. 'You will go with me back to the finish line and wait to see the outcome of this race that you engineered. Neither man is likely to be predisposed to help you.'

'But…but…the race has begun.' Crispus put his head on his knees and hit it with his hands. 'I am not there.'

'Crispus, you are very lucky.' Silvana knelt down and put an arm around her brother's shoulders. 'Aurelius Fortis could barely handle the horse around the first turn. I hate to think what it would have been like for you—made the laughing stock of Baiae.'

'That was my race.' Crispus raised his tear-streaked face to hers. 'I wanted to save us all.'

'You should have thought of that before you started drinking.' Silvana began to rehearse what she would say to Fortis. What could she say? Once again he had rescued her from a nasty situation.

'If you don't mind me saying, ma'am, your brother is in a sorry state.' Merlus twisted his belt around his hand. 'My master had indicated that he should stay here and sleep off the effects. His head is bound to ache like Hades. It would be better for all concerned.'

Crispus gave a watery smile and reached out a hand towards the former gladiator. 'You know, I like you.'

'My pleasure.' Merlus made a sketch of a bow.

Silvana screwed up her eyes tight and then opened

them. The pair were smiling at each other. Broadly smiling, as if they did not have a care in the world! And her world was about to be turned upside down as a result of Crispus's wager.

'My brother caused this mess to happen. He can see it to the end.'

'Your voice is too loud, Silvana. They can probably hear it on the other side of the River Styx. I heard you from halfway across the stableyard.' Uncle Aulus commented as he peered into the stable. 'However, I do agree with you. This sorry excuse of a nephew needs to be there at the finish to see what mischief he wrought. Gods, Crispus, you look as if you had gone several rounds with Hercules.'

Crispus slowly rose to his feet and faced his uncle. His skin held a greenish pallor, but he was on his feet, advancing towards his uncle.

'Did my team go off without a problem? I made Cotta promise there would be no loud blasts on the trumpet.'

'They did fine, nephew.' Uncle Aulus put his arm around Crispus. 'Fortis got them away. You will see. We will win in the end.'

Silvana shook her head and gave an exasperated sigh. Crispus raised his head and looked at her. A lock of hair fell over his forehead.

'I am sorry, Silvana. I had wanted to do the right

thing, but I didn't.' Crispus made no move to rise and his face took on a pleading expression. 'If you don't mind, I will go home and sleep. Jupiter could not have had a worse pain when Minerva emerged from his head.'

'Next time, think of the consequences.' Silvana put her hands on her hips and glared at Crispus. He was trying to get out of facing his responsibilities. If she gave into him, he would keep finding more reasons. '*Somebody* might not be there to get you out of the mess. *Somebody* is racing against Cotta, who will stop at nothing to win. Are you going to sit here and feel sorry for yourself or are you going to be there at the end?'

Her eyes met Crispus's and held for a long time. She willed him to back down.

'All right, all right, I will go.' Crispus rubbed the back of his neck. 'Give me some time to find my feet first. This standing business is more difficult than it looks.'

'And, Crispus, no more complaining about my scandalous behaviour, you have created a far larger scandal than I have done,' Silvana said. 'From here on, I do as I please.'

The priest of the Sibyl's cave stood outside the temple grounds with the two grooms. As Fortis had predicted to Silvana, Cotta had a team of brown horses standing by, ready.

Fortis pulled Crispus's team to a halt, and signalled for his pair of matched greys. The men rushed forward and began to change the horses. Fortis gulped down a jug of cooled mint tea as Cotta arrived with a screech of wheels.

'I did not agree to race you,' Cotta spat out as he dismounted.

Fortis put his sandal up against the low stone wall and retied the lace. 'Crispus was indisposed.'

'Why are you doing this, Fortis? What exactly do you get out of this?' Cotta leant closer. 'You no longer race. But it makes no difference, I will win.'

'Your information was incorrect. When the occasion demands, I can handle the reins.'

'But why? Did that witch put you up to it? You have to be careful with her. The men she has had. The tales I have heard would curl your ears.'

Fortis hooked his thumbs in his belt and planted his feet firmly, barely managing to refrain from attacking Cotta. It would serve no purpose. Revenge was a dish best served ice cold. He had little doubt who the main source for the rumours surrounding Silvana was. Fortis leant forward until his face was level with Cotta's.

'Why? For the pleasure of beating you.'

'That is not a foregone conclusion.' Cotta backed away and hurriedly accepted a jug of mint tea.

'Sometimes, not everything goes your way, Cotta.'

'I take exception to your tone of voice. Remember whom you are speaking with.'

'Where exactly were you on the night the pirate shipment landed? I understand some important Egyptian silver came in—special consignment carried by Draco himself.'

'Tucked up in bed with Poppea.' Cotta kissed his fingers and winked. 'Little did I imagine how sweet she would be. You try to prove otherwise, and I will see you in court. Never heard of any pirate called Draco.'

'Did I say he was a pirate?'

Cotta turned his head and berated his servants for not attaching the horses quickly enough.

Fortis regarded Cotta, who stood there with a smug grin on his face. He had something to do with the set up that had entrapped Silvana's uncle, he was sure of it, but exactly how to prove it? Cotta's connections were formidable and it was rumoured he had successfully bribed last year's Consul.

'My horses are ready.' Fortis jumped up and refastened the reins about his waist. 'Forgive me if I don't grip your arm, Cotta. May the best man win.'

'You should have a care, Aurelius Fortis. The

gods do not look kindly on such arrogance.' Cotta gave a contemptuous flick of the whip.

'I would use the whip with more finesse.'

'I will win this race, Fortis.'

'We shall see what the Fates have in store for us.'

'And Fortis…' Fortis heard Cotta's voice floating on the breeze as he flicked the reins to start the greys galloping '…mind you don't crash.'

The crowds had dissipated slightly, but Poppea still held court, seated on a magnificent gold-inlaid chair and dressed in a rich Tyrean purple gown. A variety of young tribunes and hangers-on buzzed about her.

'Ah, Silvana, come and sit a while with me,' Poppea called. 'The race started so well. Cotta handles his horse magnificently. A pity your brother appeared to have some difficulties. It was a miracle he didn't crash.'

'Poppea, how truly splendid you are looking.' Silvana fluttered her eyelashes and forced her smile to be as sweet as a honey cake. 'I take it the merchant trouble has all been resolved.'

'Most satisfactorily.' Poppea gave a languid wave. 'Find an appropriate protector, Silvana. Between your uncle and your brother, your financial position is worrisome. I know Cotta is quite concerned about it. We were speaking about it last night after dinner.'

'How gratifying to know.' Silvana waited. She had wondered how the approach about the property she had inherited from Cotta the Elder would be made. She had thought perhaps Cotta would summon her. But she should have guessed that he would use his new mistress as his instrument. 'My former stepson has never shown the slightest bit of interest in my personal welfare.'

'He mentioned to me that he would be willing to look kindly on any offer you might make, if your brother loses, for the sake of your previous association.' Poppea reached out a beringed hand. Tears shimmered gently in her eyes. 'Cotta did not seek this race, Silvana. He is fond of your brother. He has no wish to make him lose his inheritance.'

'He should have thought of that before he engineered the challenge.'

'I want to help, Silvana—as an old friend. We women have to stick together.' Poppea sounded genuinely hurt. 'Protectors come and go, but the true friends we make are priceless. I begged Cotta, but he would not listen to me. It was only this morning he bent enough to allow me to speak to you about this…discreetly. It is always best to get these things sorted.'

'The outcome of the race is not a foregone conclusion.' Silvana crossed her arms and waited.

Poppea's eyes narrowed and she tapped the arm of her chair impatiently. Her voice became much harder. 'Your brother is going to lose, Silvana. Cotta is vastly more experienced. He has won every race he entered for the last four seasons. Think about it. It is not good to dismiss a hand of friendship. You never know when you might have need of it.'

'It is not my brother who is racing. It is Aurelius Fortis.' Silvana permitted a small smile to cross her lips.

A sharp collective intake of breath resounded in her ears, but Silvana walked away from the group and concentrated on taking deep breaths. She had to remain calm. Poppea had merely confirmed her suspicions. Crispus had been set up. Fortis had evened the odds, but the outcome of the race was in the lap of the gods.

'Has either of the chariots been spotted?' Silvana asked a soldier who was standing a little way away from the main group.

The soldier shook his head. 'Bit early yet. They will have barely made it to the cave and changed their horses. It's a treacherous road, that one. Six crashes in the last two months. Me? I would have thought the road to Naples would make a better route.'

Silvana gave a nod, but her hands trembled slightly.

* * *

Fortis maintained the lead for nearly all the way back. He had expected Cotta to challenge him on the straight downhill, but nothing came. He could hear the sound of the wheels against the road, but didn't look around, believing if he did he would betray his fear of losing. Instead he kept his gaze on the road, which had started to narrow and curve.

His mouth became dry as the chariot hit a rock in the road and flew up slightly. The spot where he had crashed with Murcia was up around the next bend. A silly wager, and one that had not necessitated taking such risks. But she had enjoyed taking risks. Exactly how much, he hadn't realised until after her death, when he found the tablets detailing her wagers, debts and assignations with other men.

'Out of the way, I am coming through.'

Fortis felt his chariot move slightly, but he bent double over the reins, urging his team on. The greys' coat had turned dark from the sweat. Clouds of steam surrounded them.

'There's not room enough. You will crash,' Fortis said between clenched teeth

'I am coming through.'

The wheels of the chariot touched, sending Fortis's chariot violently rocking. The jarring vibrations echoed up the reins and along his aching arms.

The movement sent shudders through him, shudders he found harder and harder to counterbalance.

'I don't think you are.' Fortis gave a piercing whistle and his team leapt ahead again. He had to win. He had given his oath to Crispus. He had to do it for Silvana, to give her a choice about how she would lead her life. She needed to be able to decide what she would do without her uncle or brother's actions forcing her.

Cotta lifted his whip. Fortis reached out and pulled it away. 'You only get one chance, Cotta, in this life.'

A loud blast on the trumpet brought Silvana to her feet. She shielded her eyes with her hands against the bright afternoon sun, unable to see anything. The Forum had filled up with spectators again, eager to see the finish.

'What is happening, Uncle Aulus? Can you see anything?'

'They are coming back. The chariots have been spotted at the edge of town.' His ice-cold hand covered hers. 'We will know shortly.'

A great shout welled up from the crowd, building, growing until it seemed that the world was on its feet, stamping and shouting. Silvana craned her neck, trying to see as the crowd rushed forward, each one intent on being there at the finish line. She held her breath, didn't want to look, but had to. The two chariots appeared from round the bend, the horses neck and neck, eyes wild and manes flecked with foam as the two men leant forward, urging their team on.

Silvana breathed a prayer of thanksgiving. Fortis had survived. And he might even win. She yelled his name and urged him onwards.

The chariots ran parallel with each other. Neither one gaining an inch. Then almost imperceptibly, Fortis flicked his reins and his team stretched their necks that little bit further and his chariot began to pull away.

Silvana's heart stopped. She could barely stand to look.

The chant went up—Junius. Junius. Victory!

Fortis had won.

The world appeared to slow down as Fortis swept off his helmet to acknowledge the shouts of the crowd. Silvana saw Cotta lean slightly as he attempted to control his team, a determined expression on his face, bumping Fortis's chariot with great force, sending it careening forward.

Silvana's heart stopped.

Everything took an age. The chariot and Fortis flew into the air, turned. Fortis's desperate attempt to keep upright and then falling, falling.

She heard her voice scream from a long distance, started to rush forward, reaching the chariot in a heartbeat.

The trainers and stable hands were there, righting the chariot. One had already cut Fortis's reins and grabbed the horses. Fortis was attempting to rise, with a smile on his face that turned to a grimace. He held his side and stumbled a few feet away from the mangled chariot.

'You're hurt,' Silvana said.

'I have had easier endings to chariot races.' Fortis attempted a smile, but his face looked pale beneath his tan.

'We won, we won!' Crispus came up and excitedly grabbed Fortis's hand. 'A brilliant piece of driving.'

'I fear your chariot will never be the same.'

Crispus hung his head. 'I don't intend to race again. I think I have learnt my lesson.'

'I will teach you to be a better driver, Crispus, if you are willing to learn.'

'Thank you, Aurelius Fortis.' Crispus's smile lit his entire face. 'I will endeavour to learn properly this time.'

'Crispus, Aurelius Fortis has been hurt. Give him some air.'

'I am perfectly fine.' Fortis held up both his hands and drew a sharp intake of breath. 'Your sister fusses.'

'You need to have a doctor look at you.'

'Later.' Fortis gave a decisive shake of his head. 'There are things I have to do first.'

'No hard feelings, Aurelius Fortis?' Cotta came up and clapped Fortis on the back. 'My horses went wild with the noise from the crowd. There was no way I could stop them.'

Silvana wanted to scream that it was a deliberate action on Cotta's part. She had seen his face as he turned the horses into Fortis, but he'd deny it.

'These things happen…even to the most experienced of drivers, Cotta,' Fortis replied, not flinching, but Silvana knew the blow had to have hurt him as fresh beads of sweat broke out on his face.

'Quite, quite. As long as you understand, it was my horses. I shall give an order to put them down.'

'It is for you to decide.'

'I will, of course, send over your winnings. Although, such fire and determination for scraps of worthless papyrus…'

'You are too kind.' Fortis inclined his head.

The throng of well-wishers around Fortis started to grow. Everyone talking at once, exclaiming, pushing forward. Silvana watched Fortis's face grow paler.

'Aurelius Fortis needs to see a doctor—a surgeon, not one of those soothsayers, Uncle Aulus.'

'Yes, yes, no expense spared for my deliverer.' Uncle Aulus turned from a well-wisher and made a vague gesture towards a slave. 'I think a large party to celebrate, don't you?'

'Aurelius Fortis has not given you the debts yet.'

'He will, my dear. You can count on it.' Uncle Aulus wore a broad smile. 'Remember, he has his reasons.'

'You won't accept them,' Silvana said in a furious undertone.

Her uncle gave an enigmatic smile and rapidly started to greet another well-wisher. All the while, Silvana could see Fortis's skin becoming paler. But all anyone seemed interested in was congratulating him on winning the race. A sudden tug at her sleeve made her turn. Merlus was there, leading a thin Greek by the arm.

'Got him from the local gladiatorial school. Proper medicine, none of your checking the entrails for my master.'

Silvana let out a breath. 'You are a marvel, Merlus.'

'I know, my lady.'

Fortis concentrated on standing upright and breathing. Every muscle ached from the race and from Cotta's accidental bumping of the chariot—a cynical cheating move after the race had finished. There was more to it than simply losing the race and having to give up Junius Maius's debts. Cotta had disliked the mention of Draco, proving Fortis's hunch correct. Now all Fortis had to do was conclusively prove the connection. He had to keep watch and see what Cotta would do next. How would he contact the pirate? It was time Cotta paid for his deeds, rather than finding innocents like Junius Maius and his niece to frame.

All that could wait until tomorrow. Right now, he needed a jug of cold mint and a bath. Something, anything, to stop this ache in his side. Fortis tried to take a deep breath, but the pain shot through his body, radiating outwards.

'Fortis, Merlus has a surgeon,' Silvana said, coming up to him and determinedly elbowing a young tribune away.

'Merlus would. Never listens to anything I say.'

'Merlus can be very sensible.'

Fortis looked at Silvana. Her shawl had slipped off her head and her hair formed little ringlets about her face. He wanted to tell her why he had raced. But not here in front of all these people.

The world swayed, and turned black at the edges. There were two Silvanas. Then one. And two again. He wanted to tell her not to worry. She did not have to fear Cotta any more. But which one did he need to tell?

He shook his head slightly to clear it and reached

out. Silvana's cool fingers curled around his and then slipped away.

'Stay with me,' he whispered.

Chapter Fourteen

'The surgeon left opium mixed with wine, and Merlus says you refuse to take it.'

Silvana looked incredulously at Fortis, who was now lying in his bed. The bandaging that the surgeon had wrapped around his chest contrasted sharply with the golden tone of his skin. The surgeon did not believe Fortis's ribs had broken because there was no whooshing sound to his breath, but he had prescribed bed rest and opium for the pain before he had departed.

'I bowed to the surgeon's wishes and am resting. My injuries are not that bad, a few aches and bruises. I will be back to my normal self in a few days.' Fortis rearranged a pillow behind his back so he was propped up higher. A wolfish smile appeared on his face and his voice dropped to an intimate whisper. 'Should you want to join me, Silvana, you only have to ask. There is room enough for two.'

The coverlet had slipped dangerously low until it barely covered his abdomen. Silvana forced her gaze higher, resolutely staring at the red-covered walls. She was not going to think about their encounter, that was history. She had to concentrate on making sure Fortis recovered and stopped playing the strong man.

He had begun to sink to the ground and had relied on Merlus's support to get him to her uncle's litter. Then when the litter had arrived back at Fortis's villa, he had needed help to rise.

'You are white-lipped with pain,' Silvana said tartly. 'Having someone else in bed with you would not be a good idea. Your ribs need to recover.'

'It was worth a try.' Fortis had an unrepentant look on his face. He crossed his hands behind his head, giving a wince as he did so. 'The offer is there, if you should change your mind. It could be a pleasant way to pass the evening.'

Silvana swallowed hard as the cup of wine mixed with opium threatened to fall from her numb fingers. She tightened her grip and tried not to think about the images his words conjured up. And knew she wanted to mean more to him than a pleasant evening's diversion.

'You want to make me forget why I am here, and have me run for cover, abandoning any thoughts of the opium,' Silvana said with sudden certainty and advanced towards him with the cup.

'It was worth it to see your face, Silvana.' Fortis raised an eyebrow and gave a slight shrug. 'Tell me what is it about our being together that you fear? Is it me? I have dreamt of our limbs being entangled, your body touching mine as your eyes fill with passion. Have you?'

Silvana's breath caught in her throat. He had dreamt of her. She could feel the tug of his gaze, roaming over her body as her nipples began to ache and warmth started to grow deep within her. She raised her chin.

'I have no fear of it. I choose not to climb into bed with you.'

'Once again you issue a challenge.' Fortis started to reach towards her, but his mouth twisted with pain. He grabbed his side and collapsed against the pillows. 'Alas, my sea witch, my mind may be willing, but my body aches. You are safe from me.'

'You will drink this and the pain will ease.' Silvana held out the cup, but Fortis continued to ignore it.

'Later…'

'I want no more heroics. You have given Merlus a hard enough time as it is today. What could you have been thinking about, giving him orders to sit on Crispus.'

'Good place for him, sitting on your brother. He is altogether too talkative.' His eyes softened as his fingers captured hers for a brief instant. 'Silvana, your brother was in no fit condition to race. There was not even time to try to sober him up. I acted in the way I thought best. I wanted to protect your brother.'

'My brother is old enough to look after himself. No one asked you to take the reins.'

'Someone had to.' His eyes became serious. 'Would you rather that I had allowed Cotta to win by default? Ask yourself that and examine your answer. There was no time to ask your opinion, Silvana. I did what I had to do. Faced with the choice again, I would do the same thing.'

Silvana put her hand to her mouth. She wanted to tell him how worried she was about him, and how her heart had stopped when Cotta had crashed into the chariot, but the words refused to come. She pressed her lips tightly together. This was another attempted diversion.

'We are not here to discuss my brother's behaviour and your high-handed actions. I am here to ensure that you take your medicine.'

'What if I don't want to?'

Their eyes met and clashed. Silvana held her breath and refused to look away. 'You will take this, Aurelius Fortis. You know you need it.'

'What will you do if I don't?'

'I will leave.'

His shoulders slumped. He reached out a defiant hand and took the cup, drained it in one gulp. He wiped his mouth with the back of his hand and smiled, the sort of smile that made Silvana's heart turn over.

'There, I have done it. Are you happy now?'

'My happiness is none of your concern.'

'So say you.'

Silvana busied herself with straightening his covers and closing the shutters. All the little things she used to do for her husband. Now she did them to keep her mind away from Fortis. There were so many unsaid things between them. She needed to say them, but not after he had just drunk opium and wine. They would wait. Then, after she knew that he understood about the debt and how she intended to pay it back over time, then maybe there would be a chance for the two of them. Equals, not one overly dependent on the other.

'Silvana...' his voice had become slurred and sleepy. His eyes closed and his eyelashes made dark smudges on the planes of his cheeks. He reached out a blind hand, grasping for hers, but missing. 'Stay here with me. I need you here. Silvana!'

'It is all right. I am here. I have not gone anywhere.' Silvana moved around the bed and caught his fingers. He heaved a great sigh and his body relaxed back against the pillows.

'I was afraid you had left.'

'That is the opium talking. Now sleep.'

Silvana reached over, and pulled the coverlet up to his chin, smoothing it. He opened his green eyes, stared directly into her soul. Silvana found it impossible to move, let alone breathe.

'Promise you will stay here with me, Silvana,' he said in a slurred voice.

'I will stay until you wake. Then we can decide what is best for you.' She knew there would be a scandal about her being here, but it had been the only way to get him home swiftly, as he had refused to move without her. She had to put his well-being above minor considerations. The scandal would be forgotten in days. She crossed her arms. It had to be.

The corners of his lips turned up in a brief smile. Silvana stood very still until she heard the steady sound of his breathing. Then she pressed her lips to his forehead.

'Thank you,' she whispered, but he gave no sign that he had heard.

'I came as soon as I could.' Aunt Sempronia's high-pitched voice pierced through Fortis's fog of pain and exhaustion.

How long had he been asleep?

Fortis cautiously opened an eye. His bedroom's narrow shutters were closed and a single olive-oil lamp glowed at the foot of his bed. Panic struck him and he glanced about the room, searching for Silvana. When he saw her sitting at the end of the bed, half in shadow, he eased back down into the nest of the pillows, safe. Silvana had kept her promise.

All he had to do was endure his aunt for as short a time possible and then he and Silvana could speak. He wanted her to understand why he had raced and what he intended to do with her uncle's debts. He wanted her to understand that she had a choice in her life.

'Whatever could have possessed you, dear boy,' Aunt Sempronia continued, oblivious to Fortis's current health, 'to race in the place of that bumptious youth who by all accounts deserves everything he gets? I warned you that Junia woman is no good and now you are embroiled in a scandal of immense proportions.'

Her shawls and *stola* quivered in indignation as Sempronia started to outline the impropriety of his behaviour.

'Pray tell me, my dear Aunt.' Fortis levered his body into a sitting position, despite its protests. Whichever servant had allowed Sempronia in deserved punishment. He grimaced. No, he had to handle her himself.

'Exactly what sort of scandal have I been embroiled in? All I have done is to win a race.'

Sempronia's cheeks flushed slightly under the white paint she wore. Her mouth opened and closed several times. 'But your name is bandied about with a notorious family. It won't do. I refuse to stand for it. You have other people to think about. Eutychus among others.'

'My dear Aunt, may I present Silvana Junia.' Fortis gestured towards where Silvana quietly sat, reading. At the sound of her name, she placed the scroll down and stood, head bowed.

The picture his aunt's face made caused Fortis to laugh, but he immediately regretted the action as a searing pain shot through his ribs. A low moan escaped his lips.

'But you are injured, Lucius. Has she no shame? No modesty?' his aunt asked in a hoarse whisper. 'You should be resting and not entertaining visitors. If I was in charge of your household, that is what I'd do. Throw all the visitors out. And your room is much, much too light. You need to have the shutters locked tight to keep out the demons. Have the entrails been read yet?'

'I asked her to stay.' Fortis enunciated the words, taking great care to pronounce each word clearly. 'She is my guest.'

'Aurelius Fortis refused to follow the surgeon's instructions.' Silvana's clear voice resounded from the far side of the bed. The golden glow of the lamp light caught her curls and gave her an aura. 'I ensured he did and kept himself from any more danger. As you have arrived, perhaps you will take over my duties and nurse your nephew as I have my own household to run.'

Sempronia's lip curled back and her nose arched as her gaze appeared to take in Silvana's slightly crumpled appearance. Fortis gazed upwards at the ceiling and willed his aunt to leave before she caused more damage. He only hoped that she had not forgotten her manners and would not venture any more of her misguided opinions.

'Indeed.' Sempronia's tone showed her distrust.

'My brother became suddenly indisposed and unable to race.' Silvana's cheeks took on a faint rosy hue. 'Your nephew stepped in and raced, rather than allowing Drusus Cotta to win by default.'

'I must confess I had no idea that your brother was indisposed,' Sempronia mumbled to her sandals. 'I fear I may know very little of the true story.'

'Next time I trust you will endeavour to find out the true story before coming to me with salacious tales,' Fortis said. It was time to finish this interview. He wanted Sempronia to go.

'I merely wanted to find out the truth. I am concerned about your reputation, Lucius.'

Fortis gave a snort. 'The only thing you care about is the group of harridans who congregate at the Bath of Mercury. There is not one of them under fifty.'

'Honestly, if you are going to be that way, I shall have to depart. I came here out of the goodness of my heart and what thanks do I get?'

'I shall be delighted to have the peace and quiet after your departure.'

'You are cruel. Cruel, I tell you.' Sempronia's shriek hurt Fortis's ears. 'First you drive my only son away and then you take delight in tormenting me. I suppose you do not want me to nurse you.'

Fortis gave a wide smile and inclined his head. 'Your perception continues to astound me, Aunt.'

'The doctor prescribed opium and wine. Aurelius Fortis has no idea what he is talking about. Of course he will be delighted to have you look after him.' Silvana bent and started to collect her things, a determined glint in her eye. 'If you speak to Merlus, he will tell you all the things you need to know to nurse your nephew. I am certain you will find it a rewarding experience.'

'Silvana, Sempronia is not one of nature's nurses,' Fortis said quickly. She couldn't just leave him here to the tender or otherwise mercies of his aunt. He shuddered to think which he would be driven to first—murder or suicide. No, Silvana had to stay. They had too much to talk about. He needed her with him.

'Oh, I am sure Sempronia will do an admirable job. It is much more proper for a man *of your position* to be looked after by his own family.'

'You would do much better,' Fortis muttered under his breath. 'You promised to stay.'

'Only until you woke,' Silvana reminded him. 'Your aunt is here. You will both have much to discuss. I have other people who need me. Unless your aunt believes that she cannot do the job.'

'I know how to nurse.'

The two women stood facing each other like gladiators about to begin sparring.

'The main thing you need to do is keep him quiet. It will take some time for his ribs to heal. The cook is trying to procure some comfrey. Once cooked, it tastes a bit like cabbage, but is excellent for strengthening bones.'

'I had no idea you knew anything about nursing, Silvana Junia,' Sempronia said with her arms crossed. 'I thought you were more of a social butterfly.'

'Having had an elderly husband, it would be strange if I didn't have intimate knowledge of how to care for an invalid.' A tiny smile appeared on Silvana's face. 'Whatever my other failings, no one ever accused me of not ministering to Drusus Cotta the Elder properly.'

'If that is the case, I must insist you look after my nephew,' Sempronia proclaimed. 'It is your fault that he became injured. And I have my own life to attend to. They are expecting me at the baths.'

'I did not ask him to race. Neither was I the one who caused the chariot to crash.' Silvana draped a shawl over her head with shaking fingers. She had to go before she exploded. She did not have to explain herself to this woman. A dignified silence was best. 'By the same token, I am not a relative. Do enjoy Sempronia's ministrations, Fortis.'

Silvana made her way with dignity to the door, shut it behind her with a click and then stood out in the corridor, trying to get her breathing back to normal. If she had stayed one heartbeat longer she would have started a fight with Sempronia and that would not have been fair to Fortis. For all she knew, he held the same opinions as his aunt.

'Good riddance! Such an impertinent woman. The stories I could tell you about her. It would make your hair curl.' Sempronia's strident voice filtered through the door.

Silvana paused. She hated eavesdropping, but it was impossible for her feet to move.

Would Fortis defend her?

His next words were indistinct, muffled. Silvana's mouth went dry and her hands began to tremble. What had he said?

'Precisely, that is my point,' Sempronia said. 'Rumours never happen without good reason. You did an admirable job of releasing Eutychus from her claws, just make sure you are not entangled yourself. That woman has ideas. Mark my words.'

Another mumbled indistinct sentence, except for her name. Silvana swallowed hard as a wave of hurt washed over her. She had wanted him to be her champion.

'I knew you would feel that way, but remember, please, you carry the hopes of our family. You cannot afford such a liaison. Don't look at me like that. I know you well enough. The woman is poison, Fortis, your career will suffer. You can't deny it. I see by your face, you won't deny it.'

Silvana forced her feet to move. She knew what people thought of her and normally it did not bother her. Those whom she cared about understood, but with Crispus's behaviour and now Fortis… She stopped, shook her head. She refused to care about Fortis. He was another senator in Baiae, that was all. Whatever they had between them was finished. The thought caused a lump to form in her throat.

* * *

'Silvana, what do you think of my new belt?' Uncle Aulus asked two days later as Silvana read Greek poetry in the *tablinum* with Bestus slumbering in the afternoon heat at her feet. 'I spied it on a stall. The merchant has sent it on trial. I think it is rather me.'

'Uncle, what are you doing?' Silvana put down the scroll of Greek poetry and stared at her uncle in ill-disguised horror.

'I felt as our money problems are over, I should celebrate.' Uncle Aulus executed a twirl, and his scarlet tunic flared above his knees, drawing attention to the new bejewelled belt he wore.

'Our money problems are not over.'

'The race was won. Drusus Cotta has given up the debts to Aurelius Fortis. I heard the rumour in the market place this morning. Cotta handed over the debts with great ceremony and no doubt more than a little reluctance. Our family has nothing to fear from him again. And you need not worry, Silvana, I have learnt my lesson.'

'The debt belongs to Aurelius Fortis, not to you.' Silvana regarded her uncle with a fixed eye. He had to understand economies were more necessary now than they had ever been. 'We are in the same position as we were before the race, except an unknown quantity holds the debts. Cotta may have been repulsive, but we knew what he would do, what his ultimate goal was. He wanted my inheritance at a very cheap price.'

Uncle Aulus wiped his face with a handkerchief. 'You have to remind me of that, just when the jeweller is about to arrive. I don't suppose you remembered to ask Aurelius Fortis for the debt?'

'Uncle Aulus!'

'Did you? It is important, Niece. I need to know. My creditors need to know.'

Silvana reached down and gave Bestus a pat where he lounged against her knee. 'I have not seen Fortis since I returned home after the race. I was hardly likely to ask him when he lay in agony after winning a race.'

'Some women would have, and they would have demanded a present as well.'

'I am not some women. How many times do I have to proclaim it before anyone believes me? I have not asked Aurelius Fortis, nor do I have any intention of asking him. For my part, the debt remains to be paid and will be paid in full as soon as we can arrange it.'

'You are quite right, my dear. You do as your honour dictates.' Her uncle gave one last regretful look at the belt before he undid the clasp and replaced it with his own less ostentatious one. 'I do hope you don't find your principles to be a cold bedfellow.'

'What are you implying, Uncle Aulus?' Silvana's nails dug tiny moons into her palms. Sempronia's words still rang in her ears. 'You know I am doing the correct thing, the only thing.'

'Nothing, nothing. But men do not stay for ever hooked, Silvana. You have already lost Eutychus this season. Please, Venus, do not lose another suitor.'

'Aurelius Fortis has not been, and will never be, my suitor.'

'You are protesting rather violently, Silvana. Fortis did not race out of the goodness of his heart.' Uncle Aulus rocked back and forth, humming a little tune. 'But I suppose you are right, I should not be doing anything without first knowing Aurelius Fortis's exact intentions.'

'Uncle, you are planning something.'

'You know me, Niece. I am a simple man with simple tastes.' Uncle Aulus moved towards where the household *lares* stood and started repositioning the statuettes of Mercury and Venus. 'The accusations you level at my head, you would think I had asked you to become Aurelius Fortis's mistress. No, no, I merely want to confirm that his intentions are honourable.'

Silvana pressed her lips together. A terrible notion began to form in her brain. Her uncle had plans. He would confront Fortis and then the whole story would emerge. Fortis's intentions towards her were anything but honourable. They had made love once, and he had made it very clear that he wished to again. She bit her lip. She wanted to as well, to see what it would be like now that she was no longer a virgin. But she knew it would not be a permanent relationship.

How could it be?

The truth of Sempronia's outburst echoed in her brain. Someday, Fortis would return to Rome and his career in the Senate, and she'd be left here with her bittersweet memories. Then, there was her promise to her brother not to create another scandal to think about.

She should have told Uncle Aulus what was between her and Fortis just after their encounter, but Crispus had arrived and there was always a good reason why the time had not been right. And the time was certainly not right now, either. He had to stop building grand villas in the air. There was no long-term happy ending for this affair. It was not one of those Greek romances that appeared in the theatre.

'I will go to see Aurelius Fortis and ask him,' she said. 'As you want me to.'

'Did you hear me ask? Bestus, did I ask Silvana to do anything?'

Bestus tucked his head more firmly in his paws as if to say that he was not going to become involved.

'No, I am merely standing here, putting the statuettes into order. You see, Bestus agrees with me.' Uncle Aulus withdrew a small piece of cheese from the folds of his tunic and held it above Bestus's nose. At the sight of the cheese, Bestus thumped the floor with his tail.

'I know you, Uncle. All too well.' Silvana went over and kissed her uncle's cheek. 'The belt can stay, but really, you must do something about the tunic.'

'You are trying to distract me.' Uncle Aulus hooked his thumbs about his belt. He fingered his chin. 'I should be the one to go.'

'You will make the request all too formal. I believe I can inquire gently. Perhaps Fortis might be open to persuasion.' Silvana felt the heat on her cheeks rise as the image of what had happened the last time she had asked for a favour burnt in her brain. This time, such a thing would not happen.

She had to hope that she could see Fortis on his own. No doubt if Sempronia was there she would have a few choice words to say, and this time Silvana knew she would be unable to control her temper.

'Now why didn't I think of that?' Uncle Aulus

clapped his hands. 'Silvana, you are a marvel. I trust you to find out the answer much more subtly.'

Silvana stopped and regarded her uncle with a practised eye. Her uncle developed a sudden interest in Bestus's ear.

'You wanted me to go.'

'It will be good for you.' Her uncle smiled up at her. 'Fortis did ask you to stay with him after he had that crash with Cotta. It is all the invitation you need. Sometimes youth is wasted on the young.'

'I am doing this for you, Uncle.'

Uncle Aulus gave her hand a squeeze as he shook his head. 'It was something you wanted to do. I was merely the excuse.'

'Thank Hercules, you have come, my lady,' Merlus said when Silvana arrived at Fortis's villa. The manservant's hair was standing up straight and his tunic bore signs of creases and smudges, very different from Silvana's memories of him. 'I was about to send for you, to beg you to come here and deliver us.'

'Is there a problem, Merlus?' Silvana asked as she heard a loud bellow echo along the upstairs corridor.

'Aurelius Fortis is like a lion before a beast fight.' Merlus quickened the pace as they started to climb the stairs that led to the upper floor. 'He has been like this ever since you left. I do not want to count the number of times he has complained about staying in bed. Or shouted at me.'

'Does Fortis normally react in this way when he is confined in bed? He strikes me as someone who would make a very bad patient.'

'Normally, he treats all the servants with the utmost respect and courtesy. But this morning he even threatened to throw a platter of food at a servant's head after the servant dropped a cup of mint tea in his nervousness.'

'And did he?'

'The threat was enough.' Merlus gave a shrug. 'The sooner he is healed and we are back to a well-ordered villa, the better.'

'What does his aunt think of his behaviour?'

'The lady Sempronia left with her *stola* flying very soon after you did. I have never seen her move so quickly, her *stola* streaming behind her as she made for the door. My master threatened to bodily remove her if she did not.'

Silvana stifled a smile. She knew she should feel sorry for Sempronia, but could not help feeling that the woman deserved it. Another bellow echoed through the corridor. There again, perhaps not.

'I wish he would get well. Then we could leave this place and get back to our normal way of life. I told him that no good would come of remaining here and reopening the house.'

'Why does he stay?'

'He searches for the man who shields one of the great pirates of the Mediterranean—Draco of Sicily. This man, a senator some whisper, enabled Draco to avoid punishment for a long time. Aurelius Fortis vowed to put an end to his activities after he murdered a friend and his wife in cold blood.'

'So he is after revenge.'

'My master has seen how this man grows fat on the misery of others and the cost to the state treasury as the cost of grain goes up and up.' Merlus gave an elaborate shrug. 'And I for one will be glad when Draco is gone. He murdered my family and sold me to gladiatorial combat. My master promised me to help find and punish him.'

Silvana forced a smile to her lips as a sudden sharp pain struck her heart. She had always felt he was here for another reason. Pirates who murdered and bartered humans. It made sense.

'So all this about staying in Baiae for the season and helping Eutychus was smoke to hide his intentions.' She wanted to ask if his dalliance with her was another screen. She supposed it was. Eutychus had left, and he needed an excuse. He had very publicly declared his interest in her after the race. But why?

Cotta, it had to be Cotta. The race had not been about her uncle's debts or saving her inheritance, but about proving something to Cotta. 'Everything he has done recently has been a diversion.'

'You could say that and I wouldn't deny it.'

Silvana kept her head upright, even though she wanted to collapse in a ball and hug her arms tight about her knees. But she refused to. The only surprise was how much it hurt. Worse than Sempronia's unkind remarks. She had hoped that he stayed in part for her and for their growing friendship.

Friendship?

She wanted more than friendship from Aurelius Fortis. She wanted him to have some feelings for her. That was what made Merlus's careless words hard to bear.

'Shall I see if I can handle his bad temper?'

'Would you?' Merlus clasped his hands together. 'I think if I go in there, he is liable to throw something at me. And if he does…' Merlus ran both his hands through his hair, making it stand on end.

'I completely understand.' Silvana smiled at Merlus. She refused to let the words wound her. She had always known that Fortis had an ulterior motive for remaining. She had allowed her hubris to build villas in the air.

'You are a good sort, my lady. I don't mind saying

that I was totally mistaken about you. Had I known what you were really like, I would never have suggested to my master to offer you money.'

'I appreciate your honesty.'

'You are truly a great lady.'

Silvana stood, with her hand on the door as another great bellow issued forth.

Did she dare?

She drew a deep breath. She had to, if for no other reason than for the sake of his servants.

Chapter Fifteen

'Merlus!' Fortis shouted again, trying to sit up properly and failing. He gave his pillow a thump in frustration and ended up causing his ribs more pain. It was bad enough to be confined to this bed, but all his servants had taken to hiding.

Everything had gone wrong since Silvana had left two days ago and he had no way of making her return. He wanted to see her. Fortis made a face.

He knew why he was out of sorts, and it had nothing to do with the ache in his side. He had asked Silvana to stay and she had left at the earliest possible opportunity. Before he had a chance to talk to her and explain, she had escaped. Confirmation that he had ruined everything between them. He wanted to start again, to go slowly this time and to show Silvana how pleasant it could be between the two of them.

His sleep had been full of her and he woke with

an aching need for her. 'Merlus, come here immediately. Can you hear me, Merlus?'

'If you keep bellowing like that, everybody on Baiae's promenade will hear you. Someone in Rome could probably hear as well,' came the clear bell-like tones.

Fortis sank back down in the pillows, the pain in his side easing as if it had never been. He turned his head. Silvana stood in the doorway. Her shawl had slipped and she wore her hair loose about her barely painted face. Her *stola* and gown hinted at the curves that lay beneath. But the thing Fortis noticed most was the sparkle in her eye.

'You have returned to the land of the living,' she said.

'Forgive me for not getting up to greet you. If I had known you were coming for a visit, I would have made sure that I was properly dressed.' Fortis made a little gesture of welcome with his hands while his eyes devoured her form, searching for any changes. He wanted to tell her how much he had missed her, but to say it would give her power over him, and he was not prepared to do that until he knew more about what she was thinking.

'You are at least obeying the surgeon by keeping in bed.' She came over and made a show of straightening the coverlet at the foot of the bed. She then opened the shutters and let the cooling breeze blow through. 'The servants, however, are suffering from the effects of your ill temper. I heard you shouting from the atrium.'

'Are you implying that I am a difficult patient?' Fortis leant forward. 'I will have you know that I have been a model of forbearance ever since you left. I have done everything the surgeon asked of me.'

'Then why is Sempronia no longer here?'

'She has other things to do, other places to gather gossip. She found it rather dull here.' Fortis decided to gloss over the row they had had after Silvana had left. He was thankful Silvana had not heard a word of it. In that, at least, Sempronia had been guarded when Silvana was in the room.

'She was not one of Nature's nurses, you said.' Silvana's lips were drawn into a firm line.

'Did I?' Fortis ran his hand through his hair. 'I can remember very little about that afternoon. Opium often does that. It is one of the reasons I had wanted to avoid taking it.'

'But it gave you some relief from the pain.' She crossed her arms and regarded the small bedside table with its jug of wine.

Fortis desperately tried to remember what he had said that afternoon. Everything was very hazy except that she had left and in doing so had made the ache in his side worse.

'Why have you come to visit me, Silvana? To gloat at my injuries? Or to force me to take more medicine?' Fortis forced his voice to be sarcastic. If she was going to leave again, he wanted her to do it right away. 'Did Merlus send you in to torment me? The gods help me with you and Merlus in league together.'

'If that is the way you are going to be, I shall go.' Silvana tried to ignore Fortis's broad expanse of chest, the streaks of yellow-green bruising clearly visible on his ribs. She thought he would have been wearing a tunic, but it appeared he had little on.

There was no point in bringing up her uncle's debts when he was in this sort of filthy mood. Any attempt to speak of them would make her look mercenary, and she didn't want that. But equally she could not admit the true reason she had come—that she had to see him again.

'Go?' His face seemed to fall. He plucked restlessly at the coverlet. 'Yes, go. Leave me in peace with my injury. Nobody cares whether I live or die.'

'No, I fancy you will stay around simply to annoy Merlus or one of your other long-suffering servants.'

A small rueful smile showed in the corner of Fortis's mouth. 'I apologise. It is just that I am such a bad patient. Do you have to go?'

'I had only stopped here on the way to the Baths

of Mercury.' Silvana knew the words were a lie. She had come because she had to, because she wanted to see his features again and to reassure her heart that he lived and breathed.

'For the heated swimming pool.' His eyes watched her with a sudden intense green fire.

'That's right. The heated pool and I remembered...your kindness that night we first met...' Silvana regarded her hands. She was making a mess of this. She should go now while she had some shreds of dignity left. 'And I thought to see how you fared.'

'The Baths of Mercury are in the opposite direction, Silvana.'

'That's right.' Her breath seemed to catch in her throat as a sudden smile crossed his features, making him glow from within.

He held out his hand. 'It's dull in bed...alone, Silvana. Play a board game with me. Being a patient doesn't suit me. Stay here and entertain me. Take pity on Merlus and my servants, if you will have none for me.'

Silvana's heart contracted. He was here in bed and in pain because of her and her family. She had to stay. She wanted to stay. She wanted an excuse. She wanted to feel his lips against hers. Whatever was between them, she needed it to last for longer.

'I know what happened the last time we played

twelve lines.' She trailed a finger along the table beside his bed. This time, she would pay attention. She would beat Fortis at his game, and remain in control of the situation.

'You were over-confident.' Fortis put his hands behind his head while his eyes danced. 'It was easy.'

'You tricked me into thinking you were a worse player than you are.' Silvana put her hands on her hips. 'My uncle says that you have Hades' own luck.'

Fortis's eyes turned sober. His tongue ran over his lips as if suddenly it had ceased to be a light-hearted game and he was playing for something else.

'The Fates favoured me that night.' His voice caressed her ears. 'Shall we play *latrunculi* instead?'

'But no wagering,' Silvana said quickly. There would be a temptation to wager for her uncle's debts and she could wind up in a much worse position. When she reached an arrangement with Fortis, she wanted it to be for the right reasons and not because she had wagered her body against a pile of scrolls and tablets. 'I have had enough wagering.'

'Games like *latrunculi* are much better if one wagers. Come now, what shall we wager? Not money, I think.' Fortis's gaze fell directly on her mouth and her lips ached as if he touched them. 'What is your suggestion, Silvana? What little thing do you want to claim as a forfeit? I will give you anything you ask within reason.'

Silvana pressed her palms into her gown. She had not come here to trade her body for the debts. She had tried that before with Fortis and the only place it had led to was heartache. But if she mentioned her uncle's debts now, it would seem as if that was the only reason she had come.

She would play the game of kings and glass counters and hope a more suitable opening would develop, one where she could reason with him. She tilted her head and peeked at him from under her lashes.

'I learnt last time that wagering with you is a hazardous occupation.'

'But you will play.'

'If you wish…'

Fortis summoned Merlus and the game board was laid out between them with great ceremonial flourishes.

'Will that be all, master? I can bring up another jug of honeyed wine.' Merlus wore a faintly self-satisfied smile, as if he had something to do with Silvana being here.

'Thank you, you may go, Merlus. As Silvana has agreed to amuse me, I think she can look after me.'

Fortis waited until Merlus had gone and then began to set out the counters. He watched how

Silvana's hands trembled on each counter. Exactly what was she scared of? And why had she come?

He had given her the opportunity to ask about the debt, but she had refused to take it. She had to know that he held the scrolls and tablets. His hand closed over the king.

He wanted her in his bed, but she had to come to him of her own free will. He did not want her because she was trying to save her uncle or her brother. He wanted her to want him and him alone. She had to have the choice.

'Shall we begin the game or are we going to stare at the pieces?' she asked with laughter in her voice, but her eyes held a hint of strain.

'I think we shall begin.' Fortis studied the pieces and knew he was playing much more than a simple game of counters. He was playing for her trust.

Silvana stared at the *latrunculi* board, rather than at Fortis's strong hand as he moved his counters about on the board. Each movement decisive and quick as if it had all been planned several moves in advance. What else had he planned?

After two matches, neither had an advantage and they were halfway through the deciding match. She bit her lip. She had yet to find a good opening to discuss her uncle's debts. Every time she tried, he blocked her effectively. If she didn't mention them, her trip would have been wasted. And she was having trouble thinking now he was near. Her body remembered the feel of his hands against hers all too clearly. Perhaps she should have suggested another less intimate room, but she hadn't thought of it soon enough.

A faint smile touched the corner of Fortis's lips as if he knew where her thoughts were. 'It's your move.' Fortis's voice rumbled over her, silky and smooth, making a curl of warmth rise from deep within her. 'You have been staring at the board for a long while.'

'I don't want to lose.' Silvana caught her tongue between her teeth and tried to redouble her concentration. With every breath she took, the longing to melt into his arms grew. And yet, he had not tried to seduce her. All his concentration appeared to be on the counters and the board.

'It is all a matter of how you play your counters. Your king is currently at risk.'

Silvana moved her king, but her hand knocked against his, sending little shoots of fire up her arm. She drew back rapidly, placed her king down in an even worse position, if he took two counters. She lifted her chin and stared directly at him, daring him to make the next move. Was this going to be a seduction?

'Silvana.' He moved his counter, capturing two more of hers. 'You are failing to pay proper attention.'

Silvana licked her lips and glanced up at him. His face was very near. She only had to lift her lips and their mouths would meet. She turned her head and pretended to examine the board again, tried to stop her heart from racing.

She had to remember that this was only a game for him. She meant nothing to him. She drew a breath. Her heart was steady. She had regained control.

Silvana stood, and straightened her *stola,* making sure the folds fell into perfect lines

'Perhaps I ought to go…my skill is obviously not what is required.'

'The game hasn't finished.'

'You are bound to win.' Silvana gave a quick smile. If she stayed much longer, she'd beg for his mouth. It would be too humiliating. 'I should never have placed my king there. Two moves at most and I will be at your mercy.'

'And that would be so bad.' His voice was quiet, but with an underlying note of iron.

'For my king, yes.' Silvana gave a strangled laugh and noticed her breath was coming faster. She wanted him to make the first move, to kiss her, to tell her that he did care about her and that he had raced for her and for her alone. 'Have you seen the water-clock? I had no idea how much time had passed.'

'My pillow has fallen. Will you straighten it for me...before you go?' There was a faint pleading note in his voice. He gave a rueful smile. 'I would do it myself, but reaching around is painful.'

Silvana glanced at her hands. Of course, she was being naïve. He was in pain. No wonder he had ignored all her open invitations to steal a kiss. She would move the pillow and then make a dignified exit.

Silvana reached over and started to rearrange his pillows. She overbalanced slightly as she reached for the last one. His hand shot up, captured her wrist and gave a gentle tug, pulling her closer. Silvana felt her body fall and put out her other hand, connecting with his chest. His arm held her there against his body.

'I should get up.' She tried half-heartedly to pull away.

'I believe I have captured a queen of Baiae. I win the match.' His words tickled her ear and sent little sparks of happiness through her. He did want her.

'Are you going to claim a forfeit?' The words came out in short gasps as a delicious shiver ran through her body.

His thumb traced the outline of her mouth, slowly and gently as if he were handling a precious object.

Silvana felt her lips grow and begin to ache again for his kiss.

'How could I do otherwise?'

With gentle pressure on her back he reversed their positions, so that he was now above her and she was sinking into the pillows, enveloped in his masculine scent, held in his strong embrace. She could feel his arousal pushing against her through the sheet.

'It has taken me a while, but I have you in my power.'

'You planned this?' Silvana drew back slightly. She had to be careful. She had to remember what she was doing.

'Ask me no questions, and I shall tell you no lies.'

He lowered his head and his lips touched hers, exploring the edges of her mouth. Gently, but then with a firm and deliberate motion, the kiss intensified, grew in power and strength, demanding a response from her. Silvana's body melted, moulding her curves to his hard planes, glorying in the feel of his body next to hers.

He pressed his lips against her forehead and her hands curled into his thick hair, holding him close. She felt his toes push at her feet. Her slippers came off and fell to the floor with a thump. She ignored them and looked into the pools of deep mossy green of his eyes

'I ought to get up.' Silvana made one last attempt to be sensible.

'Such a serious face.' He brushed a lock of hair from her forehead. 'Tell me your thoughts. What did you think about my racing? You never said.'

'I was frightened at the end of the race,' she whispered against the strong column of his throat. 'I wanted to make sure you were alive.'

'I won.'

'Cotta attacked you. I saw you fly through the air.'

'It could have happened to anyone.'

'You were hurt.' Her hands sought his chest, but he captured them and brought them to his lips.

'It is but a bruise. I have had worse from the gymnasium at the baths.' He pulled a pin from her hair, held it in his hand. A deliberate action. 'If you were so worried about me, why did you leave?'

'Your aunt arrived.'

'My aunt wanted to cause trouble.' Fortis dropped the pin on the floor and pulled another two out, sending her carefully arranged hairstyle tumbling about her shoulders. 'That's better.'

'But—' Silvana swallowed hard and tried to concentrate on the reason she was there and not the way his hands felt as they combed out her hair. Her lips ached to be kissed, but she refused to go further down the road of becoming a courtesan. Yes, she wanted him, but he needed to know that she wanted him because she desired his body and his mind, not the size of his fortune. 'There are things that must be said between us two.'

'Hush.' He put a finger to her lips. 'I have not finished claiming my forfeit. We will speak later. Time for other things.'

His lips reclaimed hers, hot, insistent, and Silvana found that all thoughts flew from her mind except for the intensity of the kiss. She gave herself up to it and gloried in the warm slow strokes of his tongue, entering in her mouth and then retreating, stoking the swirling fire that was building within her.

His hands expertly untied her belt, slipped the *stola* and gown from her shoulders. Each move slow and deliberate, his hand caressing each inch of skin as it appeared, pushing the cloth away. A thrill ran through her. She had been wrong. He did want her in the way she wanted him. She refused to think about what might happen later—all she knew was that she needed to feel him against her now.

Her nipples had hardened and were clearly visible through the breast band. He reached out and circled them with his fingers, rolling the tender skin until they ached and her breath came in short, sharp gasps.

Then he bent his head and his teeth pulled the cloth down, revealing the dusky pink points. He captured one in his mouth and suckled. Waves of pleasure coursed through her as her hands gripped his thick hair, holding him there. Here was the man who had risked life and limb for her, in her arms. She was certain now that he had participated in the race for her. Her heart soared as his mouth explored her skin.

'Do you like?' He lifted his head and smiled down at her. 'Silvana, think of how good it will make me feel if you do the same to me.'

'You want me to—' Silvana stopped, unable to say the words. He wanted her to do more than simply lie there. The truth slowly dawned on her. He had not rejected her because she had been forward. He wanted her passion.

Had there been something else? Had she been feeling too fragile? Too uncertain?

'Yes, I want you to. I want to feel your hands on me, your mouth.' He gave a groan. 'Please.'

Her hands reached up and mimicked his pathway, spreading over his chest. Her fingers rolled his nipples. She felt them spring to life under her fingertips. Then she moved her tongue on to his chest, tasting the slightly salty tang of his golden skin, circling tighter and tighter until she heard a low moan come from his throat. A feeling of power swept over her. She had made him become like that. She was not taking, she was giving him pleasure. It was mutual and all the more exciting because they had shared each other before.

She put a finger to his lips and he nuzzled it, drawing it into the warm recesses of his mouth and holding her there with his tongue circling around and around her finger. A sweet languor filled her.

'See what you are doing to me, Silvana.' His voice was a husky rasp in her ear.

She glanced down and saw his arousal, hard and erect. Large, as large as it had been before. She gave a slight gasp as she remembered the burning pain from the last time. And yet her body wanted him inside her. She wanted to feel being taken to the edge but not the pain. Would he understand?

'I won't hurt you again,' he murmured against her hair as his hands roamed over her body, stroking and caressing her as if she were made of precious glass. A sigh of contentment rose from within her. He did understand. 'There is no need to be frightened. We will take it very slowly and you will see. Let me show you how good it can be between us.'

'I am not afraid,' she said and knew it was the truth.

He kissed the corner of her mouth.

'If I had known the last time of your inexperience, you would have been properly prepared. This time, you will be.'

His hands continued down their path, skimming

over her curls at the apex of her thighs. She gave a sharp gasp as her body remembered the sensations from the last time, but his hands continued lower, caressing her thighs and calves until they reached her feet. His thumbs made small circles on her arches, sending little tongues of fire through her body. Spasms of pleasure went up her legs to her inner core. Her body lifted off the bed as her hands entangled themselves in the sheets.

Her thighs parted, willing him to move upwards but he merely put her other big toe in his mouth and suckled it. Then very slowly his tongue traced a line up her leg, until he reached the apex of her thighs. There it lingered and played. The ache inside her reached fever pitch. Wave after wave of sensation hit, until she thought she could stand it no more. Her body demanded release.

'Please,' she cried.

He seemed to understand and positioned himself between her legs.

This time her body opened up and drew him in, expanding to take the full length of him. No pain, only pleasure. He had told the truth. She had been right to trust him. Silvana knew then that she wanted this to continue for as long as possible. She wanted to make love with him again and again and not think about anything but how he felt inside her. Her body bucked.

He lay still on top of her, not moving.

Her fingers tentatively touched his back as her body began to move, lifting against him. But he was too heavy. She gave a little mewl of frustration.

He twisted and she felt them turning together. Suddenly she was on top, looking down into his face, a face transformed with passion.

'Now, you give the rhythm,' he gasped out. 'We go at your pace.'

Silvana went still. He was letting her take the initiative. She had control. His hand intertwined with hers as she smiled.

She leant forward and began rocking as his fingers recaptured her nipples. Faster and faster, until the world was washed in a sea of sensation. She heard a cry and did not know if it came from her throat or his as he drove deep within her and she collapsed on to his chest.

Silvana blinked open her eyes. How long she had been asleep, her head resting on the golden expanse of Fortis's chest, his strong arms about her? This was where she wanted to be. The room, which had been bathed in barred sunlight, now slumbered in afternoon shadow.

'I believe you claimed your forfeit,' she murmured, laying a kiss on his chest.

336 The Roman's Virgin Mistress

'I do believe I did.' His hand raised her chin so that she was forced to look into his eyes. 'Tell me, Silvana, have you stopped running away? You will not leave so quickly this time.'

She gave a smile as his hand traced a line down her arm. 'I have never run away. It was tactical retreat. I thought you did not want me any more. That you had finished with me because I was a virgin.'

'You underestimate your charms. Once could never be enough.' His hand brought her hair to his lips and his eyes became deep pools of green. Against her body she felt his body begin to stir, calling to hers.

'You can linger longer,' he murmured against her hair. 'We can pass the afternoon and evening together. We have time.'

She turned her head and saw the sun had moved across the room, highlighting a bowl of golden quince, a fruit sacred to Venus, the sort of repast two lovers might share after they had made passionate love.

How much of this affair had been planned?

It bothered her that she didn't care. She wanted to be in Fortis's arms, in his bed. But he would get well, and go back to Rome while she would stay here. Their affair would be over and she would be left nursing a broken heart. A chill passed over her. She had stayed much longer than she had intended.

'I must go. My uncle will be expecting me. He will think something is amiss if I don't return soon.'

'And you have no wish for what is between us to become public currency.'

'Your reputation has already taken a battering because of the race. I would hate to see it damaged further.' The words tasted bitter in Silvana's mouth.

Fortis's arms fell away, and allowed her to rise. She pulled on her discarded clothes, twisting her hair into a simple knot. Quick and efficient movements. If she lingered, she would climb back in bed with him and ask to stay there for as long as he would have her.

'Do you enjoy being your uncle's hostess?' Fortis watched her face to see any sign of change.

'I enjoy the freedom it gives me.' A smile touched her lips, but not her eyes. 'You can come and dine. Perhaps we will dance in the garden again.'

Fortis examined the spot where her hair skimmed her shoulder. He wanted to talk about the debt, but things had moved too quickly. If he mentioned it now, she might get the wrong idea. He knew how much she valued her freedom and he did not want her coming to him out of a sense of duty or loyalty to her uncle. He needed Silvana to come to him without conditions. 'Tonight is not good.'

Her face fell. 'I understand.'

And he knew she did not. He had to speak to her uncle first. Before anything else, he wanted this to be done properly. He had no wish for anyone to attach any more scandal to Silvana's *stola*. 'You could stay with me. Have dinner with me. Merlus can chaperon.'

She gave a quick shake of her head. 'Impossible. My uncle needs my help.'

Silvana reached for her clothes and started dressing.

'You will come and visit tomorrow. We can play another game of *latrunculi*.'

She paused in tying her belt. Her cheeks grew rosy. 'I would not want to disturb your convalescence.'

Fortis gave a hearty laugh. Silvana was exactly the balm he needed. It was only a matter of time before she was back in his bed and then he would work on convincing her that she needed to stay in his life for good.

Chapter Sixteen

Silvana sat, one eye on her loom and the other on the long line of clients that had assembled to see her uncle this morning. She had been unable to speak to him last evening when she had returned from Fortis's. The house had been filled with well-wishers and hangers-on. One would almost think that her uncle had won the race on his own. Crispus, thankfully, had kept a low profile.

She had to explain to her uncle that nothing was settled, and she had no idea when it would be. The trust she and Fortis shared was too new and fragile. She had no wish for it to be poisoned with the talk of the debt. But she needed to explain without revealing the affair. Her uncle would not understand why she felt the need to become Fortis's lover.

'My lady, these have arrived for you.' Dida the

porter came into the atrium carrying an assortment of tablets and scrolls.

'Letters from admirers, Silvana?' Uncle Aulus asked as he strolled into the atrium, having successfully dealt with the last client. 'You should see the number of tablets I have received. I *told* you that Crispus's decision to race against Cotta was a good idea. I am glad *I* thought of asking Aurelius Fortis to help when Crispus fell ill.'

Silvana pressed her lips together. Her uncle appeared intent on re-inventing the race and the aftermath to suit his view. Or, maybe, it was an attempt on his part to deflect scandal. If he told the story to enough people, maybe the gossip would die down. She tied off a thread and attached another one. She had not noticed the ways in which her uncle attempted to protect her before.

'Who knows?' she replied lightly. 'Maybe more demands from Cotta to buy the property.'

'Had you not better open them and see?' Uncle Aulus leant forward and pointed to the first scroll.

Silvana broke the seal and unfurled the scroll. Her heart stopped. The words swam in front of her eyes. She quickly flipped through the rest of the tablets. All the debts were all there. Every single last one of them. But nothing else. No note and no offer— honourable or dishonourable.

All last night she had had this fantasy that Fortis was going to make an offer of marriage for her, that his feelings for her were close to hers for him, that despite the possibility of scandal he wanted to spend the rest of his life with her. The wisps of the dream had clung to her senses throughout the morning, and she had been full of hopeful anticipation.

She looked again at the many bills and promises to pay. The full sickening reality crashed in on her— he had sent the debts as payment for her *services.*

Fantasies had no place in Baiae. She should know that. Illusion was everything, but illusion held no place for dreams. This was not a prelude to marriage. These tablets were something else entirely. She could not accept them, not given like this.

Yesterday, they had made passionate love and this morning he had returned the debt—to her. A payment for services rendered. What they had shared became not beautiful, but twisted. After all they had shared, he still thought of her as a mercenary Baiae widow.

She wanted to sink down and weep for her dreams. Then she straightened her back. She could do this. She would see him and explain the situation. He needed to take back the debt. Her uncle would pay it back properly. She had not gone into his bed expecting to be paid. She had gone because she wanted to be with him. Surely he would understand her reasoning after what they had shared?

'Silvana? You have gone pale.' Uncle Aulus reached for the scroll. 'If someone has sent you a curse, I will send for the augur. He can deal with it. I will not have you being upset.'

'Not a curse, not in the way you are thinking.' Silvana wrapped the scroll up. How could she explain what had passed between her and Fortis, and why he had sent these scrolls? 'I need to borrow the litter.'

'Where are you going? You are being very mysterious suddenly. You still have not told me what Fortis said about the debts. Will he give me time to repay them? Tell me everything that passed between you two.'

'Uncle—another time.' Silvana glanced pointedly at the last stragglers in the atrium.

'Can you tell me please what is going on?' her uncle asked after he had shooed the clients away. 'You did manage to secure the debts, didn't you? That was the important thing—the debts.'

Silvana regarded her uncle. She had always thought him a fair man, but now she could see how fundamentally selfish he was. He had no wish for the debts to be cleared in order to provide a secure home for her or Crispus, but to be able to start afresh with his creditors. Did he care that Fortis thought she had traded her body for them?

'Uncle, Aurelius Fortis has sent me all your debts.'

She stood with eyes downcast, waiting for the inevitable question of how she had managed it.

'But that is wonderful, my dear woman, all our troubles are over. Slightly out of the ordinary, but I am willing to overlook that in a suitor for your hand. Has he sent an offer as well?' Uncle Aulus opened the brazier's door and gave the cold coals a poke. 'Shall we burn these? I can get a fire going in here in next to no time. Nasty things to having lying around. They might fall into the wrong hands.'

'There is no offer. Nothing but the debts. No note, nothing.'

'It makes little sense to me, but they are here, and why shouldn't we get rid of them?'

Silvana gathered the tablets and scrolls up, hugging them to her chest, daring him to take them. Their eyes met for a long time. Uncle Aulus's hand fell slowly to his side. With a distinct click, he closed the brazier and turned away from it.

'I can't accept these, you know I can't.'

Uncle Aulus's eyes became sad, but he nodded as if he understood. 'What are you going to do with them?'

'Return them.'

'Shall I do it for you?' Uncle Aulus stretched out his hand. 'If he repulses you, it is kinder for all concerned.'

Silvana hugged the scrolls and tablets tighter to her chest. 'Uncle, it is not as if I mistrust you, but I feel that it would be better if I returned these personally to Aurelius Fortis. As you said, these things have a nasty habit of falling into the wrong hands. He needs to understand why I am doing this.'

'I suppose you are correct, my dear.' Uncle Aulus wiped his forehead with his handkerchief. 'Do give Fortis my regards and tell him that it was your idea and not mine. All gifts of money and the like gratefully and wholeheartedly received.'

It was far easier to tell Uncle Aulus that she was going to deliver the scrolls and tablets than to actually do it, Silvana thought as she followed Fortis's porter into the villa.

Instead of leading her towards the atrium or even Fortis's study, the porter led her to the *tablinum*. The air tasted of newly painted plaster and the walls vibrated with all the colours of a summer garden. A small fire burnt in the brazier. Fortis sat, dressed in a snow-white tunic with his hair gleaming, as if it had been newly washed. He was writing, but put the stylus down and stood as Silvana entered the room.

Her eyes hungrily feasted on him as all thoughts

of the speech she had prepared vanished. She longed for him to sweep her into his arms and kiss her the way he had done yesterday. But he simply stood, making no move towards her. He was not making this any easier, but he had to understand, she was not a courtesan. Yesterday, she had come to him freely without any expectation of monetary reward. It had been a meeting of equals. With this between them, she became a courtesan, no better than Poppea.

'Silvana, I have been expecting you.' Fortis gestured towards the couch. 'Have a seat, and a drink of cool mint tea. Honeyed wine, if you prefer.'

'I…I'm not thirsty.' Silvana clutched the scrolls and tablets tighter to her chest. The words she had carefully prepared stuck in her throat.

Fortis raised an eyebrow, but other than that betrayed nothing of his feelings. Silvana found herself searching for some sign, something that showed that he thought of her as someone other than a mercenary Baiae woman who would sleep with anyone simply to get a fortune. She wanted to know that he thought they had a future together, and that he cared about what happened to her. She knew she was selfish but she wanted more than an affair. She wanted his heart, and if he was not prepared to give it, she would have to walk away.

'The decorators have recently finished this room. I think it is much more restful with garden scenes rather than nymphs and Bacchus on the walls.' He gave a rueful smile but she noticed he seemed ill at ease. When she did not reply he continued, 'You see what a slave I am to Merlus. He has allowed me up as long as I keep warm.'

'We need to speak.' Silvana held out the scrolls and tablets. She had to take control of the conversation. What has passed between them yesterday was too new and raw. She had no idea of how to act. She wanted to walk in to his arms but it was no longer possible, not with the debt between them. 'These belong to you, I believe.'

'I sent them to you.' Fortis's eyebrows drew together in a frown. 'They belong to you now.'

'Why have you given them to me?' Silvana asked, her voice barely above a whisper. Her stomach trembled. She willed him not to say the words.

He tilted his head to one side, assessing her, and then he gave a little shrug.

'To do with as you pleased. The race was won. You deserve the spoils. A laurel wreath was enough for me. I meant to give them to you yesterday but other things intervened, and you had left by the time I remembered.'

'It is a small fortune.' Silvana forced the words from her throat.

'I know how much it is.' Fortis's face turned hard. 'Cotta gleefully told me. Your uncle was rather unwise.'

'Why not send them to my uncle?'

'They belong to you.' Fortis turned away from her. 'It was what you came for yesterday, wasn't it?'

Silvana stared open-mouthed. It was as she feared. He thought she had gone to him because she wanted the money.

'I am returning them. We will arrange a payment schedule.' Her throat closed and she found it impossible to say anything more. She held out the scrolls.

Fortis made no move to take the items. He stood there, regarding her with an unfathomable expression. Silvana put them down on a small table. She arranged them in a neat little pile, taking care that each was laid out properly.

'I made an accounting of them.' She forced her voice to remain steady. He had to understand what she was doing and what she intended to do or otherwise there was no hope for them. The debt would be like a cancer that would grow. 'Five hundred gold pieces is what we owe you. Obviously we don't have that sum of money to hand, but I am willing to negotiate a good rate of interest.'

Silvana shifted in her sandals, waiting to see his response. He had to say something. He looked her up and down and then strode over to the jug and poured himself a cup of cool mint.

'Does your uncle know you are here?' he asked at last. His voice was hard and sent shivers of ice down her spine.

Silvana stared at him, unbelieving. What did her uncle have to do with anything? She had come here to sort out this problem, not to be questioned about her motives.

'He does, and he wanted to burn them in the charcoal brazier but I have convinced him otherwise.' She crossed her arms.

'Your uncle shows a certain amount of sense.'

'You sent the debt to me. I am returning it to you, and we will discuss how it will be repaid. I want to show Crispus that wagering does not do anyone any good at all. The way my uncle is going on, you would think he won the debt.'

Fortis gathered up the scrolls and tablets and threw them into the brazier, directly on the hot coals. Instantly the flames licked the dry wood and papyrus, curling around them.

'What are you doing? Have the Furies attacked your mind?' Silvana rushed forward, preparing to pull the tablets out of the braziers. 'Do you know how much money is there?'

'Burning them.' He turned to her, eyes glowing. In his cheek a muscle jumped. 'It is my money and I can do what I like with it.'

Silvana watched in horror as the fire burnt brighter. It seemed as if all her dreams were going up in smoke. He was refusing to listen to her. She put her hand to her throat. He had to understand what he was doing to her. 'But it's not what I want. You can't just burn them. We owe you that money.'

'I have. Your uncle's debts are no more.'

'They are still there.' Silvana put her hands on her hips. 'Burning the pieces of papyrus and bits of wood changes nothing.'

'You will obey me in this matter.' Fortis's voice allowed for no refusal.

'Why?' Silvana tilted her head in the air. 'You are not my husband or my guardian. You have no control over my actions.'

'I am your lover,' he said quietly as he held his arms out, a tender expression on his face. 'I want to look after you, Silvana Junia. Let me.'

Silvana closed her eyes. She thought she would feel elated once the debts were gone, but now something very different hung over her head. She wanted Fortis, but not like this. His actions cheapened what they shared. She shook her head. 'I can't. You haven't bought me as your mistress. I am a free woman. The debt and what we shared…yesterday. They are not connected.'

His hand reached out and grabbed her shoulders, giving her a gentle shake, making her open her eyes. She stared into his deep green eyes. 'Silvana, I am giving you a choice. I wanted you to be with me because you want to, not because you feel some sort of misplaced loyalty to your uncle.'

Silvana ignored the tightness of her throat. She wanted to lay her head against Fortis's chest and draw strength from him, but he had to understand why she had to refuse his gift.

'It has nothing to do with my uncle.'

'Your uncle's debts are the reason you came to spend time with me yesterday.'

'After what happened yesterday, I am amazed you could even think that. Let alone say it to my face!' White hot anger filled her body, blazing up inside her. 'Do you think so little of me, of yourself to think that I would come to your bed because of my uncle? It is why I never mentioned the debt, and my plan for getting rid of it.'

'You did before when you wanted to stop your uncle from being crucified.'

'That was different, I was trying to save his life.'

Silvana bit her lip. He had to understand the difference. That what had passed between them yesterday was something out of the ordinary.

Fortis's hands loosened their grip, turned gentle to caress down her arms. 'Why should I think any differently? Are you going to deny that you came here yesterday to speak about your uncle's debts? That you only came to amuse me in my hour of need?'

Silvana stepped away from him. She had to think clearly. He had no understanding of what this meant to her. She was tempted to give a laugh and deny the reason, but she could not lie. 'You knew.'

'I knew why you came, and I decided to play a waiting game.' He leant forward, his face intent. 'If you did not make love with me for your uncle's debts, why did you? Why did you leave without asking for them?'

She wanted to tell him that it was because she loved him. But the words would not come. How could she when she had no idea of his feelings? She turned her back on him, went over to the *lares* and picked up a statuette. When she was sure that she was in control of her emotions, she faced him again.

'You will get your money back. The Junius family always repays its debts.'

'What debt?' Fortis opened the brazier's door and used a poker to destroy the small pile of white ash.

'I see no debt. There is no more debt. Whatever debt there was, it has been paid in full. I am more than happy to write a note out with those words on it. Can you stop this game, Silvana? We shall speak of it no more.'

'Don't treat me like a child with no mind.'

'When you insist on acting like one, how else can I treat you?'

Silvana stared disbelievingly at the pile of ash. He had burnt the debt, destroyed it.

What sort of man burnt that amount of money? Didn't he understand that this debt was a point of honour for her?

'I intend to pay you every copper *as.* I kept an account of it.' She pulled a thin tablet out of her belt and held it aloft.

Fortis reached over and plucked the tablet from her fingers. It burnt brightly in the brazier until it too joined its fellows as a pile of white ash.

'Let me take care of you, Silvana. Come with me to Rome.' He held out his arms. She wanted to run into them, but not when he had done that. If she did, where would it stop? The walls of the room seemed to close in on her, to stop her from breathing. She wanted to believe that he was doing this because he cared about her, but she had been wrong before. And if he cared about her, he would have listened to her and understood how important it was for her to pay him back. She had vowed not to take handouts long before now.

'I have had enough of being taken care of. I stand on my own two feet. I refuse to be an ornament for a senator's arm, to go back to the sort of life I led with Drusus Cotta. You have no idea of what I went through.'

A flash of pain crossed his face. 'I have never asked you.'

'But that is what you want. You keep trying to push me into a mould, some place where I don't want to be. You simply assumed.'

'You dislike people helping you, Silvana.'

Silvana stared into the charcoal brazier. 'I have no wish to go back to being a living statue, if that is what you mean.'

'You are a stubborn lady, Silvana, but you will come around. You will see what is best for you.'

'I had years of being told what was best for me. How I had to dress, what I had to talk about, to think. If you have learnt nothing about me, learn this—my independence has been won.' Silvana slammed her fists together. 'You understand nothing about me.'

Fortis stood straight. His chin held high in the air.

'I was going to make an offer for you.'

Silvana's mouth twisted. All too clearly she remembered Sempronia's words and how Fortis did not deny them. He might not feel ashamed of her now, but in the future, how would he feel? And when he did, how would she feel? He already held a large part of her heart. To see him turn away from her in disgust was something she could not bear. No, it was far better to end the thing now when they both were in the throes of passion, rather than letting it fizzle out.

'Your family would never accept me, Aurelius Fortis. You care too much about what the world thinks of you. I saw Eutychus's pride at your success. I know what Baiae does to people. How it turns their heads. It is a pleasant dream and not the harsh reality of Rome.'

'I care about you.'

'That is only pride speaking, because you can't have me. Don't you worry, in a few months you will return to your well-ordered life and you will have forgotten that I ever existed.'

'But I want you, Silvana.'

'You want a dream of me.' Silvana shook her head. 'Forgive me, Fortis, but our association is at an end.'

She started towards the door. It seemed to take a much longer time than when she had first arrived.

Each step, an aching age. Her heart kept telling her to throw herself into his arms and beg forgiveness, but her pride would not let her.

'Why do you cling on to the past so hard, Silvana?' he called after her. 'Why are you frightened of the future?'

'I have no idea what you are talking about.' Silvana paused, her hand on the door, not daring to turn and face him.

'Why are you unwilling to take a risk? We could be good together.'

But for how long? Until the rumours caught up with her and he began to despise her? She had to be hard now to save herself from heartache later on.

'I do take risks.' Her knuckles shone white against the door handle. If he took her in his arms, she'd melt. Silvana forced her body to remain still.

'You are a coward, Silvana—content to live in this cosy world you have built for yourself. You are afraid of your feelings. You play at being a great hostess, but really it is to mask your empty life. Why are you letting yourself be haunted by the ghosts from the past? When you are ready to grow up and start living, we can talk.'

Silvana paused, hand on the door.

'Every last bronze denarius, Lucius Aurelius Fortis, every last one.'

* * *

Silvana paced the small antechamber of Cotta's villa where she waited with Lyde. Fortis was correct about one thing. She had hung on to the past. She had held on to the property at Capri not out of loyalty to her dead husband, but out of pride. Now she owed Fortis a debt she could not pay without getting rid of it.

Fortis had exorcised his ghosts when he had raced against Cotta. Now she needed to do the same. She had to let go of the past. She could do this. Selling the property was the only way. She wanted to go forward with Fortis, not be dragged back into the past. She wanted to live and to give Fortis and her a chance together. A clean start.

She walked over to two large urns. The last time she had seen them, they had stood in her husband's atrium. It was where he had liked to hide the amphora of wine that the doctors had forbidden him in his last days. Thinking about it brought a smile to her face. Had Cotta hidden anything in here? More wine? Or something else that he wanted to keep away from Poppea's acquisitive fingers and the world at large?

Silvana stood on tiptoe and peered in. Something silver gleamed back at her. She pulled out a bracelet near the top and looked at the markings—hieroglyphics. Egyptian silver. The memory of her interview with Fortis flooded back. He had been expecting her uncle to land a shipment of Egyptian silver. And the next day, Poppea had been wearing some new trinkets. She had been blind not to see it before. Silvana dropped the bracelet like an asp. And it fell with a heavy thump, rolling just out of reach behind the urn.

'My lady, are you feeling all right?' Lyde stood respectfully to one side. She had not uttered one word of complaint the entire time they had been there, although she had worn a long-suffering expression. 'Perhaps you would be better off at home. Your uncle warned me that if you should go to Drusus Cotta, I was to urge you to return home as no good would come of it.'

'Where is Cotta?' Silvana clasped and unclasped her hands. She had to do this now, before she found another excuse. It was the only way. 'He has to be here. The porter said that he would come out directly.'

The maid put her head to one side. 'I can hear voices. We should go. It was a mistake to come here. I can feel it in my bones.'

'I am going to conduct a little business with my stepson, that is all.'

'The last time…'

'The last time, I was not prepared to sell the property, now I am. My circumstances have changed.'

Lyde wrung her hands. 'I have no idea why you left Aurelius Fortis. He is a good man, and this one... No good will come of this. I have a bad feeling about this place. You should never have come here. It is...unsecmly.'

'You worry too much, Lyde,' Silvana said with more assurance than she felt. 'Once Cotta has finished with his client, he will be ready to listen. He wants the property. Poppea said that to me at the race. Now, hush, Lyde. He is coming.'

Heavy footsteps sounded in the hallway, and the door to the vestibule where Silvana waited was flung open.

'As I was saying to you, Draco, this deal will be a good one for both of us.' Cotta's voice boomed out.

Silvana swallowed hard as the two men appeared from Cotta's study. Her flesh crawled as she saw the man standing next to Cotta. Draco—the pirate captain. The one her uncle had been accused of helping. Only it hadn't been him, it had been Drusus Cotta all along. Every instinct in her body told her to run, but her feet seemed to be rooted to the ground.

'Exactly who do we have here?' Draco drawled. 'Are you entertaining more women than the delightfully expensive Poppea? It was a mistake, you know, Cotta, to give her that bracelet.'

Cotta stopped. His lip curled back to an evil snarl. 'My former stepmother. It is indeed a pleasure. I wonder that no one told me you were waiting. What brings you here, Silvana? Have you come to gloat? Your lover won.'

Silvana rearranged her shawl. She refused to let Cotta see how his words cut into her. 'You're busy, Drusus Cotta, it can wait.'

'I'm never too busy to speak with my stepmother. Come and sit a while. You visit all too seldom and have a way of disappearing before I can properly say goodbye.' Cotta's smile widened a little further. He made an expansive gesture towards the stone bench. 'My friend and I were discussing you. My stepmother is the woman Aurelius Fortis raced for.'

'Indeed, perhaps you are right, Drusus Cotta, the Fates are kind in the way they twist their thread.'

'I really think I ought to go.' Silvana put on her best hostess manner, one that had seen her through innumerable nights. 'When you have some free time, Cotta, we must speak, but not until then. At your convenience.'

Cotta smiled, but it reminded Silvana of a shark eyeing a tasty piece of meat. 'I would not dream of letting you depart, Silvana Junia. Not without enjoying some of my fabled hospitality. And I do believe we shall get word of it to your lover. He will be most interested to hear of your whereabouts.'

'Lover?' Silvana gave a hollow laugh and threw her shawl over her shoulder. 'Such a fanciful notion. I have no idea what you are speaking of, Drusus Cotta. Over the years you have made some wild accusations, but this is the wildest. I have no lover.'

'Call it a lucky surmise.' Cotta tapped his teeth as his eyes raked her form. 'I think some token to show him that we have you. Yes, you will finally serve me well, Silvana.'

'Are you sure that will work, Drusus Cotta? Your last fail-proof plan ended in disaster,' the pirate captain drawled. 'And the time before that, we only just got the silver on shore.'

Cotta flushed and began to bluster.

As the two men started to discuss plans, Silvana saw Lyde cowering between the two urns, and gave a nod towards the doorway. Lyde had to understand.

Agonisingly at first Lyde did nothing but crouch down. Then she started to move silently towards the opening.

Silvana watched, hardly daring to breathe. Lyde had to make it. Now while Cotta and his pirate friend were arguing about the best method.

'There was another woman here,' Draco said. 'Where has she gone?'

Silvana released her breath. 'Run, Lyde, run like the wind! Warn Fortis.'

Lyde scampered. Silvana could hear shouts and cries. Then nothing. One of Cotta's henchmen returned carrying Lyde's shawl, but that was all.

'She got away. She got away.'

'For now, but we will find her,' Draco said.

'That was not very wise, my lady,' Cotta sneered.

'You can do what you like with me.' Silvana turned to face her captors. 'But you will not prevail.'

Chapter Seventeen

Fortis stirred the ashes in the brazier one more time. He would give Silvana a little while longer and then he would go to her uncle. Between the two of them, they should be able to make her see sense. He had handled the gift of the debt badly, but he refused to allow one mistake to end their relationship. This was about much more than money, prestige or status, this was about his future happiness. He wanted Silvana, he needed Silvana and yesterday, he had been certain she had felt the same way.

'Aurelius Fortis, there is a woman here to see you,' Merlus said. 'And the porter is quite insistent that you see her. I know you asked not to be disturbed, but it may be important.'

Fortis's heart leapt. Had Silvana come back to say she was sorry? Then his heart plummeted to the tops of his sandals. Behind the porter stood

Silvana's tire-woman. Her face showed red marks and her clothing was torn in several places.

'My cousin, Lyde,' the porter murmured.

She rushed to Fortis and grabbed his hands. 'Forgive me, sir, I did not know where to go. Junius Maius and Junius Crispus would be no help at all. I had to come to you.'

'Why me?'

'Because the garrison would not listen. Silvana told me to come and warn you, and I hope you will help her. You are the only one who would, the only one who can save her.'

'What has happened, Lyde?' Fortis resisted the temptation to shake the frightened woman. 'You did well to come here. Tell me what has happened and I will do my best to rescue Silvana from whatever fate has befallen her.'

'They have taken my mistress and I am afraid for her.' The woman dissolved into noisy sobs.

Icy cold washed over Fortis. He struggled to remain calm and not to shake the woman, but hysterics were not going to help anyone. 'Tell me quickly. What is going on? Where is Silvana?'

'Silvana, my mistress,' Lyde said in between sobs and hiccups, 'went to Drusus Cotta. She wanted to sell her property and pay you back all the money her uncle owed. Cotta was there with another

man—someone named Draco. And they decided…
she knew too much.'

Fortis closed his eyes. He had thought to spare
Silvana any hurt or problem, but had driven her
straight into the hands of Cotta. He never dreamt
that she'd take it into her head to confront Cotta. He
cursed under his breath.

'Where is Silvana? Why did you leave her?' His
hands curled around his belt as anger filled him.
This woman had left Silvana in danger!

'She wanted me to go. She begged me with her
eyes.' Lyde put her hands together. 'I swear this
before Jupiter Optimates and all the rest of the gods.
If I lie, may they strike me dead.'

Lyde raised a fist in the air and stood there.

'No one will strike you, Lyde. You are quite
safe here. How did you find your way without
being attacked?'

'I sidled to the door and ran. They chased me,
Cotta's porter and others, but I grew up in this
city. I know the back alleys of Baiae and I made
my way here.'

'Where is Silvana now?'

'She is with Cotta and the other man, a pirate, I
think. They were plotting your demise. I have no
idea where they will take her. They were not going
to keep her there.'

'No, you are right about that. Cotta will have moved her. Probably in a closed litter.' Fortis banged his fists together. 'I want my sword and dagger, Merlus.'

'Master, what are you going to do?' Merlus blocked his way, his hands on his hips. 'The surgeon has not said that you are well enough.'

'Rescue her.' Fortis put his hand on Merlus's shoulder. 'I have had enough of doctors and their treatments. Let me pass.'

'But how?'

'Leave that to me, Merlus. Now is the time for acting, not discussing strategy.'

'He is not coming. Aurelius Fortis will not come for me,' Silvana said from where she sat with her hands tied and her back against the far wall in the main cabin of Cotta's well-appointed yacht. She was dressed only in her gap-sleeved gown as Cotta had taken her shawl and *stola* for other purposes. 'You are making a terrible mistake.'

'I don't think we are. He will come to rescue you.' Cotta gave a superior smile before he ordered his henchmen to let out the sails more.

'I am nothing to him.' Silvana closed her eyes as she forced the words from her throat.

It was the truth. How could Fortis ever forgive her

for the words she had said to him? She had willfully misinterpreted his actions, because it meant giving up part of herself. She had destroyed whatever trust there was between them.

'He raced for your debts.' Cotta's fingers pinched her chin, forcing her to look at him. 'If that isn't proof of devotion, I have no idea what is.'

Silvana jerked her head away from his grasp and focused on the row of Greek vases behind him. Her whole body started to shake with uncontrollable shudders. She wanted to curl up in a ball and hide her head. Silvana forced the air between her lips. She had to concentrate. She had to reason with Cotta and make him understand. There was still time to take her back to Baiae. They could both forget this had ever happened.

'Not my debts. My uncle's!' she cried. 'He raced to provoke you…because he knows who you are, Drusus Cotta. Because of you and your association with Draco, a close friend of his died. He swore revenge. His actions had nothing to do with me.'

'Brave words, and what you say may be the truth. Aurelius Fortis did make a point to goad me about Draco when we stopped at Cumae.' Cotta ran a finger down the side of her cheek. Silvana forced her body not to jerk away in revulsion. 'But you have been a thorn in my side for long enough. And this time, my sweet stepmother, I am prepared for your tricks. I shall be glad to get rid of you.'

Silvana ran her tongue over her lips, moistening them as she tried to ignore the cold sweat making her gown stick to the back of her neck. 'Where are you taking me?'

'Capri. It is as good as place as any and, as you seem unaccountably attached to the estate, you might as well end your days there. Make no mistake, your lover will come for you and you both shall enjoy its charms.'

'How will he know?'

Cotta pulled out his portable sundial and held it aloft. 'He should be getting my message about now. Your shawl and *stola* came in useful, my dear.'

Fortis hung on the rails of Pio's ship and willed the sails to fill. 'Can you make this crate go any faster?'

'How do you know she is out there?' Merlus asked, coming to stand beside him. Like Fortis, Merlus wore a sword belt and in his hand he carried a dagger.

'Cotta's yacht has gone, slipped the mooring just before we got down to the quayside.'

'Yes, but what does that prove? The bay is wide.'

'He is heading for Capri. For some reason that

estate is important to him, and he knows I know it. He will expect me there.'

'Why not wait for the garrison? These men—they are not fighters. If Cotta means for you to follow, he will contact you.'

Fortis turned and stared at his manservant. Merlus had no understanding. Silvana was in jeopardy because he had inadvertently sent her to Cotta's house. He had to find her before anything happened to her. 'I know my instinct is correct.'

He called to Pio to let out the sail slightly and the craft picked up speed, sending spray into his face, blinding him.

'Sail to the starboard,' came the call.

Fortis wiped the seawater from his face and peered out. He could just make out the distinctive lines of Cotta's yacht. He turned back to Pio's assembled crew and the men from his household. A motley crew, but they would have to be enough. 'Be prepared to board the yacht at my command, and my command only. Remember, there is a woman on board. I want her unharmed! We can do it! The gods are on our side.'

A rousing cheer rose from the assembled crowd.

'As you were saying, Merlus.' Fortis turned back to his manservant.

'I would follow you anywhere, master, even into the depths of Hades as the gods do truly love you.'

* * *

'Why do you want the estate?' Silvana asked as Cotta turned away from her. Anything to keep him talking and to keep her mind from wondering what would happen to her once they arrived on the island. She had visited it several times before, but not often, as the little villa had an oppressive air.

'It is a perfect inlet for unloading boats, and, of course, you failed to sell it to me when I requested.'

'Your adopted father, Drusus Cotta the Elder, asked me to keep it.'

'He was dead!'

'I promised,' Silvana said quietly. 'I promised I would keep it until my hour of need. Cotta the Elder loved me in his own way, I know that now.'

'You have humiliated me for the last time, Silvana Junia. Ponder on that as you prepare to cross the River Styx.' Cotta turned his back and strode away from her, barking orders as he went.

Silvana swallowed hard as the shudders returned, hard and faster. She watched helplessly as the yacht started to pick up speed and go further out into the bay.

Diving off the side of the boat was impossible with her hands tied. Her skirt would drag her down and there was no way she could swim to shore without using her arms. Silvana laid her head against her knees, wanting to give up, to surrender. She rested like that for a while and then the anger filled her. She refused to give in to despair. Maybe in some way she could prevent Fortis's death. Had she not been stubborn, none of this would have happened.

She felt along the side of the boat, hoping for a nub of sharp iron to rub the rope against. Anything to make her feel less helpless. Her thumb found a sharp spike, not much but a start. She began to rub the rope along it.

She was going to die. She knew that. When would Cotta and Draco decide she was no longer of any use to their plans, that Fortis was not coming to rescue her? It was ironic how easily she could accept it. No tears. No hysterics, just the cold reality.

She wanted to say goodbye to her uncle and Crispus, but most of all she wanted to tell Fortis how much she loved him and that she was wrong. She should have known that what he had done was not to make life harder for her, but to make it easier. She should have been big enough to accept his generosity. If the Fates ever allowed her to see him again, she would say it; she knew, with her last breath, she would whisper his name.

The ropes slipped slightly and Silvana started to ease her wrist out. She could almost do it, but then her hand stuck, and she felt the small trickle of blood where she had cut her wrist. Silvana closed her eyes and willed the pain to go away. She had to have a chance. Back and forth, back and forth, as no one was paying attention to her now.

The wind had died and the sail flapped uselessly. Cotta made furious gestures while Draco made several pointed remarks about his efficiency as a sailor. Silvana watched with satisfaction as Cotta's face reddened and he demanded all attention be paid to getting the boat moving again. Silvana worked feverishly. She was certain the slippery ropes were about to give. If her arms were free, she would stand a chance.

A sudden sickening thud made her stop as the ship rocked violently from side to side. All became confusion and pandemonium. The tiny cabin emptied except for herself and Cotta. Silvana watched Cotta's face grow white.

'We have been boarded!'

'You told me that this yacht was the fastest boat on the bay!' Draco yelled as men started to stream on board.

Cotta began screaming obscenities as he wildly gestured about him. Screams and bellows filled the air. Silvana worked feverishly to free her hands but the final few threads refused to budge.

'You always did overestimate your abilities, Drusus Cotta.' Silvana heard Fortis's slightly sardonic tones. She stared as Fortis strolled into the cabin as if he had come to share a cup of honeyed wine, seemingly unflustered by the sounds of fighting going around him. In his hand, he carried his unbloodied sword.

She relaxed against the side and closed her eyes. Everything was going to be all right. Fortis was uninjured.

'You have a strange way of coming to call, Aurelius Fortis.' Cotta did not move, but stared at him. 'I must ask you and your band to leave this yacht immediately. I shall be lodging a complaint with the Senate about your high-handed and unsupportable behaviour.'

'I believe you have an unwilling passenger.'

'I have no idea what you are talking about.' Cotta held out both his hands. 'I must ask you to leave my yacht immediately or I shall not be responsible for the consequences.'

'You are a liar and a thief, Drusus Cotta, and you always were a poor loser.'

'You are hardly in a position to be calling names.' Cotta put his hand on his sword hilt. 'I demand you leave this boat at once. You have no right to be here. This time you have gone too far, Aurelius Fortis. I shall report you to the Prefect, and I will pursue you in the courts.'

'I shall depart once I have your unwilling passenger.'

'I see no unwilling passenger.'

Silvana scrambled to her feet, and stumbled forward, swaying slightly with the motion of the boat. 'I'm here, Fortis.'

'Unharmed?' He glanced over to her and she saw the anxiety in his eyes.

'A bit shaken, but I am fine except for the ropes that bind my wrists.'

He nodded. 'It is a strange way of behaving, to tie up willing passengers.'

'You have no idea of the games my stepmother likes to play.'

There was a loud crack as Fortis laid a blow across Cotta's face. Cotta put his hand to his mouth, wiped away the trickle of blood as his merciless smile increased. 'You will be punished for that, Fortis.'

'Do you give Silvana to me or do I take her?' Fortis's voice was cold.

'Take her,' Cotta said, drawing his sword. 'I have waited for a long time for this, Aurelius Fortis. I plan to see you in Hades before this day is out.'

'As have I.' Fortis drew his sword and concentrated on Cotta's swinging blade. Every muscle tensed as he waited for the first blow. Cotta swung wildly, and the blow was easily blocked.

Fortis lunged forward with his blade, engaging Cotta. 'Run, Silvana, run. Get to Pio's ship.'

Round and round they circled in the small cabin, blade meeting blade. Fortis's side ached from the earlier injury, but he had to give Pio's men time. 'Are you ready to give up, Cotta?'

'Never!' Cotta surged forward, striking at Fortis's side.

The blow impacted on Fortis's bruised side. Burning pain shot through him. He clutched at the sword and refused to lose his footing. Cotta brought his sword down a second time, again connecting with Fortis's side. Fortis's arms went numb as he staggered to the right, searching for something to grab on to. He heard a clang as the sword dropped to the ground.

Silvana watched in horror as Cotta raised his sword again. The sword hung in the air, gleaming as Fortis lay unprotected on the ground.

She had to do something!

She refused to let Fortis die!

With every ounce of energy that she possessed, she strained against her bonds and felt them break. Cotta's back was to her as he stood sneering over Fortis. She reached for one of the Greek vases, and brought it down on top of Cotta's head. The vase shattered against Cotta's skull. Cotta turned and advanced towards her. Her hand blindly reached for another vase.

'Fight a man, Cotta, not a woman,' Fortis called out. 'I have a score to settle.'

Silvana felt the smooth wall of the cabin trap her as Cotta advanced toward her. She lifted the vase and brought it down on Cotta's sword arm. He stepped backwards and Fortis hit him again on the base of his skull. He gave a low moan and lay still.

'Have you killed him?' Silvana asked.

'It would be a shame if I had.' Fortis prodded him with his foot and there was a grunt. Fortis put his foot firmly on Cotta, holding him down. 'He's not dead. He will face trial, Silvana.'

'And the rest?' Silvana gestured to the outside where the sounds of the battle still raged.

'Merlus will see to it. He has a family to avenge. He has waited a long time to find that particular pirate.'

A great shout went up on the boat and then silence. Silvana moved towards Fortis. Had Merlus and his men been beaten? Merlus appeared in the doorway with a bloodied sword.

'My family's honour is restored, Aurelius Fortis,' he said, wiping blood from his face. 'A violent man met his end. I am at peace.'

'Pio, Merlus, take this boat back to the harbour. I believe the Prefect will be very interested in the prisoner,' Fortis said as he securely tied Cotta.

'And if he does not believe you, tell him to investigate the large urns in Cotta's atrium. They are full of Egyptian silver,' Silvana said. Silvana looked at Fortis and all words failed her. She wanted to tell him what he meant to her, but not here with all these men around.

'Silvana, you continue to amaze me.' Fortis smiled down at her. 'All the time and wasted days I spent, searching warehouses from here to Naples, and the goods were stored in Cotta's house all the time. He was very sure of himself.'

'He knew the authorities would never dare search his house.'

'Right, you,' Merlus said, raising Cotta to his feet. 'Off to the hold with the other scum of humanity.'

The room emptied and Silvana was left facing Fortis. 'You have got what you came here for.'

'What did I come here for?' he asked, lifting one eyebrow.

'You came to find Draco and to ensure Cotta was punished.'

Fortis made no move towards her. 'Is that really why you think I risked life and limb?'

'Yes,' Silvana whispered, as her heart started to

race. 'Merlus said it is why you stayed after Eutychus left.'

'Eutychus left long ago and I knew Cotta was the man I sought fairly soon after I arrived. Before we made love for the first time. I knew the Prefect had not caught the right men. The shipment was too small. I had seen Cotta do things like that before.' Fortis ran his hand through his hair, making it stand on end. 'If Cotta survives, I will see him prosecuted to the full extent of the law. He no longer has the power to harm you or your family. You have my promise on that.'

Silvana nodded, not trusting herself to speak. This was goodbye then. He was going to walk out of her life. She turned from him and started to pick up the shards from the vase, anything to keep from blurting out her true feelings for him.

His hand closed round hers, holding it in its warm grip.

'Cotta was not the reason I stayed.'

'But Merlus said—'

'Merlus talks a great deal too much, Silvana. I stayed for one reason and one reason only. And it had nothing to do with chasing pirates or looking after my cousin.' He raised her to her feet, and put his hands on her waist, holding her.

'Why did you stay?' Silvana's breath stuck in her throat.

'You.'

'I don't understand.'

'Silvana Junia, I want to spend the rest of my life with you, as infuriating as you are.' Fortis lifted her chin so she could stare in his eyes. 'I knew I wanted you since the first moment we met. Later I discovered it was not just your body I wanted, as lovely as that is. It was your mind and your courage. Even when you are beaten, you fight back. You saved my life just now when most women would have been a crumpled heap of tears. I owe you my life.'

'Then we are even. I owe you mine.'

'You are maddening,' he said against her hair. 'Why will you never take a compliment?'

Silvana leant back against his arms. 'I am maddening? You are arrogant, overbearing and a bully.'

'But you love me just as much I love you.'

Silvana stared at him, convinced she had heard him wrong. 'You love me?'

'I have been trying to show it to you. Words are cheap and promises easily broken. It is why I burnt your uncle's debts. It was not to make you a courtesan, Silvana, far from it. I want to spend the rest of my life with you, but only if you desire it as well. When I make a marriage offer for you, I want you to be able to choose freely. You saved my life not only today, but the first day I met you. You were right. I was sleepwalking through life. We need each other, Silvana.'

'What are you asking me?' Silvana's heart contracted. The breath stopped in her throat. Every sinew of her body strained to hear his words.

'Will you marry me, Silvana Junia, and be my wife?' He raised her bruised wrist to his lips and kissed it.

'I have no choice, Lucius Aurelius Fortis,' she said, cupping his face with her hand. Her heart soaring as she could finally say the words. 'I cannot imagine a life without you. You are in my heart and my soul.'

'Good,' he said against her mouth. 'I want you with me always by my side, in my bed and in my life. My life would be worthless without you to share it with.'

'But your career? I am a scandalous widow and my family notorious. Your family will despise me. You said as much about Eutychus and me. Why should it change for you?'

'Silvana Junia, my life would be meaningless without you.' Fortis lifted her chin and stared into her eyes. 'I said a great deal too many things that morning. I was jealous. I can admit that now. I have wanted you for my own since I first pulled you up on to the harbour wall. As for my family, if I led my life according to their wishes, I would have no life.

Now, say you will be my wife, my partner, my one and only love.'

'I will.'

Silvana gave herself up to his embrace, safe in his arms and secure in his love. Home at last.

Historical Note

Baiae (modern-day Baia) was the seaside resort where the wealthy Romans went to play and relax away from Rome's fierce summer heat. Its heyday was during the mid-first century BC, but it remained a popular resort for most of the Roman period. The Emperor Hadrian went there for its waters at the end of his life. It was a place known for its bending of rules and easy mixing of classes. Here, it was possible for an *adulescens* (the Romans used the term to mean a not fully mature man, rather than a teenager) to socialise with a senator or one of the many power-brokers in Roman society. It was a place where fortunes could be made or lost. There was a saying in Rome that more divorces were made on the sands of Baiae than anywhere else.

Because of its active social life, it was one of the few places where women could gain real political power. The most notorious of the Baiae hostesses was one Clodia Mettalia, who has been immortalised as Catullus's mistress and demonised by Cicero when he attempted to defend her brother. According to Cicero, she was all go in the dining room and no go in the bedroom. Like other Roman aristocratic women, she could read and converse in both Latin and Greek, play the lyre, and could do geometry, but her real crime was to dance better than an honest woman should. Dancing, along with goatee beards and flowing dining robes, was frowned upon by more austere members of Roman society. To display any of these tendencies was to mark a person out as a 'loose belt' or, as we might say, a dandy. Julius Caesar, before he conquered Bithynia, was perhaps one of the most famous loose belts. Once he tore down a newly built villa because the workmanship failed to reach his exacting standards. This attitude put him in direct conflict with Cato, and would eventually lead to a polarisation of Rome.

Among other things, Baiae was responsible for the creation of underfloor heating and hanging baths, which some scholars assume to mean showers.

A fresco of Baiae's waterfront during the Roman Republic was discovered in Pompeii's House of Marcus Lucretius Fronto. If the time period interests you, Adrian Goldsworthy's new biography,

Julius Caesar, is worth a read, as is Tom Holland's *Rubicon.* The following books I found useful when I was researching the book.

Broadman, John, Jasper Griffin and Oswyn Murray (eds), *The Oxford Illustrated History of the Roman World* (Oxford University Press 1986) Oxford

Butterworth, Alex and Ray Laurence, *Pompeii—The Living City* (Weidenfeld & Nicolson 2005) London

Grant, Mark, *Roman Cookery: Ancient Recipes for Modern Kitchens* (Seriff 1999) London

Goldsworthy, Adrian, *Caesar—The Life of a Colossus* (Weidenfeld & Nicolson 2006) London

Holland, Tom, *Rubicon: The Triumph and Tragedy of the Roman Republic* (Little, Brown 2003) London

Lane Fox, Robin, *The Classical World—An Epic History from Homer to Hadrian* (Allen Lane 2005) London

Woolf, Greg (ed), *Cambridge Illustrated History of the Roman World* (Cambridge University Press 2003) Cambridge

HISTORICAL ROMANCE™

LARGE PRINT

NO PLACE FOR A LADY
Louise Allen

Miss Bree Mallory is too taken up with running her successful coaching company to have time for pampered aristocracy! But then an accidental meeting with Max Dysart, Earl of Penrith, changes everything… Bree's independence is hard-won: she has no interest in marriage. But Max's kisses are powerfully – passionately – persuasive…!

BRIDE OF THE SOLWAY
Joanna Maitland

If Cassandra Elliott does not escape from her brother, the Laird of Galloway, she will either be forced into marriage or confined to Bedlam! Desperate, she turns to a handsome stranger and begs for help in the most unladylike manner. Captain Ross Graham *must* help her flee across the Solway to safety. But neither Cassie nor Ross expects a desire as wild as the Scottish hills to flare between them…

MARIANNE AND THE MARQUIS
Anne Herries

Sheltered innocent Miss Marianne Horne had come to Cornwall to care for her ailing great-aunt. Surrounded by smugglers, spies and plots, Marianne hardly knew whom to trust. Instinctively, she turned to the handsome Mr Beck. But Mr Beck turned out to be Andrew, Marquis of Marlbeck, who would *surely* never look twice at the daughter of a country vicar…so why was he paying Marianne such flattering attention?

MILLS & BOON®

HIST1207 LP